A Plague of Scoundrels

by

JON CORY

KOMENAR
publishing

Cover design by KOMENAR Publishing
Interior design by BookMatters

A PLAGUE OF SCOUNDRELS.
Copyright © 2008 by Jon Cory.

Special book excerpts or customized printings can be created to fit specific needs.

For information, address KOMENAR Publishing, 1756 Lacassie Avenue, Suite 202, Walnut Creek, California 94596-7002.

Library of Congress Cataloging-in-Publication Data available

ISBN 978-0-9772081-8-0 (Hardcover)

ISBN 978-0-9772081-9-7 (Trade Paperback)

First Edition

10 9 8 7 6 5 4 3 2 1

Printed in the United States of America

To Jan and Steve

Acknowledgements

My wife Jan for her love, unfailing support and encouragement along with discerning editing of my rough drafts.

My son Steve, my chief cheerleader who contributed his ever-present sense of humor and valuable perspective.

Charlotte Cook and the Wednesday Writers group, including Jill Hedgecock, Leslie Burton, John Randolph, Tom Ward, Jane Booth, Cheryl Spanos, Marianne Lonsdale and Keith Wheeler. Special thanks to Laurel Hill and Elisabeth Tuck for their skillful editing and astute comments. To this whole group of talented writers, past and present who wouldn't let me kill off Gumby.

To Dereck Love for reviewing my manuscript and providing insight into London and old England.

To the professionals at KOMENAR Publishing for their support, dedication and contributions.

And, of course, CJ, Jim, Jody and Jenifer.

A Plague of Scoundrels

ONE

The Man
in the Feathered Hat

I had encountered some peculiar characters in the roommate-and-landlord maze of San Francisco apartments, but never a man dressed in a medieval costume. This man's garish Robin Hood attire belonged in Merrie Old England in the time of lords and ladies, knights and kings. He postured before me in purple doublet, lime-colored tights, and a formless green hat adorned with a cock's feather while I stood outside the open door of his Chinatown rental, striving to appear trustworthy.

"Sir," he said, his stance that of a bantam barnyard rooster. "I assume you have responded to my Internet posting for a renter with discretion and a tolerance for the bizarre." He tilted his head. "If so, come in."

"Yeah," I said. I needed a cheap apartment to fit my bare-bones budget. I would like to claim that I'm a successful stand-up comedian. One day I will be, but for the past twelve years my career ladder has had a few rungs missing. "Already sent back your renter's questionnaire."

I stepped inside but kept one hand on the doorknob behind me. The little oddball didn't appear dangerous, probably a harmless eccentric. If he caused any trouble, my six-foot, two-hundred-pound physique would take care of matters. But I didn't need any trouble with the local constabulary. A quick sprint up the outside steps would take me from this basement-level apartment back to the Chinatown alley off Grant Avenue.

"Welcome to my castle," my potential landlord/roommate said.

He bowed and swept his hand in a flourish. Halloween was months away, so he was either a Shakespearian actor or just plain daft. No matter which. I needed an abode of my own, cheap and quick.

I gazed over the man's shoulder, which wasn't hard since he was about five feet tall. A living room filled the center space of a T-shaped apartment. An efficiency kitchen occupied one corner, with a bathroom on the other side. Through an open door, I could see an unused bedroom on the left. The closed door behind him must lead to another bedroom.

Thick velvet drapes covered all the apartment's small basement windows, totally blocking all natural light and any outsider's view into the place. A desire for privacy or a fear of sunlight? Maybe both, considering this odd little man's sallow complexion and strange attire.

"I am Edward Bockman." Bockman stroked his sandy-colored Van Dyke while inspecting me with darting glances. "Sir, God's truth, I will offer low rent to the right person."

Low rent, what did that mean? According to the application letterhead, Edward Bockman was the sole owner of PST Corporation. Whatever that was. I clasped my arms behind my back like an awkward kid meeting his distant relatives for the first time. Modern executive or medieval Robin Hood, I didn't care. All I wanted was to have that vacant room at the lowest price.

"Pray tell me your name."

"Vail, like the ski resort," I said. "Elliot Vail."

He joined his hands and nodded his head as if I had said something important. The cock feather in his hat made it hard to take his demeanor seriously. Where did his imaginary life take him? What far country? What distant year? In my hometown, gender confusion was one thing, but century confusion quite another.

"I've decided to offer you free rent," he said, "for one bedroom plus use of the kitchen. Providing you agree to the strict conditions I impose." He made no attempt to explain his outlandish attire or why he changed his mind. "Think of it. Free rent, Mr. Elliot Vail."

"Free is good," I said. "Seriously good."

In fact, a perfect rent. My budget could expand to include eating two meals a day. He hadn't yet stated his strict conditions, but anything short of sex or murder for hire would suit me fine. I could handle anything, except—

"Do you have cats?" I asked. Any hairball would be a deal breaker. Even for free rent.

"No cats." Bockman seemed amused. "Nor hounds, falcons or gerbils."

"I can do without a litany of the animal kingdom." I extended my open palm like a traffic cop.

The cliché "Beggars can't be choosers" had been my mantra while seeking a low-rent apartment. The cheapest rental I had found still had exceeded half my monthly income. That one had required keeping seven cavalier cats happy while their owner was away. I lasted there only forty-five days. The cost of my allergy meds had offset the savings on rent.

Bockman quit yakking and fussed with the shoulders of his close-fitting jacket. He avoided eye contact. Guess he wasn't used to guys like me, sarcastic comedians who can be annoying while being funny. Or maybe not so funny. My career "showed promise"—my agent's faint praise. My bank statement showed depletion. I needed to cinch this deal.

"I'm good at honoring conditions," I assured him. Should have added, as long as I agreed with them. But "free" could take the edge off my attitude. "My stint in the army taught me not to question orders." Unless those commands were arbitrary intrusions on my personal well-being. Still . . .

He smoothed the front of his jacket. I swallowed any thought of saying something wiseass. Both of us were a bit nervous about each other. But I sensed each wanted the deal settled here and now.

Then he smiled, his eyes wide open, and spread his arms in welcome. The effort extended a bony wrist from his sleeve, revealing his watch. He checked the time.

"How stupid of me," Bockman said, smacking his palm against his forehead. "I could be burned at the stake." He loosened his wristwatch and tossed it onto a small table. "I'm running very short of time."

"What are your conditions so I can abide by them?" I attempted to grease the skids to my immediate occupancy of that vacant room.

"My rental conditions are few, but each is ironclad and must be followed to the letter." He lifted a three-quarter-length cape off a chair back, wrapped the garment around his narrow shoulders, and stood arms akimbo. "Never, ever," he thumbed over his shoulder, "try to open the door to my room, my inner sanctum, office and computer center. I keep it locked at all times. Don't forget, this is my home. You are the renter."

The trouble with having a landlord as a roommate is that they act like they own the place. I was tempted to rattle his cage by tossing out a line my ex-wife had once used on me during our settlement negotiations. "*Su casa es mi casa*—your house is my house." Hah. But Bockman probably wouldn't appreciate my offbeat humor.

"See this wooden chest beside me?"

My new landlord used one ribbon-tied shoe to nudge a sturdy

box covered by a flat lid. Considering Bockman's quaint costume, I wouldn't have been surprised to see a pirate's chest. But it was just a plain rectangular box made of smooth boards.

"Whenever it appears outside my locked door," Bockman said, "look inside for a list of my needs. Purchase the items and leave them in the box. Same-day service would be appreciated. Especially if you do this before you retire for the night. My requirements will be limited. I have taken care of almost everything."

Yeah, like when my ex convinced me she had paid off all her credit card charges. They kept showing up for months after she left. I wasn't going to be suckered again.

"Sorry," I said. "My limited finances won't cover front money for someone I know, let alone a stranger in lime-colored tights."

"Okay." He blinked his owlish eyes at me. "There's fifty dollars in the tea container on the kitchen counter. Take that."

"And if that's not enough?" I'd learned to hammer out monetary details before moving in. Free rent couldn't change that.

"Here." Bockman pressed a sheet of paper into my hand. "My accountant, Mr. Perello, is handling my finances while I'm away. Perello's telephone number is included in these instructions."

There was that corporate PST letterhead again. Below the fussy font Bockman had noted his accountant's contact info, followed by a reiteration of the locked-room-and-box instructions. Then began an odd list of personal preferences on items to be purchased. My new landlord insisted on such trivial things as spearmint, not peppermint. Chocolate instead of vanilla, and vitamin tablets, not soft gels—-and never in plastic blister packs. Fifty bucks wouldn't buy much if Bockman stayed away for long.

"I can't see pestering Perello for pocket money," I said. "Accountants and lawyers are two professions I avoid. They charge you for saying hello."

"I'll try to send some more money." Bockman exhaled through pursed lips. "It will be in the box. Don't be surprised to find old English coins."

"I've never found anything wrong with good old American money," I pushed back at him. "Lots of people accept it, kind of a worldwide phenomenon."

"Sell them to a coin dealer." Bockman's shoulders worked uncomfortably beneath the fit of the cape. "They will be valuable." He tugged at his sagging stockings. "I have a collection . . . I'm, ah, I'm a numismatist."

The little guy was all jumpy, twitchy. He kept glancing at his wristwatch on the table, as if he was worried he would miss the last train. He ran a finger under his nose. He was working pretty hard to wrap up our deal and didn't seem to be trying to put anything over on me. I shot him a quick smile and put up another open palm to settle him down.

"We won't be talking again," Bockman said, a grateful smile appearing. "No telephone or cell number to reach me. Now, repeat our understanding."

"Check for the box," I said. "Buy what's on your list, put the stuff inside and leave it outside your locked door at night." I couldn't resist a tag line. "And don't peek."

"Important." He raised his index finger. "My oak box is the only container you can use. No plastic or cardboard. Furthermore, if you write a note to me, it has to be handwritten. No computer printouts."

I screwed my face into a Gomer Pyle expression and resisted the temptation to add, "Golly, Mr. Bockman." Then I added my sure-fire closer: "And I won't tell anybody."

Tension seeped out of Bockman. His drawn shoulders relaxed like warm pudding. He tilted his head down as he let out a long breath of relief.

"To tell the truth," I said, "I don't really care about other people's problems. My curiosity is nil."

Not exactly true. Strange happenings and wacky people were my comedy source material. So I fudged a little. But Bockman needed reassurance, and I needed free rent.

"I'll be your box-jockey," I added.

"I'm not certain how long I will be away," Bockman said. "But then, I issue my own return ticket."

He smiled at some private joke. I felt like putting a headlock on Bockman and giving him a noogie like I used to do to my kid brother whenever he annoyed me.

"Now, Elliot, do we have a deal?"

Bockman rummaged in a leather sack-purse tied to his belt and extracted a key. He put it between his teeth while he tugged a pair of black leather gauntlets over his small hands. Then he spat the key into his right hand.

"Well?"

"Works for me, Bockman," I said. "Just so you know, I do stand-up comedy. Some improv. Late hours. Sometimes I get out-of-town gigs. My schedule is erratic."

Bockman fussed a gloved hand across his forehead. He still held the key, so he looked like he was winding his brain. Cracked me up.

"Perfect," Bockman said, his face lighting up like a kid being offered ice cream. He flipped the apartment key over to me. "Fare thee well, Elliot."

"Wait," I said. "One little question."

I felt Bockman owed me a tidbit of information in exchange for me being his flunky. If nothing else, I might have to defend myself to the cops if Bockman went missing or was fished out of the Bay. Or if they came knocking on our apartment door searching for him, and me knowing little more than my landlord was peculiar.

"I'm curious," I said. "What does your PST Corporation do?"

"Particle Shift Technology," he enunciated. "Leading-edge science. Futuristic." He affected a smug smile. "Or not."

Technology? Science? Not of any interest to me. In my opinion, particles should stay put and not move around. The little man was having too much fun with this. Was he making a joke at my expense? Yeah, well, my business was comedy, and he didn't know dip about that.

"Now, our business has concluded," Bockman said. "You can move in tomorrow. Excuse me. I have a rendezvous with Lady Greyhurst. I wouldn't say she's a fair maiden, but then the ex-mistress of a king is always a lady."

Another flourish of hand and cape as Bockman steered me across the threshold and closed the door. I chewed on this last enigmatic exchange at the bottom of the sidewalk stairs. From somewhere behind his closed door, a jumble of sounds, fading clicks and whines, reverberated as if a volume control was being adjusted. Then I understood.

Bockman was like a Star Wars fanatic. Costumed, in character, to play some super-graphic computer game set in Old England. An image of the skinny Bockman hunched over a game console, stroking his joystick, conjured up a deep belly laugh. I walked up the Chinatown alley that was now my neighborhood, turned right at Wing Fu's corner restaurant, and headed off to pack my meager belongings.

TWO

The Disappearing Box

Three days after I had moved my stuff into Bockman's San Francisco apartment, I retrieved a voice message from my worthless agent. His fake bonhomie instructed me to get some new material, something funny, and report for a four-week gig at the What's Up? Comedy Club. I would be one of several second-string comedians that rounded out the bill. Hippo Hyman was the headliner.

Working with Hippo was fine with me. Our professional careers had crisscrossed for years. We ran the same race, but he was the track favorite, while I was the dark horse. I considered him sort of an overstuffed mentor. He admitted to weighing three hundred fifty pounds. Hippo would quip he achieved the results by adhering to a strict vegan diet. I liked his humor, and he liked me. He referred to our comedic friendship as Fatman and Robin.

— — —

"Elliot, my man," Hippo bellowed at me when he appeared backstage after the final Saturday night show. "You murdered them tonight." Hippo was dripping sweat onto the floor. "Best performance I've heard you do in a year. You had tonight's audience by their privates. Let's celebrate with a case of beer."

"I have nothing against drinking except my empty wallet." I

turned my pants pockets inside out and let them dangle. "No filthy money soils my artistic integrity."

"My treat."

Hippo made good money and had a quick hand for the check. This rare combination of traits endeared him to me. We walked a half-block to his favorite bar. To put a fine point on it, I walked, Hippo waddled. He rationed his walking, but not his consumption. I admired his priorities.

— — —

Later that night, I counted it a major victory to have found the right Chinatown alley, considering my inebriated state. Wing Fu's neon sign was out of focus, and my feet had developed a tendency to stray, both consequences of Hippo's generous bar tab. I executed a precise ninety-degree turn and marched down to my new pad in Bockman's basement apartment.

My landlord hadn't turned on the welcome-home light, and the reflected glow from Wing's beacon did a poor job of illuminating the apartment entrance. The stairwell was an inky black hole. Toes down, I searched for each step edge and made it unscathed to my door. Wonder of wonders, I inserted the key in the lock on my first try.

The living room ceiling fixture cast a feeble glow. Shadows pushed back at the gloom—dark color where the furniture squatted, light gray in the open spaces. I vowed to replace the underachieving light bulb with the highest wattage I could screw into the overhead socket. After all, the electric bill was my landlord's problem.

Then there it was—the box. Bockman's wooden crate rested against his locked door. The box had disappeared the same day as Bockman. I hadn't heard from him since he had left that day to meet Lady Greyhurst, whoever she really was. Probably nothing more than a computer-generated girlfriend for that lonely nerd.

I detoured over to the box and pressed one ear against Bockman's door, listening for any sound. Nothing. Did some secret delivery service have a key to the apartment? I did a cursory search of the kitchen, bathroom, and my bedroom. Nothing seemed missing or amiss. Not that I had anything worth stealing, but the thought was disquieting.

The top cover of the box looked a bit charred around the edges. I lifted the lid, more out of duty than anticipation, and stirred my hand around the inside of the box without hitting anything. Then my fingertips touched something on the bottom.

I fished out a rolled-up scroll neatly tied with a black ribbon. A glob of red wax secured the message. A circle of etched roses surrounding the initials EB was pressed into the seal—Edward Bockman, my landlord.

I retreated to my bedroom and flopped on the sagging mattress, broke the seal and unrolled the letter.

Mr. Vail:

I must share my adventure. Missed my stop and found myself in the English countryside by mistake. A local peasant woman assisted me in getting to London, where I have leased a quaint wooden house in the teeming city. It is from these dwellings that I venture forth to meet Lady Greyhurst. Exciting times. The trip was a bit rough on the body. Send a large bottle of extra-strength aspirin via the box.

Your humble servant,
E. Bockman.

Why use this particular box for delivery? That was weird, but then, everything about Bockman had been off-kilter. I held his note up to the light. The message was written on vellum, not paper. From the appearance of the ink script, Bockman could have scrawled the note with a quill pen. The guy was really into authentic trappings. Where did one go nowadays to buy sheepskin parchment and quill pens? I rolled the message back into a tight cylinder and retied it. Bockman had forgotten to ask me to buy a screwdriver to fix his loose screws.

I splurged for a super-sized container of aspirin for my first delivery to Bockman. It looked kind of lonely in the box, so I added a bottle of Ibuprofen as a bonus. I scooted the box over against Bockman's door. When I returned after the show, someone's night-time delivery service had picked up the box from inside my locked apartment.

— — —

A week after it disappeared, the box showed up again outside Bockman's door. Enclosed was another request list of everyday items that he could have bought for himself at any drugstore. My landlord must be hanging out in the boonies.

That afternoon at the Club, I showed Bockman's list to Hippo and tried to interest him in my mystery. But he made jokes out of everything I said about the absent Bockman and his Robin Hood costume. Hippo had no respect for my story. He considered the whole event as a new comedy routine I was trying out on him.

"You want merry men? Try the Leather Lounge in SoMa," he said. "I want to be Friar Tuck. Now, where did I put my monk's robe?"

I gave up and went shopping at the local drugstore. Six rolls of double-ply toilet paper, three large bars of strongly scented soap, and ointment for head lice. I returned to the apartment, tossed the purchased items into the box, and knocked on Bockman's door. No one answered.

I kicked off my shoes and lay back on the bed to grab a nap before heading over to the What's Up? Club for my evening performance. Questions about Bockman jumped all over my attempts to snooze, like horses in a steeplechase. Bockman's box defied logic by shuttling back and forth without evidence of anyone's intervention. Something goofy, other than Bockman, was going on.

— — —

Thanks to good reviews and the month-long gig at the Club, my career as a comedian was picking up. My agent managed to book me into some comedy clubs in Reno and Las Vegas. Truth be told, by the time I got home from my travels and performances, my sole interest was to sleep in a familiar bed with my head nestled in a goose-down pillow.

Bockman and I continued to play box-tag on and off for three weeks, always following the same routine: check the list, buy the stuff, and send it off. Bockman neither wrote an explanation of why he wanted an item nor any personal details. Then, a few days after fulfilling his latest order, the box returned, looking more beat-up than usual.

Bockman had reinforced the corners with iron straps, held in place with handmade square nails. He had also penned a letter. The greeting had become more personal. Maybe he was getting homesick.

Elliot, my dear friend:

Reality intrudes on romance. When in love, one must take the bad with the good. Send the following:

1. Room air freshener. Solid.

No aerosol spray.

2. Rat traps. Four.

3. Two large tubes of anti-yeast-infection medicine. Maximum strength. (King Charles II may have had a good reason to secure a new mistress.)

I am annoyed to discover the hotheaded Lord Weston believes he has a prior claim on Lady Greyhurst's affections. Sorting this all out. London streets so narrow my house almost touches the neighbor's. Might return home sooner than planned.

Bockman.
PS: Send a dozen rolls of breath mints.

I estimated what it would cost to fill his latest order and came up short. I handwrote a brief note requesting additional funds, doubling the amount so I wouldn't have to fuss with money issues anytime soon. Bockman was already dealing with bad news. A little more wouldn't hurt.

— — —

No snooze alarm for me. I depended on overpowering urges for bladder relief as my alarm clock in the morning. Imprecise but reliable.

I emerged from the bathroom and headed to the kitchen to switch on the coffee pot. I was in the midst of my morning routine—combing my hair with my hand, rubbing my eyes, stretching and scratching—when I noticed Bockman's box had returned sometime during the night. The stealthy delivery service was up to its old tricks.

Fortified with caffeine, I opened the crate. A linen-wrapped bundle lay on the bottom. The package's weight surprised me. I moved to the kitchen countertop and unfolded the cloth, spreading it out on the surface. I'm no expert on old-time lingerie, but the garment sure looked like a woman's petticoat, slip, shift, or whatever ladies used to wear under their long skirts. This garment didn't look like underclothing my ex-wife or female friends wore.

I did recognize the contents, though. A silver teapot, a pewter charger and Bockman's gold signet ring with the initials EB carved into its face. A rolled-up slip of parchment was inserted through the ring.

Vail, old buddy:

Sell these items. Keep half the money for expenses. Send my share in gold or silver bars. No coins or paper money.

Many parts of London are filthy and disease-ridden. The city is a disaster waiting to happen. It is far worse than I anticipated. One must be careful.

Bock

I toted Bockman's treasures to the A-2-Z Pawnshop. The owner, Abe Zimmerman, had a reputation for screwing you fairly. Lots of out-of-work actors will testify to that fact as well as a few struggling comedians.

"Elliot." Zimmerman looked up from his computer monitor with an earnest smile. "You don't have to answer my questions if you prefer to play dumb." He caressed the teapot with tenderness reserved for newborn babies. "My database of silver antiques shows a similar teapot at the Potter museum in London. This is seventeenth-century, Charles II, English silver. A rare find."

"How about the charger and the signet ring?"

"Perhaps, Mr. Vail, we can do business," Zimmerman said. He took out a silver polishing cloth and buffed the teapot with a gentle rub. The finish shone as if it were new. "God forbid I should ask questions about these items. And, if anybody asks, I have a bad memory."

Zimmerman struggled to keep a poker face, but I sensed his excitement. Why else would he call me Mister? I kept glancing out the window, half expecting a cop to charge through the door in response to some silent alarm Zimmerman might have triggered.

"Well," I said, "how much will you give me for them?"

"You have a choice," he said in a fatherly voice. "I can give you a fair price, and we can do a lot of paperwork. You can answer questions on provenance . . ." He left the word hanging in the shop's musty air.

"I thought Provence was in southern France," I quipped. Zimmerman stayed business serious. "Okay," I said, "I assume cash right now moves the price's decimal point."

"Of course."

Zimmerman selected a pen from a coffee cup filled with a half-dozen cheap pens. The type retailers keep next to the cash register so customers can steal them without guilt. His choice was a bright-green pen with Foggy City Motel printed on the side.

I rubbed my thumb and index finger together, giving him the universal money gesture. He gave me his most reassuring-the-customer smile as he cupped his hand over a notepad. To shield his writing from the shop's security camera mounted against the crown molding. I lifted his hand off the pad just enough to see the price he had written.

"And the charger?" Maybe it would be worth more than I thought. We did another round of dollar hide-and-peek. Zimmerman was winning this provenance game.

"Changed my mind," I said. "The gold ring isn't part of the deal." Bockman's signet ring had to have a special place in that little guy's heart. My ex and I had been through the anguish of giving and getting rings back again. "It's a family heirloom."

My voice had an unexpected hard edge to it. I'd save the ring for Bockman. Besides, if he didn't show up, I'd have a memento of Robin Hood and His Magic Box. Abe shrugged. He must have seen lots of raw emotion in the pawn business.

"This very minute is a good time to decide," Zimmerman urged with palms uplifted.

"Okay. But the money has to be right now and in gold or silver ingots," I said. "You got any squirreled in your safe?"

Abe didn't blink an eye. Nodded as if all his customers wanted bullion instead of dollars. He probably melted down any unclaimed jewelry.

I tightened the waistband of my sweats to make sure my pants would stay in place and put my share of the small gold bars into one pocket, Bockman's share into the other. The gold felt heavy, substantial, in my pocket. There was comfort in that feeling. Toting gold in my pants was a new experience.

Back in the apartment, I wrapped Bockman's ingots in the petticoat and laid the bundle in the bedraggled box. I wanted to ring a bell or press a button to let Bockman know his stash was available. Instead, I headed out to the What's Up? A man has to earn bread to eat.

THREE

Chained and Detained

Hippo was headlining at the Club again. After the last show he arm-twisted me into barhopping with him. My weakness of character resulted in blurred vision, a thunderous headache, and an unsteady gait. When I got home I noticed Bockman's box, filled with items I had purchased the day before, still parked outside his door. I puzzled over the box's erratic delivery schedule, then fell asleep on the living room sofa.

A sour stomach and a spinning room awakened me from a troubled dream of performing to an audience of stone-faced Amish elders. They had neither honored the two-drink minimum nor uttered a single laugh. I lurched from the sofa to the sink, dropped a tablet into a glass of water and watched the fizz. After chugging my drink, I returned to my refuge on the couch cushions. Thank God for darkness. The very thought of light was unsettling. Sleep finally returned.

An alert from my subconscious woke me wide-eyed and fully functioning. A bluish light flickered from underneath Bockman's bedroom door. Chains rattled and bolts slid. The door opened, and an eerie glow washed over the sofa. I pushed myself upright.

Bockman's bent figure stood in the open doorway, his beard long and disheveled. The once-proud cock feather dangled from his cap. His clothes were faded. A long rip in his over-jacket had been sloppily mended. Bockman could have passed for Coleridge's ancient mariner.

He reached out trembling hands, grasped the box and tugged it inside the room. Fluorescing particles trailed from around his body like smeared paint fading into thinness. Before I could yell at him, the door slammed and the locks reset.

I bounded from my seat and tried to force my way through the closed door. Yikes. I jerked my hand back. The handle was too hot to touch. What the hell was going on? Was any of this real?

Cold water on my head seemed like a reasonable recovery tactic for a delusional drunk. I centered my scalp under the faucet and turned the handle wide open. Water cascaded through my hair and down to my neck. I cupped my hands under the flowing stream and splashed my face. Then I pushed my head back and shook it like a wet spaniel.

Had I imagined the glowing image of Bockman retrieving his box? I looked at Bockman's door to reassure myself that the box was still there. It wasn't. I stuck my head back under the cold water.

— — —

Two days later Hippo pulled me aside during the first What's Up? intermission. He seemed more serious than his usual buoyant self. Did he have a negative critique of my performance?

"Elliot, I need a favor," he said. "Benny bailed on me. He was supposed to open for me on a cruise-ship gig. Can you pinch hit for him?" He reached over, ran his ham-sized hand over my head and messed my hair. "Good money, endless food, oodles of spare time. Also lovely and lonely ladies to entice a handsome bachelor like you. Fourteen days, free cabin, clean sheets."

My mind was still befuddled from Bockman's strange appearance. My preoccupation had affected my act. Even though I couldn't see the audience in the darkened room, I could sense I wasn't connecting with them. Laughs had been hard to come by. Maybe a little working vacation would help me sort things out.

I gave feeble consideration to Bockman's lists and his battered box. But if the guy wanted to be a hermit and play erotic fantasy computer games behind closed doors, it was not my problem. Besides, Hippo had said all the right words in the right sequence: ladies, free room, and maid service.

"You're on, Fat Boy," I said. "As long as I don't have to room with you."

— — —

My tanned body manifested outer evidence of my inner health. A couple of shipboard romances had added some spice and boosted my male ego. The cruise had lived up to its brochure's promises, a rare feat. I slammed shut my Chinatown apartment door with my foot and bowled my luggage across the floor in the general direction of my bedroom. Then I saw it.

The wooden sides were a wreck, scarred, cracked, and split. The top had been covered with cowhide tacked into place with bronze studs. The sideboards had turned the color of black walnut. Bockman's box awaited me.

The lid was jammed. A couple of well-placed kicks knocked it open. A scrap of parchment rested in one corner. Ink splotches and smears littered the paper. A shaky hand had scribbled a terse message.

> E: Urgent. Lady Greyhurst is playing Lord Weston for a fool at my expense. Send an instruction book on dueling with swords. Make haste. B.

The note could have been two weeks old. I pictured Bockman

in a royal twist because I hadn't jumped on his request. I needed to get right on it.

I googled "How to duel" and found an out-of-print book titled *Defending Your Honor with Sword and Dagger.* Paid extra to have it overnighted to me. I tucked a brief note of apology between the pages and tossed the book in the box.

Days passed but Bockman never retrieved the book and box. Then one morning I woke to find the box had disappeared. All these strange happenings made me question why I bothered to stay involved with Bockman. The reason must have been my fascination with odd people and quirky situations, a dependable source for my comic routines. But I hadn't yet found a way to incorporate Bockman's antics into my act.

Then Linda, a luscious lady from the cruise ship, called. We chatted, joked about our first meeting and recounted our fun times together. She invited me to play house with her. How could I say no to a romp along with free rent? I threw some clothes into a suitcase and headed out the door to give her my acceptance, person-to-person.

Two days later, a nagging voice in my head reminded me that I needed to tidy up some loose ends and collect my belongings. I returned to my old apartment. Uh-oh. Bockman's box was propped against his bedroom door.

The lid half gone, the leather covering peeled and ripped. One iron strap was missing. Several wooden sideboards were split, blackened, and scorched. What had caused all the damage? The to-and-fro trips had always been rough on the box, but now the container looked like it had been hit by a Kansas tornado.

Bockman had always tried to repair his mail bin. Had somebody else dispatched the box on its latest journey? Not my problem. I didn't belong to the Save-The-Box League. I needed to end my rental arrangement and get away from Bockman's preposterous scenario. Besides, lovely Linda from the cruise awaited my attention.

I backdated a two-weeks termination notice to my absent landlord, deeming it a proper way to end our agreement. I put the note and door key in an envelope. I dangled the envelope over the open box and looked inside.

Pages from the sword-fighting book lay scattered on the bottom of Bockman's box. I found a crumpled ball of parchment scrunched in one dusty corner and retrieved it. Maybe Bockman had sent me a belated thank-you note for sending him the gold. Didn't matter. Long-term commitments weren't my style. I was through with the phony Robin Hood.

Except, I couldn't ignore this note. I smoothed out the vellum scrap. The writing looked like it had been done with the end of a charcoal stick.

Help.
Chained in dungeon.
Break down door.
Believe what you see.

— FOUR —

Through the Door

I needed to jump-start my strategy for rescuing the imprisoned Bockman. I tracked down a half-full bottle of English gin that languished in the kitchen cabinet. I filled a tumbler with ice cubes, grasped the gin bottle by the neck, and parked myself on the sofa to evaluate Bockman's strange message. By the time the second glass was empty, I had settled my mind on three facts and a couple of "what ifs?"

Fact one. I hadn't seen Bockman since the night he stood in his doorway, trailing glowing particles. The problem? The reliability of my sighting was on par with that of a hunter encountering Bigfoot. In my drunken state, hallucination had to be considered. But since that spooky night, I hadn't found a scrap of evidence that Bockman had visited our shared living space. No dirty dishes, trash, or misaligned sofa cushions. Conclusion: He really had disappeared.

Fact two. Bockman was a strange duck, all wrapped up in Old English lore. Eccentric, yes. Stupid, no. He was astute enough to be the founder of Particle Shift Technology Corporation. That implied he had filed California incorporation papers. The state was tight-assed about proper business registrations.

Fact three. Bockman, or someone, had put the silver teapot and pewter charger in the box. Zimmerman validated that the items were genuine seventeenth-century English antiques in pristine condition. Explain that. And Bockman's gold signet ring had also been included in the shipment, a foreshadowing of trouble.

Bockman's note claimed he was being held captive in a dungeon. He assumed or prayed that a plea for help would get through to me. The only link between the two of us had been the box that appeared and disappeared. Now he was raising the ante?

But if Bockman were locked up, who could have sent the box? A romantic soul would yearn for Lady Greyhurst's involvement. Some part of me wanted to meet the ex-mistress who inspired two guys to fight a duel to win her favor, or favors. No matter how it turned out, this adventure offered a rich vein of comedy material to be mined from Bockman and Lady Greyhurst's misguided love affair. Based on what? I had no details. Even my free-rent agreement wasn't in writing. Not even a handshake.

But what if all this was a ploy? Bockman's plea—and the box shuttle—merely part of a silly computer game. What if I broke down his door and found him sitting in his baggy tights, laughing at my naiveté? Was he testing me to see if I had followed his instructions? If so, I could claim that my attempt to rescue him entitled me to lifetime free rent, a worthy payoff. But if he were gone, where would I go? Given my history of short-term relationships, I couldn't count on staying with Linda the Cruise Lady.

I went over to my bedroom door and measured its thickness with my fingers, an inch and a half at the most. Bockman's should be identical. Now, where was my toolbox? I dropped to my hands and knees and groped under the bed. Every bachelor has a set of handyman tools. You never knew when you could earn extra points by fixing some gal's broken whatever.

I lugged my kit into the living room and took out my favorite battery-powered reciprocating saw. Revved the motor to the max and set to work cutting a hole in Bockman's locked door big enough for me to step through. Maybe his dungeon also had a wooden door. Piece of cake. I had my tools. And thanks to my gin-induced buzz, I needed both hands to steady the saw.

The blade chattered a downward arc through the door's panel. Sawdust fell onto the floor, covering my shoes. Neighbors must be wondering about the daytime racket. Bockman didn't impress me as a guy who made loud noises. Chirping was more his style.

I guided my vibrating blade through the six o'clock position and circled back towards twelve. The fresh-cut section hung in place like a super-sized porthole without hinges. My cut was now complete. Not bad for a blitzed handyman. And just in case something dangerous lurked inside Bockman's inner sanctum, I had better take my trusty power saw with me.

I kicked the circular cut as hard as I could. Wood flew inward. I stepped through the hole in the door and did my best imitation of a cop entering a dark, unknown danger zone. I crouched with my improvised weapon in front of me, ready to drill anyone who might threaten me. Actually, saber-saw him.

"Bockman?" I called.

No response. On my right, a man-sized form hid in the shadows. Danger. My finger tightened, and the saw surged to full power.

"That better be you," I yelled and turned to confront the threat.

My eyes adjusted to the room's dim light. Mounted on the right wall was a larger-than-life movie poster. Its wood frame spanned from floor to almost the ceiling. The colorful theater poster heralded *Technicolor*. Red words against a brown background proclaimed the message: *The Adventures of ROBIN HOOD. STARRING ERROL FLYNN*. My shadow man was an old movie portrait of a Hollywood actor.

"Clear," I shouted.

No Bockman. No threat. The room was empty. The absurdity of my actions brought me down from my adrenaline high.

Bockman had claimed the locked room was his inner sanctum,

office and computer center. This hideaway was hardly larger than a common workstation cubicle. The desktop held a standard computer setup. An olive-drab futon in one corner of the room was the only thing that qualified as bedroom furniture. The whole cubicle, complete with the black metal chair resting on an oversized plastic floor mat, looked like it had been lifted out of a failed small business.

I paced around the small room looking for another exit, a backdoor that would allow Bockman to come and go without being seen or heard. Perhaps hidden stairs leading to a courtyard or a trapdoor, something, anything. I struck out. My fresh-cut porthole through the door was the only entrance.

Iron security bars filtered outside light through a smudged window high on the room's back wall. I reached up to the grime-coated window ledge and hoisted myself up for a better view. I saw an interior courtyard littered with trash. I craned my neck and looked towards the rooftops. The only street-level exit was on the courtyard's far side. A heavy, padlocked chain secured a rusted iron gate. Bockman hadn't gone through there. I let myself drop and landed back onto the floor without falling over.

I definitely needed to revise my strategy for finding my absent landlord. Printed flyers might work. Stick them on neighborhood telephone poles or fences. *Missing. Small man. Height: Around five feet. Last seen wearing a black cape and lime-green tights. Sandy-colored hair. Van Dyke beard. Tends to be out of focus.* Probably would get a few responses in San Francisco. Most likely requests to meet him.

I dusted dirt and a dried fly off my hands, pulled out the desk chair, and sat down. If this entry-level computer setup were any indication of his game-center capabilities, then the runt was playing with himself. I'd seen better workstations at the local library. Bockman's grand Robin Hood adventure must be his imagination run amok. He was as phony as my ex-wife's orgasms.

I studied the old, oversized movie poster. Above and behind the title lettering, a costumed Flynn pulled a bow and aimed an arrow at the movie audience. Olivia de Havilland stood behind Robin, her dark eyes lusting after her hero. Now I knew what Bockman's funky medieval costume had been patterned after. Poor guy's bird legs could never fill tights like Flynn's. And his ribbon-tied shoes were a limp contrast to Robin Hood's macho leather boots. Bockman had one detail right though. The jaunty cock feather in Robin's hat.

Something about the room nagged at me. Doing improv comedy taught me to pick up on details that define a scene. That experience had given me a sense of stage setting. I swiveled in Bockman's chair. What didn't fit?

I had expected to find Bockman's corporate office packed with high-tech gear. Instead, I had found a pedestrian plain-Jane office. Hell, Bockman's computer center didn't even have a bathroom. How had he managed? I never heard him use the one in the apartment. Only thing out of the ordinary was the Robin Hood poster.

An idea popped into my head. Happened to me on rare occasions. Bockman didn't run his company from this setup. This office had been staged for effect if someone intruded into the locked room. Designed to be ignored. Put down and dismissed.

"Can't fool me, Robin Hood Bockman." I held my portable power weapon in a gunslinger stance, trigger finger poised. "You devious little twerp."

With my best devilish grin I revved up my trusty saw and thrust at the poster. I aimed at Robin Hood's hat, cut deep and trimmed off the feather. The blade kicked. I pulled it free and jumped back. The violated poster emitted a pulsating beam of blue light.

FIVE

The Vial Stuff

My legs stumbled backwards without any command from my brain. I flung the power saw over my shoulder. Crash-smash sounds blasted from behind me, followed by a bright electrical flash. I crossed outstretched hands to shield my face from the throbbing light. A laser beam from that cut poster might drill out my eyeballs. Acrid smoke assaulted my nose. I fell into the chair with momentum that sent it rolling into the desk.

I squeezed my eyelids shut. Red spots danced in my closed eyes. Then I opened my eyes the absolute minimum squint required to see. The light from the saw-cut slit cast a blue slash on the far wall. The intensity of the color rose and fell as if it were breathing. I spun the seat around, away from the laser-beaming poster.

My whole body shook worse than during my last hangover. I buried my head in my hands. Hey, I'm no wimp. But how was I supposed to react to an unprovoked attack by an inanimate movie poster?

"Damn," I said. "Bockman, you pint-sized bastard."

Time for damage assessment. Arms and legs still attached? Check. Brain? Addled. Check. I was unharmed, a modest but important victory. Reassured for the moment, I raised my head and surveyed damage to the cubicle area. My portable saber-saw was embedded in Bockman's computer monitor. Its power-pack handle jutted from the broken glass screen. That explained the noise and electrical flash.

I congratulated myself for having the fortitude to keep my feet firmly planted and not to run away. My worry about a crazed killer waiting behind Bockman's door had been overblown. And, best of all, I now had a clue. The movie poster concealed the source of the blue light—another room. I rubbed my hands together in exaggerated glee like an old-time silent-screen actor. Now, how best to proceed with my adventure?

"Bockman, never fear," I shouted at the poster. "Your knight in shining armor is about to charge forth to your rescue."

False bravado. Errol Flynn wasn't impressed. Neither was Olivia.

So, did Robin Hood hide an entrance? I stood beside the poster, avoided the cut, then thumped my fists around the picture's framing. The fifth whack, right next to Robin's quiver of arrows, did the trick. Click. The poster frame popped open an inch, like the hood on a car allowing access to the inside latch. The pulsating blue light slowed, then settled into a low-intensity glow.

I ran my hand behind the poster, found the latch and pulled. Robin Hood swung aside. If Bockman's hidden room was based on his fantasies, the place might look like Sherwood Forest. I took a deep breath, covered my eyes with one hand, and stepped over the threshold.

I counted to ten, then separated my middle fingers for a guarded view. I stood on the command deck of the Star Ship Enterprise: controls, displays, computers mounted everywhere. Soft blue light bathed the control room.

"Captain Kirk," I called out in my best imitation of an authoritarian voice. "What have you done with Bockman?"

The blue light stirred and swirled to the sound of my words. A grid of red lines scanned me from head to toe. The computer was gathering information about my body, measuring, and testing.

"You are not Bockman," the computer's flat guttural voice declared.

Bright lights raced around the edges of one wall-mounted monitor like some garish casino sign. The screen was cabled to a serious-looking computer that dominated the center wall across from the entrance. Must be the boss machine.

"Not Bockman," the voice added. "No entrance."

What's this, Club Bockman's surly electronic bouncer? Maybe I should have affected a Scottish brogue and asked to be beamed up—or in. I stepped forward to test its security.

"Warning. Do not advance," the machine-generated voice ordered.

The hair on the back of my neck stood at attention. I was ready to salute, but to whom or what? My standard method of dealing with aggressive people was to joke with them. Say something funny to break the tension. I have talked my way out of two muggings and three DUI stops. I'm good at schmoozing.

"Ah, hello, Mr. Computer. Chill," I said. "I am here to rescue Edward Bockman."

I spoke each word with forced clarity. My experience with help-desk voice-recognition systems suggested this essential tactic. Problem was, I had no response buttons to press. So I listened for instructions just in case the menu had changed.

"I'm sorry," the voice said. "The word rescue is not correlated with Bockman. Try another word."

The computer was being helpful. Sounded like something Bockman would have programmed. I briefly considered asking to be transferred to the machine's supervisor. But a different vocabulary might do the trick.

"Benefit." I waved my hand in a cordial greeting. "Save. Assist."

"Warning, warning. Do not advance. Danger."

The computer was being obstinate. If I ignored the order, would I be zapped by a death ray? Bockman didn't impress me as the kind of misanthrope who would fry an intruder. However, the way he was immersed in playing Robin Hood, he might twang an arrow at me.

"Help. Lend a hand." I was running out of synonyms. "Throw a life preserver."

"Negative. Leave." The blue light shifted along the color spectrum. Moving from royal blue to indigo. "You have sixty seconds. Counting."

A whirring sound accompanied the computer command. A red laser beam centered on my chest and created a bull's eye over my heart. Wonderful, I had managed to piss off a computer. That was a first for me.

"Okay. Hold your fire." I held up my hands. "I'm leaving. Sorry I ever met Bockman. Let him rot in his dungeon. I'm tired of being his box jockey."

"Box?" The whirring diminished. "Welcome, Box. You are free to enter."

The blue light settled down like a vigilant guard dog called off by his master. I sauntered into Bockman's computer center, pretending I belonged.

"Same to you," I said. "Thank you. Gracias. Merci." Who knew what Bockman had programmed into his gatekeeper routines? "And up yours," I muttered, just to cover all bases.

"You are welcome, Mr. Box." The computer-generated voice was placid, a far cry from its original bullying tone. The surrounding light softened to baby blue.

A super-sized reclining chair sat in front of a monster monitor.

Two joysticks flanked a keyboard. Above them, a junior version of a jumbo-jet instrument panel crowded with an intimidating array of gauges, switches, and displays. All hidden in Bockman's basement apartment. He must have had a device to measure every important variable, including two oversized digital clocks labeled "Now" and "Then" mounted directly over the main monitor.

I eased onto the command seat, taking care to keep my hands away from any switches or buttons. An impression of a human hand was molded into a square metal unit mounted into the right armrest. *Bio-metric Labs* was stamped onto the metal frame. Beneath it, a printed label: Fingerprint Scanner Model XC-352. The biometric security should have ended my quest to find Bockman. But leave it to my kooky landlord to have done something off-the-wall.

A yellow Post-it note stuck onto the fingerprint read: "Problem: My particle shift technology scrambles fingerprint patterns. Things to do: (1) Program bypass routine. (2) Get refund from manufacturer." Bockman had penciled himself a reminder. No fancy ink script this time.

What was I getting myself into? The whole setup reeked of unknown dangers and unpredictable technology. Bockman had ended up in a dungeon. I didn't want to join him there. I settled back in the command chair, put my hands behind my head and rested against the cushioned seat.

Now what? My instincts advised me to avoid this weirdness. But the disabled fingerprint device could also be an omen to move forward. Based on Bockman's Post-it note, anyone could now access the system. My mission, should I choose to accept it, was to go where Bockman had gone before. Locate the imprisoned techie goober, free him, and get us both back safely. Then present my bill for services rendered.

Dungeon. The very word turned me off. Weren't dungeons dark, dank, and full of rats? The only character I could recall who had escaped from a dungeon in fine fettle was the Count of Monte Cristo. The author, Dumas, had his bedraggled hero, assumed dead and tossed into the sea, then emerge both wealthy and titled. But Bockman was a kook, not a count.

I decided to take a tentative step forward, like testing the surface ice on a frozen lake. It couldn't hurt to communicate with my landlord's high-tech gatekeeper. I might even get him to reveal Bockman's whereabouts.

"Hey, Blue Light," I said. "Wake up."

No response. The color didn't change. The pale-blue light must be taking a siesta. Or I was being ignored. I needed to bond with this inanimate bucket of chips, circuits, and codes. But how to establish rapport with my landlord's electronic sidekick? Maybe Bockman had assigned a code name to the computer. Perhaps he had selected one of Robin Hood's buddies.

"Friar Tuck, Little John, Will Scarlet," I offered. Nothing. Not even a computer-generated response of "You talking to me?" I switched sexes. "Maid Marian." How about a good guy? "King Richard." Bad guys? "King John. The Sheriff of Nottingham."

No reaction. The computer was not buying my initial approach. Same problem I had with pickup lines in a bar.

"Box," I said.

The light moved in a lazy pattern, like a person waking from a sound sleep. A visual version of "Hmmm, what?"

"Identity confirmed," the disemboweled voice acknowledged. "Yes, you are Box."

"Box equals friend," I said.

"Entry accepted."

It didn't sound too impressed. Kind of like the way restaurant hostesses treat me when I walk in with confirmed reservations. Might as well go for the power. I smiled a plastic greeting like a loan officer.

"Friend equals command," I said.

"Negative. Bockman One equals Command." The light intensity remained level, as unemotional as a polite but firm security guard.

"Well, Command has got himself in a pickle," I said.

"No food served during transmission," the metallic voice countered.

A flippant computer, just what I needed. The computer must have wanted me to think logically, which for an improv comedian like me was the kiss of death. Time to turn the tables.

"Bockman Computer. What is your name?" No more Mr. Anonymous. Cough up. Confess, you binary bastard. I tried a fake German accent. "You vill gif me your name."

"Bockman Two." Formal, like we had never been properly introduced. The light was as unemotional as a Norwegian minister.

"Bockman Two same as Bockman One?" I could hear a glimmer of hope in my voice. Maybe I could interchange control commands.

"Affirmative."

"Hallelujah," I declared. Now I was getting somewhere.

"Hal bad computer." The blue color shifted along the spectrum to a purple hue. Held the shade for a moment then morphed to azure. "Bockman Two good."

"Enter new name," I said, putting as much authority as I could muster into my voice. "Computer new name equals, ah, Blue," I said. The moniker was the first thing from my lips. Spontaneous.

Good thing I had never named kids. "Blue equals friend equals Box."

"How may I help you? Mr. Box Friend?"

"Tell me what the hell is going on," I said.

"Hell not currently in database. Try another location and time. Current location entry is England. Please enter exact dates and GPS coordinates. Caution. Incomplete entries could be hazardous to your health."

The clocks above the monitor lit up. The "Now" clock displayed the current date and time. The "Then" clock showed July 7, 1665.

"Yeah, sure. 1665," I mumbled.

I needed to find Blue's user manual. Should be close by the command chair. Next to my right knee was a wide compartment. I opened the door and rummaged through the drawers. Success. I found a white three-ring binder filled with Bockman's notes, computer printouts, and a sketch labeled Lady Greyhurst's Garden.

The first page was a downer. Red border around a capitalized, bold-font warning. DANGER. HYDRATION IS ESSENTIAL TO TIME TRAVEL. DRINK ONE VIAL PARTICLE ENHANCEMENT LIQUID THIRTY MINUTES BEFORE LAUNCH.

This was all too much to comprehend. I needed help. Just in case I had flipped out and didn't realize it.

"Blue." I struggled to control my breathing. "Tell Box Friend the truth," I said. "Date and location of Bockman One?"

"London, England. Year, 1665."

Wow, Bockman really had devised a method of time travel. Then I tapped on my mental brakes. Step by step I was letting myself be sucked into a high-risk attempt to rescue my whacky landlord. I had engaged in wild adventures when growing up. But once I started making my own living, those carefree days had faded away.

Did I really want to chase after Bockman in some convoluted attempt to recapture that youthful excitement? Let's face it. My current life as a second-rate comedian with a string of temporary girlfriends wasn't too exhilarating. Boring, in fact. That was another reason I liked Hippo as a friend—he never made me face my obvious faults.

"Blue," I said. "Where is Particle Enhancement Liquid?"

Off to my left, a wall panel slid open. Hanging in the narrow enclosure was a bandoleer. The over-the-shoulder soldier's belt should have held cartridges. Instead, slim glass vials were inserted through the loops where bullets would have been. According to the manual, this was essential travel juice.

I reached over, took the bandoleer off the hook and placed it on my lap. After a few deep breaths to steady my hand, I used my thumb and index finger to wiggle one of the vials free. I tilted the glass tube. A yellow-greenish liquid moved. Loathsome, vile stuff that looked like cloudy urine mixed with pond scum. Toxic waste left over from some environmental disaster. I was supposed to drink this crap? Maybe the solution was to add alcohol to the slime. Mix the first slime martini.

Creating a palatable Particle Enhancement drink was only the first step. Blending into the local scene of 1665 was going to be critical. Going back to year 1665 required historical research, period clothing, and authentic money. I didn't want a mob of irate citizens hounding my alien ass through the city's dark streets like a pack of pitchfork-wielding peasants chasing Frankenstein. Or burning me as a warlock.

I needed a historian who would not report me to the medical authorities as a nut case. Hippo Hyman, my comic mentor, was the right man. I slung the bandoleer over my shoulder.

"Blue?"

"Yes, Box Friend?"

"Box exit now, return later," I said. "I must talk to Hippo."

"Hippo," Blue said. "Scientific name *Hippopotamus amphibious.* Greek for River Horse. Large, short-legged mammal with broad, wide mouth."

"Yep. That's my man," I said. "Blue. Open address file." I had to find a local contact, a friendly person to aim me in the right direction to search for Bockman. "Subject: Bockman One Personal. 1665. London, England. Names."

"One matching entry." The blue light started its simulated breathing rhythm, faster and faster, building towards a crescendo.

"And who might that be?" I said. "Chips ahoy, Blue. Spit out the digits, cough up the syllables."

"Lady," Blue purred, "Greyhurst."

SIX

Tripping the Light Fantastic

I found Hippo in the What's Up? Comedy Club's lounge. Hippo's favorite table was off to one side of the room, underneath a lighted wall sconce. He liked to camp there during that downtime between lunch and dinner, while the staff cleaned up the noontime mess around him and prepped for the evening show.

Hippo scowled at me as I approached. I learned long ago that during the day he preferred to sit alone, read, or sketch on a small pad. Hippo welcomed neither company nor interruption.

"Oh great Master of HOHO HAHA." I went down on one knee and genuflected. "Your humble servant begs an audience. See, I have brought a bag of fresh-baked pastry as an offering."

People assumed because Hippo was fat and funny, he was not serious or smart. Hey, the man had two degrees, history and fine arts. I had once asked Hippo why, with all his education, he got into stand-up comedy for a living.

"Elliot," he had said. "I can't fit into office cubicles, pose for underwear ads, or impress clients. But I can laugh at myself and laugh with people."

Hippo placed a bookmark between the pages of an oversized coffee-table book. I glanced at the title. He was studying *Toulouse-Lautrec, 118 reproductions with 55 in full color.* The cover picture featured a woman flashing her long red stockings while she danced.

"Looks like a hot babe." I gestured at the colorful book jacket. I affected an exaggerated leer. "Can you introduce me?"

"Not unless you happen to be in Paris at the Moulin Rouge in 1890." Hippo patted the book cover to emphasize his point.

"I just might be able to arrange that." I pulled up a chair across from him and tore open the doughnut sack. Fanned my hand back and forth to nudge the aroma toward him. "History, one of your favorite subjects," I said. "And I'll tell you something so crazy you won't believe me. Science-fiction stuff."

"Let me smell your breath." Hippo wrapped his oversized hand around my neck and pulled me closer. "If you're plastered, I might be a figment of your imagination and you're really talking to yourself."

Then he poked a sausage-sized finger through the holes in two doughnuts and examined the skewered treats. He took a huge bite out of the first tire-shaped goody. I relaxed a bit.

"Pretty please," I said. "Hippo, I'm prepared to grovel and whine."

"I'll give you five minutes per doughnut, half hour, a half-dozen. Deal?" He mouthed his offer as powdered sugar fell from his lips onto the table.

"Okay, but don't interrupt me." I reserved one glazed doughnut for myself, pulling it to safety. "Assume what I tell you is true. The technology exists to transport me back in time," I said. "How do I pass for a citizen of the era? How can I take advantage of being in 1665 to make some money? Buy cheap real estate or something."

"And when is your fantasy novel due to be published?" Hippo wet one finger, sponged fallen crumbs from the tabletop. He tried to look bored, but a flicker of interest twitched at his eyes as he polished off the sugary debris.

"Work with me on this, Hippo," I urged. "Suspend disbelief."

Hippo moved his jaw round and round while his brain grappled with my problem. At least, I hoped that's what was happening. He could be working on a new comedy routine about a delusional friend who believed in time travel.

"I suppose," Hippo agreed, "I could give you a history lesson.

"Can you think of any way for me to make my fortune while I'm back there?" As long as I was risking my life for Bockman, I might as well take advantage of the situation. "Something that would pay off when I returned to modern time?"

"Can you bring objects back?" Hippo asked. He had an open-mouthed expression while examining the ceiling like he was expecting an answer from heaven.

"Yes, in the box," I said. "Hippo, it's all very complicated."

My voice lacked confidence. My depth of knowledge was shallow. I believed Bockman's technology worked. But I didn't understand how, kind of like a kid riding in a car.

"As long as you are backdated to old England," Hippo continued. "I would seek out several famous artists who were not yet recognized by their contemporary critics. Buy their paintings cheap. Bring the best back to today. Then subsequently have them discovered in an old attic or maybe mounted behind a modern painting in an old frame. Both are time-tested techniques for changing a dollar into a couple hundred thousand, or even millions."

"Give me some guidelines," I said. "The only art I know is a talent agent named Art Felder down in Los Angeles."

"I can give you a list of artists' names." Hippo broke a doughnut in half and stuffed a piece in each cheek making his already puffed face look like a super-sized chipmunk. "Of course," Hippo mouthed, "if you want big bucks, get your hands on portraits of King Charles II or any of the royalty." He swallowed with an audible gulp. "Better still. Miniatures. It was the fashion for high-society men and women to have themselves painted in miniature.

Samuel Cooper, for example, did one of Lady Castlemaine. The Queen of England owns it in her royal collection."

"Miniatures," I enthused. "Perfect size. A whole lot would fit into the box."

Now I had an attainable goal other than rescuing Bockman. And I already had a contact at the royal court. Lady Greyhurst. She should know which local artists painted miniatures of lords and ladies.

Sometime while I wasn't paying attention, my glazed doughnut had disappeared. I rummaged around the table legs trying to see if I had accidentally knocked it onto the floor during my animated discussion. No such luck. Hippo had exceeded his caloric quota.

"Okay, Elliot," Hippo said. "I'll give you a bit of history about the 1660s and old London." He finger-tapped his forehead. "Even at the risk that you are currently dwelling in Fruitcakeville."

"Don't forget King Charles II," I reminded Hippo.

"Old Rowley was his nickname," Hippo said. "Called him that after one of his breeding stallions. The jolly monarch had a reputation as a stud. Fathered a dozen or so bastards."

"I hope to have a date with one of his mistresses," I said.

"Can't help you there." Hippo said. "Your track record with women has not been marked with great success." He secured his Toulouse book under one arm and pushed his chair back. "However, as to finding correct period clothing, I will give you the address of Alice Ho. She's a seamstress who makes many of the local Renaissance Pleasure Faire costumes. She also sews for the opera and Shakespeare Theater." He waved a paw in the general direction of the What's Up? bar and pantomimed chugging a beer. "I'll buy the first round."

"My doughnut went missing," I said. "Only a guilty man would be so generous."

"This period in English history is called the Restoration," Hippo pontificated, ignoring my quip. "Young Charles II was declared King seventeen days after his father lost his head for real, not figuratively—in 1649."

Hippo was off and running. With words, not motion. I trudged after him while mentally patting my pockets for a pen. I should take notes.

— — —

Alice Ho's shop was squeezed between two Chinatown retail stores. The narrow, wood-framed door featured an upper-half window. A small sign taped to the glass said *Theater Costumes and Dressmaking*. I knocked on the door to announce my arrival, twisted the knob and walked in.

A petite Asian woman, dressed in black pants and a matching boat-collar blouse, perched on the edge of a low stool. Screeching and discordant music assaulted my ears. She looked over the upper rims of her spectacles, nodded a greeting, and turned off the radio.

"You the comedian," she said.

Not a question. A statement. I hadn't uttered a word, and she didn't fit the typical customer profile at my comedy performances. How did she know me?

"Hippo must have called," I said, "and warned you."

She covered her mouth and tee-heed behind her hand. She ducked behind the counter and reappeared holding a long cardboard box.

"This you lucky day," she said. "I have costume for you. Need alteration so pass for sixteen-hunnut period."

She tugged off the cardboard top and displayed the outfit. Then she put the box on the countertop and whipped off the thin white measuring tape that dangled from her neck. She held one end and positioned it level with my bellybutton.

"Hippo said measure you. Take off yo pant."

The things I did for Bockman. I unbuckled my belt. She placed one delicate hand on my arm to stop me, then doubled over with laughter.

"Hippo Hyman is a dead man," I said.

Alice went right to work making the necessary modifications to my costume. She mumbled and chatted to herself while she sewed. Twice she had me standing around in my boxers while she pinned and measured the outfit.

Forty-five minutes later, I emerged from the store. Tucked under my arm was a polyester version of a more-or-less historically accurate English gentleman's costume, wrapped in pink tissue paper. I hoped no one got close enough to my neck to read the label.

Hippo had given me a crash course on life in the 1660s and also the reign of King Chuck Two. He straightened me out on one thing. Bockman had gotten so carried away with his fantasy costume that he messed up his history. Robin Hood was more thirteenth century than the seventeenth. Richard the Lionhearted and Mr. R. Hood of the Sherwood Forest subdivision preceded the reign of Charles II by four hundred years.

A puzzlement. Smart guy like Bockman had to have known the difference. No wonder they had locked him up. I'd have to ask Bockman about that little historic inconsistency when I sprung him out of the dungeon.

Then I had a bad thought. Real bad. What if Bockman's time travel computer program had a glitch, over- or undershooting the target date? I needed to ask Blue to clarify the program's degree of time accuracy for hours, days, weeks, months, years, decades, and centuries. What color did Blue's light turn if he told a lie? Or withheld vital information?

SEVEN

Riding the Blue Express

Blue greeted me as Box Friend when I returned to the control room. I slouched in the command chair trying to fathom the launch sequence. Bockman's flight manual was a collection of computer printouts, handwritten notations and yellow sticky notes. Grammatical errors and misspellings littered page after page. No helpful hints like Start, First, or Step One. His scribbled notes were reminders to himself, not to others. Time seemed to melt like ice cream in August as I pored over the contents of Bockman's three-ring binder.

My personal skill-set didn't include advanced technology. I did an eeny, meeny, miney, mo routine and picked a couple of displays that looked important. I boned up on their functions and ignored the other devices.

"Blue," I said. "Question. First launch. Was there a malfunction in the time setting?"

"Calibration error." Blue confirmed. "Target, 1265 Delivery, 1665. More or less. Programming error corrected in Beta Version 6.2."

That dubious assurance knotted my stomach. Now, where in the computer center could I find the box's storage site? It was packed with items I might need for survival. Was there a bin for the box? I searched for an hour and almost gave up. Then I noticed four L-shaped brackets screwed into the platform behind the command chair. Box's corners fit snug against metal guides.

My search for the exact launch site for myself proved fruitless. No instruction sign in the computer room said "Stand Here." No arrow pointed to "Launch Area. No Smoking." I had the nagging feeling Blue was chuckling his chips at my incompetence.

The computer had forecast that optimum launch time would occur in six hours. In my mind the word *optimum* and *less danger* were synonymous. Bockman had posted warnings against lightning, rain, or wind shear during launch. Optimum better be concerned with more than the weather if I was going to be safe.

"Blue, Box Friend, help," I said.

"Scheduled maintenance. Twenty minutes until completion."

The monitor displayed a cartoon character of Bockman with a busty woman. She stood on the edge of a swimming pool, applying sun tan lotion to his back. He wore his feathered Robin Hood cap and nothing else. The pool steadily filled. A yellow rubber ducky floated on the surface. Depth markings calibrated in time intervals were painted on each side of the pool. I watched the rising water level cover the twenty-minute marker, then fifteen minutes, and finally ten. The countdown was ten minutes longer than my patience.

"Blue. Box Friend. Help. Now," I insisted.

"Yes? Yes? Box Friend."

It was like I had interrupted him. Can computers be annoyed? Tough, it was my ass on the line.

"Identify launch location," I ordered. Four hours remained. I had to find the pad. Store the box.

"No such entry in index. Modify search. Check spelling."

I got up from the command chair and walked to the center of the room, spread my arms wide and tilted my head backwards.

"What, Bockman? What am I supposed to do?" I shouted. "If you were here, I'd tie you to a chair and force you to listen to four hours of bad jokes. Then I'd shove you on stage and make you open for my act."

"OPEN." The display screen flashed the word in large, bold letters. Light around the base of the walls intensified, ascending like a stage curtain being raised. The bluish glow crept up the walls, then flowed onto the center of the ceiling to condense into a six-foot-wide circle. Shimmering ribbons of light appeared, luminous streamers of color. An aurora borealis of charged particles.

The sight triggered a cascade of emotions. Awe, fear, and joy coursed through my body. The lights formed concentric circles spinning faster and faster. A rainbow vortex hovered two feet below the ceiling. Now I understood. The entire room was the launch pad. What to do next? God, I was confused. What if I pushed the wrong button and vaporized myself?

"Enter launch initiation password," Blue advised.

Password? I didn't know I needed a stinking password to launch. And I wasn't dressed for the seventeenth century. I couldn't show up in jeans and T-shirt. I still had to drink the Particle Enhancement slime and find the damn password.

"Blue, discontinue launch program," I said. "Reset. Hold your horses. Stop."

"SEQUENCE HALTED." The aurora faded away.

"Blue," I said. "Box Friend. Exit."

I picked up the launch manual in one hand and slipped the bandoleer across my chest. As I headed for my bedroom, I swore I heard the word "Rookie" uttered.

"Behave," I threatened, "or I'll unplug you."

I positioned my pillow behind my head and leaned back against the headboard and opened Bockman's launch manual. I had to locate the hidden password. Somewhere, the code word waited for me. I kept returning to the final countdown page. Bockman had drawn a picture of a medieval siege machine.

Nice try at hiding the password, Bockman, but I'm a visual kind of guy, better with images than numbers. I smacked the manual shut with a satisfying noise. Hooray. I had the word. Catapult. One last hurdle ahead.

"Attention, world," I shouted. "Mr. Super Comedian is on his way to rescue Bockman."

If I didn't get creamed in the process.

— — —

Ready to go. I had crossed every item off my "To Do" list. And decided not to clean out the refrigerator. Even my costume looked good on me, although I was a bit self-conscious wearing tights under my breeches. Alice Ho's costume didn't include long silk stockings for men. And she had replaced the elastic with a drawstring.

I retrieved the bandoleer from the headboard, where I had draped it for safekeeping. Six vials remained in the bandoleer. I needed one for the upcoming launch. The five remaining vials should be plenty to get both Bockman and me back from 1665. Of course, accompanied by my Buddy Box full of valuable miniature paintings.

One-thirty in the afternoon, the final half hour before launch. My nostrils flared at the mere thought of taking a full-strength dose of Particle Enhancement Liquid. I wiggled one vial free from the bandoleer and removed the stopper. This time was for real.

I held my nose and shut my eyes. Three. Two. One. I opened my mouth and poured. Bitter, acid, rancid. Gulp. The initial assault on my taste buds gave way to nasty impressions of wet newspapers, nail-polish remover, and burnt rubber. The old movie images of good Doctor Jekyll turning into evil Mr. Hyde paraded through my mind.

The mirror in my bedroom reflected a stranger. Some guy dressed like a Shakespearian actor looked back at me. Eye pupils dilated. Wired. A little disoriented. Spacey. An electric energy coursed through my veins. I balled my fists, threw mock right and left jabs. The same good-luck routine I always did before doing my comedy act. Then I hurried to the command center.

The sturdy oak box, packed with the slime bandoleer and survival items such as a butane lighter, compass, first aid kit, and water purification tablets had been secured in its floor clips. The sack purse attached to my waist contained the small gold bars I would use for money. Bockman's notes had claimed that gold could be transported with the time traveler. I liked the feel of it there. Timeless money.

I wiggled myself deeper into the command seat. How long would the launch take? Would some secret government agency clear me for take-off? Should I go to the bathroom? "Fasten Seatbelt" was one reminder I didn't need.

I patted the lap-and-shoulder harness for the umpteenth time, then double-checked the GPS coordinates and time/date settings. Reassured, I mouthed my mantra: 1665, London, Lady Greyhurst's garden. 1665, London, Lady Greyhurst's garden. An odd question occurred to me. What was Lady Greyhurst's first name? No matter now.

"Blue," I commanded. "Open."

The curtain of light arose. The aurora came to life.

"Enter launch initiation password," Blue intoned.

"Catapult," I yelled as if Blue were hard of hearing. I lifted my face toward the ceiling. The circle was forming, moving like a living being. Then it condensed and started spinning. I was on my way.

CAUTION. The monitor flashed a warning. DO NOT SEND HUMAN AND TRANSPORT BIN SIMULTANEOUSLY. PARTICLES MAY CROSS CONTAMINATE.

My heartbeat zoomed. The box's body and mine merging? Talk about ending up with a genuine English oak woodie.

"Blue. Confirm Box and Box Friend are safe." I couldn't keep the tremor from my voice. My feet were tap dancing.

"Sequence correct," Blue responded in his official tone. "Box transports nine minutes after Box Friend."

Bless your little blue light. I exhaled in one long expulsion of air. No problems so far.

"Box will be delivered in Year 1665 to home address stored on file." Sounds hummed from the computer.

"Wait. What address? Where does Bockman live?" I demanded. All my survival stuff was packed in Buddy Box. I struggled against the seat harness, but the straps held me secure. "Where is Box going?"

"Bockman One's London house," Blue announced. "Please sit back and enjoy the flight."

"Fat lot of good that does me. Tell me the street address," I pleaded. "Stop the train, let me off."

"Do not bother the Captain." Dials registered, displays sprang to life, gauges calibrated. "Seat Belt Sign is on."

The aurora whirled. Brilliant points of light arced across the color spectrum like shooting stars. Riveting. Beautiful and scary. Tears ran down my cheeks. The perfection of time. If I got through this, I'd stop drinking. Get a real job.

Static electricity raised the hairs on my arm. I should be wearing a crash helmet. Knee pads. The monitor turned red and flashed the warning:

Virus Protection License Has Expired.
Do you want to renew?

"Countdown initiated. Ten." Blue's voice was dictatorial.

"Wait." What the hell? Could a hacker hack me?

"Nine, eight," the computer droned the countdown.

"Buy, authorize, renew," I said. My head jerked. My teeth chattered. "Extend." My mind scrambled for the correct words. "Okay. You bet. Right on."

"Seven. Six. Five."

"Oh, hell, yes," I shouted.

"Four." Blue sounded anxious.

"Subscribe," I yelled. The light circles above blurred, spinning faster and faster. The console was a riot of sounds, sights, and motion. Then music blared, "As Time Goes By."

"Three . . ."

The screen displayed: "Thank you, Mr. Bockman. Your Visa Card account on file will be billed immediately. Would you like to receive emails regarding new products?"

"Two . . ."

"I'll buy one of everything," I screamed.

"One. Launch."

My feet disappeared below the ankles. Particles trailed away from my hands, like smoke. My senses dulled, drained. My gut was gone. Oh, God. I was coming apart. In front of me, a vision of bright sun melted snow on a river's edge. And my essence flowed into the river of time.

— EIGHT —

Lady Greyhurst

My first view of the landing site was obscured by an apple hanging three inches from my nose. I pulled aside leaves and tilted my head around the branch for a better view. Bockman, that Minion of Merrie England, had claimed in his notes that his particle shift technology avoided solids so the time traveler wouldn't end up inside a tree trunk or stacked-stone wall. The risk of emerging among semisolids, apple tree branches, for instance, must be somewhere in his footnotes.

From my vantage point high in the tree, I saw roofs of wooden houses and taller stone edifices. An unclouded sky and mild temperature promised a comfortable day. The clip-clop of horses' hooves resonated along with smells that suggested a multitude of people living too close together.

I didn't know if Bockman's computer had correctly delivered me into Lady Greyhurst's seventeenth-century London, but the city perspective seemed appropriate. Now, what else could I see? I twisted half-circle for a different view.

A stone wall surrounded an orderly garden below my perch. Geometric paths lined with low, well-trimmed boxwood and square flowerbeds filled with colorful blooms. Fruit trees, including the one I now inhabited, grew along the back wall. A small stone bench nestled near a fountain. If I accurately recalled the drawing in

Bockman's launch manual, the scene matched his sketch of Lady Greyhurst's garden.

Blue had delivered me to the right location, but my poor navigational skills had caused me to overshoot the garden pathway by ten feet and to land in the apple tree along the garden's back wall. I shifted position, and my footing gave away. Uh-oh. I fell through the branches. My flailing arms tried to slow my descent. I grabbed a limb and dangled above the ground. My arm muscles protested the weight of me. Then my hands slipped. I landed in a stumbling roll among fallen fruit.

I gathered myself and leaned against the tree trunk to take stock of my body parts and to get my bearings. All in all, my maiden voyage hadn't gone too badly. I could have emerged on a bell tower to dangle high above a cobbled street or done a freefall from a hundred feet above the ground.

"Pray, sir," a woman's soft voice inquired, "what are you doing in the garden behind my house?"

The voice startled me. My head jerked around. I'd been too busy gawking to notice I was not alone. A young woman dressed in a full-skirted outfit frowned at me. Her pale-yellow, off-the-shoulder gown exposed tantalizing cleavage. A deeper shade of yellow silk trimmed the bodice. Her hairstyle featured thin wisps of loose curls cascading on either side of her head. A single spit curl dangled over the center of her forehead.

"Would you believe my workers sell fruit in the market?" I shook a squished mess of rotten apples from my hands, plucked a ripe apple from a low-hanging limb, shined it on my sleeve and took a bite. "As the landowner, I insist on personal taste-testing for quality control. Your gardener said I could sample a few fallen apples."

"Well, then," she said. "You will have no trouble telling me what variety it is."

Slender arms protruded from puffed sleeves. Her skin showed a clear and glowing complexion. Late twenties, I'd guess. All in all, a nice package of youthful femininity. A mischievous smile from her full lips pressed me for an answer. But what did I know about apples except those that I had seen in the supermarket?

"Red Delicious," I ventured, "or maybe Granny Smith?"

"Is it a Devonshire or Nonpareil?" she asked. "Tell me which one was Queen Elizabeth's favorite apple." Her hands rested on her slender waist. "Come, sir, what say you? Turn around so I may see that you hold no hidden weapon with which to harm me."

I had no choice but to humor her request. I rotated in a slow circle, hands out from my sides. I gave her my best smile, a ploy that seldom worked to my advantage. But explaining my presence would only get me into more trouble. I could hardly say I'd popped in from the twenty-first century, looking to invite my buddy, Robin Hood, to our class reunion.

"You do realize the cheeks of your arse are wet with squashed apples?" Her hand moved to cover her mouth, but a giggle escaped. "You are a tall fellow and well-proportioned." Her eyes sparkled and seemed to hold no malice. "Play no more games with me. What is your name, and why do you sneak like a thief into the garden of my home?"

"Elliot of Vail," I said. "A traveler from Carolina in the New World." I did the bow and the arm-sweep thing I had seen Bockman do in his apartment. "I must confess this is my first visit to London. I lost my way and wandered into your garden. I am ignorant of the proper way to conduct myself."

"Carolina?" she said. "King Charles awarded those lands to his eight friends who assisted in restoring his monarchy. Methinks his gesture a reward far too vast for so small a service. They and their friends will reap riches from the King's generosity."

I didn't doubt for a moment that monetary calculations swirled inside her pretty head. I munched on the apple and waited while she mulled over the prospect of my being a beneficiary of estates and vast lands. She announced her decision with a slight bow.

"I am Lady Greyhurst," she said. "Perhaps I should venture to know you better, Elliot of Vail. But there be more to your tale than you profess. You might be a spy in the service of the French or Dutch. Prone to bribe good citizens like me for information from inside the court."

My body was starting to complain. The joints of my knees and arms ached. My muscles seemed like mush. Must be the aftereffects of a slime hangover and time lag. Bockman's equivalent of jet lag.

"To tell the truth," I said, "My travels have left me sore in body and parched in throat. Please give me a moment to recover." And time to make up some plausible tale.

"Indeed. You do look weary," she said. "Pray rest upon the garden bench."

I hobbled over to the stone bench and eased myself onto the seat. Lady Greyhurst kept a safe distance as she tapped her lips with a delicate finger, until she reached some conclusion about my presence in her garden. She gave me a civil smile, then joined me on the bench.

"It is pleasant here among the flowers." She sat next to me and struck a demure pose, hands folded in her lap. "Tell me of the New World. I have heard stories of thick forests filled with wild red Indians. Last September, the Dutch surrendered New Amsterdam to our Colonel Nocolls. I am curious about the city which has been renamed New York.

For a king's ex-mistress, she seemed a captivating lady with no hard edges. No wonder Bockman was enamored with her. But wait. I wasn't here to delight in Lady Greyhurst's attractions. My landlord needed rescuing, and Lady G had vital information. Time to listen. And ask a few discreet questions.

— — —

The muted rumble of wagons, shouts from drivers, and a horse's neigh merged with the buzz of city dwellers, providing a background for our conversation. The high stone walls made Lady Greyhurst's garden a peaceful refuge. The garden walkways led to her house, where a carved archway sheltered a half-opened Dutch door. The only other opening from the garden was along the back wall, where an iron-hinged gate, partially hidden by climbing ivy, promised an unobtrusive exit to the street.

"Elliot of Vail," she said. Her words were controlled, but nervous hands that adjusted and readjusted her sleeves evidenced inner tension. "When first I heard your strange words and odd Carolina accent, the sounds did grate upon my ears. But now I find its foreign nature somewhat charming."

Charming accent. Well, that was good news for the likes of me. I needed to sweet-talk her into taking me into her confidence. Top priority was getting her to direct me to Bockman's London house, where Blue had delivered Buddy Box filled with my survival gear.

"I would be most grateful," I said, "if you would tell me of King Charles and the court. We have no such royalty or culture where I live."

Not exactly true. San Francisco had its own cadre of queens and offbeat life-style. But I'm sure she wouldn't understand. Anyway, for some thirty minutes she chatted away, dispensing stray bits of information about the King and life at Whitehall Palace. The royal digs had a couple of thousand rooms. The King even had his own brewery. You got to love a palace like that.

"The only reason Charles married Catherine of Braganza,"

Lady Greyhurst said, "was because her father, the king of Portugal, enticed him with a large dowry. He even included the seaports of Tangier and Bombay as a sweetmeat in the agreement." She fingered a single strand of pearls that circled her slender neck, and added a coy smile for effect. "I should say, for the sweetmeat."

"All I know about Charles II," I said, "is what I have been told by a friend who is familiar with Samuel Pepys' observations." Hippo Hyman had quoted from Pepys' diary about the King's ladies. "He seems to be keeping a score on all the King's mistresses."

"And what," she said, "does Mr. Pepys, mere Member of Parliament and lowly naval administrator, say about me?"

Damn, I had blundered into her gotcha. Hippo's briefing had been vague on specifics. The depth of my knowledge about current events was as shallow as my annual New Year's resolution to quit drinking. But I had to coax information from her if I had any hope of finding Bockman.

"I . . . he . . . is most complimentary and discreet," I hoped she wouldn't press me for details.

"Discretion is scarce" she said. "Gossip is plentiful at court."

A grimace hardened the corners of her mouth. Anger flared the nostrils of her pert nose. Lady Greyhurst seemed put out that people talked about her putting out.

But she soon relaxed and seemed to appreciate friendly ears that didn't judge her status as ex-mistress of King Charles II. From what I had been told, it wasn't like she had suffered from any performance failure. England's Charlie the Duce went through his paramours like a conductor through a passenger train. *Next. Let me punch your ticket, my dear.* The King just had a short attention span.

"When he first laid eyes on Catherine," Lady Greyhurst said, "she wore her hair in corkscrew braids protruding from each side.

The King confided to Lady Castlemaine that his bride-to-be looked like a bat."

"And who is Lady Castlemaine?" I asked.

Lady G jerked her head, eyes on full alert. Her smile froze on tightened lips. Apparently, every upper-class gentleman, including the newest arrival from the colonies, would know Castlemaine's status with the King. I had made a serious blunder.

"She has been his mistress since the Restoration in 1660." Lady Greyhurst spaced her words like she was talking to someone for whom English was a second language. "Her reputation, shall I say, for variety implies both physical flexibility and an adventurous spirit."

That description jogged my memory. I did my best to recover. "Oh, of course. I know her as Barbara Palmer," I said. "I call her Babs . . ."

Palmer had convinced Charles to make her husband an Earl. Which to my way of thinking showed she had her spouse's best interest in mind. Best laid plans, or plans best laid, so to speak.

"What is a Babs?" she asked in a frost-tinged voice.

The way she leaned away from me telegraphed her suspicions. I was a man not to be trusted. My brain kept shouting "Distract her. Distract her."

"Lady Greyhurst, you are a beautiful woman, and I can see why you are so well connected at Court. What a lovely garden you have. Do you come here often?"

Lady Greyhurst was not buying my babble. Her hazel eyes studied me with dreaded scrutiny. In spite of seamstress Alice Ho's best efforts, my twenty-first-century costume was not meant for close-ups. Explaining polyester fabric with a Made in China label would be tough.

"You seek to fool me," she accused. "Pretend one thing but

deliver another. Beneath the King's codpiece is a scepter of substance. As I can vouch from personal experience. But you, Elliot of Vail, are not what you appear on the surface. I have a mind to shout an alarm."

She stood up and edged away, keeping her face toward me. Not good. I had bombed with audiences before, but the risk of being beheaded in the Tower of London for deceiving a royal mistress had never been the penalty. I had to do something fast.

"Bockman," I said.

A toss of her tight chestnut curls was her response. The rise and fall of her delightful half-bared breasts was like a bellows gathering air. A prelude to her summoning a manservant to manhandle me?

"Wait." I fished in my sack purse. My fingers closed around my only hope, Bockman's signet ring.

"Gold," I said. The one word I hoped would short-circuit any perceived threat from me. A King's mistress didn't lift her skirts for pure love.

"Gold?" She placed her index finger alongside her cheek to accent a dimple. "A royal treasure that, once given, leaves the bedchamber with its new owner. Pray explain yourself. Be brief, Elliot of Vail. I will not place my life in danger for one such as you."

"Catch."

I tossed her Bockman's gold ring. She snatched it midair, like a major league shortstop on the front end of a double play. She examined the ring between thumb and index finger. Her eyes opened wide. I heard the sharp intake of her breath.

"Lord Edward's signet ring," she said. "Have you come to free my poor little cockerel from his dungeon?"

— NINE —

Pouring Out Troubles

Bingo. I had said the magic word. Now was the perfect time to make my pitch. I leaped up from the bench.

"Yes," I said. In great agitation, I waved my hands and clutched my chest in exaggerated gestures. "I'm on a secret mission to rescue Lord Edward of Bockman from prison. That's why I've ventured across the ocean. We are from the same city." I held my arms outwards in case Lady Greyhurst wanted to throw herself in my general direction. "We used to hang together."

"You were both almost hanged?" A perplexed countenance clouded her face. Her hands covered her mouth to suppress a outcry. "But here you are, Elliot of Vail, safe. God's grace must be on your side."

She lowered her hands to shoulder height, but didn't step forward. We stood facing each other, three feet apart, in a "What? What?" pose. I needed to come up with an explanation and fast.

"Lady Greyhurst," I said. "To save Lord Edward's body and soul, I must take you into my confidence. I swear you to secrecy, for I lay my life in your hands. These are desperate times."

Corny. Hey, I never said I was eloquent. Whatever worked.

She fiddled with a stray lock of hair, twisting it between nervous fingers. Conflicting thoughts must have been whirling behind her beautiful hazel eyes. Whether to listen to me or summon help. Lord

Edward on one side of the scale, gold and a suspicious stranger on the other.

"If we are going to rescue Lord Edward," I said, "you must hear me out. Otherwise, he is doomed to rot in that dungeon."

"How do I know you are not a spy, or worse?" she said. "Someone sent by my enemies to test my loyalty to the king?"

The lady might be the King's ex-mistress, but that high honor was not a position gained by a fool. She had played in the major leagues.

"Would that person be so lacking in skill or concoct so shallow a story?" My "so" defense. I was so bad I had to be good.

Lady Greyhurst fidgeted while she debated my future. She toyed with her finger rings while deciding. She was a wary survivor of court intrigue. Choosing the wrong side of shifting political and religious alliances could get a person banished from court or conveniently disposed of. Even worse, shipped to far-off America. I hoped she would trust her instincts.

"You speak and act in a foreign manner," she said. "The only reason I do not immediately call for my manservant is that your speech reminds me of Lord Edward."

My guts were in that state of panic that always beset me before I went on stage. If Lady Greyhurst didn't help me rescue Bockman, I couldn't find the location of his London house. No house, no Box. No Box, no Particle Enhancement or launch pad to return me to my own time. If she ratted me out, I could end up hanging by my thumbs in some dark jail cell.

"I may regret my decision in your favor," Lady Greyhurst said. "I can be a victim of my strong emotions." She favored me with a coquettish smile. "Wouldst thou like something to quench thy thirst while we talk?"

"Wouldst thou happen to have a beer handy?" I accommodated my wobbly knees by returning to the bench.

"Indeed. Fine English ale made in the Dutch style with hops," she said. "Many at court have taken a liking to this new flavor. Even the King partakes after his robust tennis exercise."

She left me waiting on the bench while she walked up the garden path to her house. I hoped she was going to fetch a six-pack and some munchies. Lady G was back in less than a minute. Alone but empty-handed.

"Just my luck," I said. "No beer."

"My maidservant will attend to us shortly." Her superior look conveyed one word—peasant.

We sat side by side and made small talk. Fun topics: London's foul air, how horses and carriages jammed narrow streets, and the ever present raw sewage that overflowed the gutters. Especially unpleasant were rumors of a deadly disease plaguing London's poor.

"Could we change the subject?" I said. "I've had a hard day's journey."

Lady Greyhurst relaxed and shared the latest court gossip about the King's love life.

"The King's new mistress, Frances Stewart, maid of honor to Queen Catherine, has shocked even the most jaded," Lady G said. "She is an odd combination of virtue and temptation."

Maybe Lady G was jealous. Or just liked to talk shop. I encouraged her to continue. I might learn something useful. To keep my host talking until the brew arrived, I smiled and went tut-tut when appropriate.

"Frances announced that she dreamed of being in bed with three French ambassadors," Lady Greyhurst said. "Isn't that shocking?"

"Which?" I said. "Three or French?"

"This June past was not a good time for Charles." She fiddled with her middle finger, sliding a jeweled ring up and down. "He is reluctant in pursuing the Dutch war. Our navy has provided one happy event for the poor dear. His brother, James, the Duke of York, was victorious over the Dutch fleet in the Battle of Lowestoft. I myself stood on the waters' edge and heard the distant sounds of ships' cannons."

She turned at the sound of a door being shut. Lady Greyhurst struck a haughty pose, nose in the air. Lady G might be beautiful, but her arrogant façade annoyed me. I stifled a sarcastic putdown. Gaining her friendship was more important then my feelings.

A serving girl approached, carrying a pitcher in one hand, a bread and cheese tray in the other. She held the heavy clay pitcher with ease. A small white cap perched atop a mop of brunette hair. A pocketed apron covered a long, drab-brown skirt. A sturdy lass.

"My maidservant comes ever so slowly," Lady Greyhurst chided.

The closer the maidservant strode towards us, the more her personality showed. No downcast eyes or subservient posture for this gal. She held her head high, shoulders squared, with jade eyes that challenged. She exuded an air of quiet confidence. She might be a lowly servant, but her demeanor didn't match her social standing.

Lady Greyhurst pointed a delicate finger at the empty space between us on the bench. The maid first put the pitcher down, followed by the tray, and two glasses retrieved from her apron pocket. She took a long kitchen knife from her apron. Raised the blade high above her head. *Thunk*. She pinned the loaf of bread to the wooden tray. The quivering knife handle protruded from the crust.

"Will my Lady be needing anything else?" the maid asked in a mock innocent voice.

Her bulging cream-colored peasant blouse was accented with a red ribbon around its neckline. She was a bit top-heavy for my taste in women. Nice slender waist though.

"No, you are free to go." Lady Greyhurst waved a dismissive hand.

The servant girl turned and left us in the garden. Lady G had offered neither greeting nor introduction. I didn't like that.

"Young lady." I called out to her retreating servant. "Do tell me your name. I am Elliot."

She turned, looked at Lady G with guarded eyes, seeking permission from her employer. Then she gave me a hint of smile.

"Lilly." She left it at that.

My gaze lingered on Lilly's figure as she returned to the house. She paused before stepping through the doorway. I would like to think Lilly favored me with an extra swing of her hips.

"Just a farm girl," Lady Greyhurst said. "She does kitchen work, cleans, and is my maid. She is rather insolent. But useful and discreet." Lady G lifted the pitcher with two hands and poured warm, frothy ale into the glass nearest me. "Here, stranger from the New World. This will quench your thirst and cool your thoughts."

My eager anticipation of a refreshing quencher was dashed with my first taste—warm, bitter liquid, and cloudy to boot. The only thing worse than this ale was no beer at all. Of course, any drink tasted better than Bockman's Particle Enhancement Liquid. Ah well, I might as well get used to English ways. I kept a pleasant smile on my face while my taste buds struggled.

Subtle scents of rose and lavender lingered in the air around us. Herbal notes of rosemary and sage intruded when a stray breeze stirred. Bees hovered over gray-green clumps of borage. I hadn't seen tall spikes of bell-flowered foxglove since I played in my grandmother's garden. A fond memory retrieved by sight and smell. Two glasses later, it was time to get serious. Both Lady G and I had been tiptoeing around the Bockman issue. We had tested the waters with polite conversation. Now we would be more direct with each other.

"How did Lord Edward end up in a dungeon?" I fired the opening volley. "Who put him there? Where is he being held?"

She reached over to grasp my arm. Her tightened lips and reserved manner burst open.

"It is my fault," she said. "Lord Weston was pressing his advances on me. I was uneasy and fearful of his reputation."

"And what reputation would that be?" I asked. Bockman had complained about a Lord Weston in one of his notes.

"His fiery temperament is provoked by jealousy." She sat back with folded arms. "Also, he is mean-spirited, conniving, and seeks to build his fortune at the expense of others." Lady Greyhurst pouted. "And he is not a faithful companion."

"Other than those minor character faults, does he have any redeeming qualities?" I asked.

"Well, he is a good dancer. Some gainsay a handsome man who has an engaging manner when it suits his purpose. He holds high rank within the army. Fought bravely in the Scottish border wars. He maintains a troop of mercenary soldiers called the guardsmen. Knows his way around Whitehall Palace's back hallways."

"How did he and Bockman, I mean, Lord Edward, cross paths?" Based on the note I had found in the transport box, I already had a good idea, but I wanted to hear Lady Greyhurst's version.

"Lord Edward and I have been friends ever since he came into my life at a time when both my fortune and self were sorely stressed."

She stood, then walked to the fountain and ran her hand under the stream that fell from the statue's vase. She fingered through the water like she was playing a keyboard. I followed her to the water's edge.

"The King had discarded me for another mistress," she said. "Nonetheless, Charles is a cheerful and kindly monarch. He granted me this house and a small stipend for my past services."

"Let me guess," I said. "You used Lord Edward as an excuse to dump Weston. Or did you merely want to make him jealous?"

She cupped a handful of water and threw it in my face. Not as bad as it sounds. All that hit me were cooling droplets. My laughter at her failed insult enticed a reluctant smile from her lips.

"Lord Weston sent men to spy on my house," Lady G said. "They reported that Lord Edward was a frequent visitor. These reports stirred Weston's rage. He took umbrage that I preferred a man of Edward's stature."

"There must be more to Lord Edward of Bockman," I said, "than meets the eye."

"Indeed," Lady Greyhurst said, "he is very skilled and does not disappoint." She waved away a honeybee attracted by the ale. "Lord Weston kept his disdain for Edward secret while pretending to be our friend."

My little landlord had run afoul of a jealous lover. I hefted the pitcher and refilled my glass. Lady Greyhurst placed jeweled fingers on top of her glass and rejected a refill.

"What triggered their duel?" I said.

"Lord Weston intercepted us while we were walking one evening in the park." Her words tumbled out. "Weston set a trap, incited an incident, and Edward took the bait. A terrible row ensued. Lord Edward insisted on defending my honor. Cruel Weston taunted him by declaring I had no honor to defend."

I had a mental picture of my Robin Hood-costumed landlord standing on tiptoes to look his opponent in the eye.

"Weston further inflamed Edward by making disparaging remarks about his old-fashioned attire. And saying Edward's hat adornment was the only part of a fighting cock that he could claim kinship to."

I understood how that taunt would set Bockman off. Defending his Robin Hood feather was something my oddball landlord might consider honorable. Or perhaps Bockman felt his bantam rooster reputation was at stake.

"Their ensuing duel was to be fought on the sheep-grazing grounds at Spindledown, a small village north of here." Lady Greyhurst indicated the general direction with a wave of her delicate hand.

"What happened?" Bockman had sent me a plea to dispatch, post haste, a book on dueling. But he had never retrieved it from the box.

"I know not the details. I was not present on that day." Lady Greyhurst turned her head, looked around the garden to reassure herself that no one lurked nearby. Her gaze lingered on the half-opened Dutch door leading to the house. "Press me not for information."

Now she evaded my questions. Each time I demanded information regarding Bockman's exact location, she skillfully changed the subject. Lady Greyhurst became over-cautious. There was more to this story than she was revealing.

And I wasn't totally buying this dustup between Weston and Bockman. Hippo had cautioned me to steer clear of seventeenth-century politics, religion, and plots that circled about the monarchy. This whole affair reeked of court intrigue more than spurned love.

"Well, then," I demanded, "who does know?"

"Lilly," Lady Greyhurst said. "Lilly was there."

TEN

Sealed Deal

"Then," I said, "I must talk to your servant about Lord Edward. Excuse me."

Lady Greyhurst started to protest my rudeness, but after an exasperated glare at me, released me with a curt nod. I strode along the garden pathway back to Lady Greyhurst's house. I could see the kitchen area through the open upper half-door. Iron pots and pans dangled from a rack mounted above a polished wooden table. A brick fireplace filled one corner of the kitchen.

"Elliot," Lady Greyhurst called after me, "do calm yourself. You are too late."

I glanced over my shoulder. Lady G made no effort to hurry toward me. Her actions provided tangible evidence of my low ranking on her priority list.

"Lilly," I yelled, "please show yourself. I must talk to you about Lord Edward."

I vaulted over the lower half of the closed Dutch door and landed inside the room. No one greeted or challenged me. The kitchen was empty.

"My, but you are an impetuous man," Lady Greyhurst said, to announce her arrival.

I turned around and faced back to the entrance. Lady G bent at the waist and leaned her elbows on the top of the Dutch half-door. Her stern expression stopped my intended search of her house.

"If you desire that we join forces," she chastised me, "you must cool the fevers that addle your brain. Otherwise, you are of no use to me. Your rash words and manner will only serve to gather trouble for us. I need a man with valor and wisdom if my plans are to go forward."

Her plans? Ah, the real reason she had been so tolerant of my foreign ways and sudden arrival. Warning signs flashed in my head. I had no doubt that hidden entanglements lurked in any dealings with Lady Greyhurst. But regardless of the risk, the lady was right. I had to settle down if I hoped to find Bockman and also make my fortune.

"Okay." I bobbed my head.

"Hokay? Is that an expression used in the Carolinas?" she asked. "I assume it means your favorable approval of my advice." Lady G opened the lower door and beckoned me forward. "Now, come back outside. I prefer that my enemy's ears not be close by. The sound of the fountain both soothes the spirit and masks our words."

I trailed after her like a chastised puppy. We sat side by side on the wide stone rim of the fountain. Lady G scooted herself next to me. Only a few inches separated our bodies. She bent her head towards mine and spoke softly. Her closeness short-circuited my concentration.

"I permit Lilly to return to her father's farm, north of London," Lady Greyhurst began. "She spends several months here with me as my servant, and I allow her to visit her family as suits my purposes." Her arrogant attitude seemed well-rehearsed.

"I can see you have a heart of gold." If my remark sounded critical, it was because I intended it to be.

"Far more generous than other ladies of my station," she flared.

"Your ignorance shows once again. I have heard reports of how New World owners treat their indentured servants and blackamoor slaves."

"Why the big hurry for Lilly to leave?" I changed the subject back to finding Bockman. Lady G's explanation was logical but far too glib. She reached out and rested one hand on my leg. If her intention was to interrupt my questioning, she accomplished her purpose.

"Sometimes you remind me of Edward of Bockman," she said. "Simple everyday events often confused him. Yet from when we first met, I sensed he kept knowledge hidden from me."

Lady, if you only knew, I thought. Things like time travel, computers, San Francisco's Bay-to-Breakers annual running circus, airbags, microwaves, and vitamins. "You haven't answered my question," I said. "Why did Lilly rush off?"

"I am willing to trade one answer for another," Lady Greyhurst said. "I have need of some truth from you."

She pinched the top of my thigh muscle right through my Made-in-China tights. My leg did an involuntary Irish jig in response. I was out of my league. Lady G pulled her hand away and rubbed her thumb against her finger tips, puzzled by the feel of polyester. I didn't need any closer examination of my phony costume. I crossed my legs and scooted back from her.

She played with a strand of her chestnut hair while mocking me with a super-sweet smile. "Lilly dashed off to join some farmers returning to her father's village. They bring produce and flour to the city. A simple explanation."

Lady Greyhurst stood and, with a swish of her skirt, stepped away from me. She smoothed the folds of her dress and brushed both hands behind her to dislodge the stray dust and leaves accumulated from sitting on the fountain's edge.

"Now, Elliot of Vail"—she wiggled a rebuking finger at me like some scolding nun—"did you really come to rescue Lord Edward? Or is there another reason you mysteriously appeared in my garden? Speak the truth. I am no fool. In my experience, there are but three things that move men like you to great effort: power, wealth and the bedchamber. There are none of these gains for you from this venture."

"Why do you say that?" I asked.

She was starting to irritate me. I stood to jam my hands into my pockets, only to realize my tights didn't have pockets. The result was to stand in front of her with both arms straight down along my sides, like a rigid soldier at attention.

"There is no reward," she said, "to be paid for Edward's freedom. No political advantage, and certainly no amour."

Did she have to say "certainly?" Was she referring to herself? I conceded her last point—for now.

"You're wrong on two counts," I said. "Lord Edward of Bockman owns property in the far western reaches of the New World. I will occupy that land free of taxes and expenses if I return him to his home." My edited version of a lifetime free rent in San Francisco. "As for the other reason, I confess that I do want your miniature."

A sharp intake of her breath indicated I had commanded Lady G's attention. Her eyebrows rose. Then she gave me a mischievous smile.

"And those of your friends at court," I said.

She pulled back a bit. I leaned into her body space and gave her my naughty-boy smile. Might as well go all the way. "A variety would be best. Titled women. Also a duke or count, if they are available."

"You are indeed a lusty lad to state your intentions so openly," she said. "Yet, there are those ladies who prefer a bold man to a timid one. I cannot speak for the men."

"Paintings," I clarified. "Miniature portraits by talented artists. I have New World buyers awaiting my return. I will grant you a commission on each painting you help me acquire."

"Oh." Lady Greyhurst sounded disappointed. "A business arrangement, hand in glove with Edward's rescue." Her eyes scrutinized me with a newfound interest. "I suppose we can work together. I, too, am pursuing a little private venture wherein you might be useful. What is my commission on the paintings? We must negotiate our positions before we proceed."

Sounded like Lady G had lots of experience in setting forth conditions in advance. I suppose a mistress benefited from that personality trait.

"Does this little private business scheme of yours happen to be illegal, dangerous, or treasonous?" I said.

She raised her nose in the air as if to show that her affairs were none of my concern. I turned away. A short stroll around the garden should clear my head.

I had a strong desire to keep my skull attached to my body. From what Hippo had told me about seventeenth-century English justice, the charge of high crimes and treason covered a wide swath of behavior, some of which would be considered mere misdemeanors in modern times. For all I knew, "pissing off the King" might be a capital crime in this London.

Lady Greyhurst intercepted my walkabout, linked her arm around mine, and fell in step beside me. Whatever perfume she was wearing must have been called eau de desire for its potent mixture of male brain-fogging chemicals. The garden flowers and her feminine scents mingled into a heady potpourri.

"In ever-shifting political alliances, treason is determined by which side wins," she elaborated. "Illegal varies depending upon which country's laws are applied, and the degree of risk depends upon the proper balance of preparation and execution."

"It's that last word I'm having trouble with," I said.

Lady G stopped, pulled me close, tilted her head and planted a kiss on my lips. I wish I could make more of her unexpected smooch than it was. Spin some romantic fantasy about how we were instantly drawn to each other. Or at least we shared a passionate, illogical moment of lust. To be honest, her kiss was more like stamping an invoice "Sold."

"I guess that seals our deal," I said. "We are business partners." I held her at arm's length. "Let's make one thing clear. My first priority is to rescue Lord Edward. My second priority is to corral, I mean collect, a batch of paintings to sell back home, and then I'll see what I can do to help you."

She shook my hands off her shoulders, her hazel eyes fixed onto mine. This fair maiden had a steely core wrapped in creamy skin, full lips, and very fine figure.

"I will undertake the task of securing the miniature portraits of my friends at the court," Lady Greyhurst said. "I will visit the studios of the painters Santuros, Glaven, and Thomas, and will buy their finer works at low prices. They are talented but out of favor at the moment. We must set to work immediately."

"All right, you do the artists," I said. "I'll start the hunt for Lord Edward. Now, tell me what your scheme is."

"I will share my plans with you at the proper moment." Lady G stomped her foot in agitation at my probing. "Suffice it to say that information you do not know, you cannot yield under torture. You may not succeed in freeing Lord Edward."

Oh, that was a comforting thought. My new partner was already mentally writing me out of our deal. And she made it sound like torture was just a normal business risk. I had to pinpoint Bockman's London house, and fast. I desperately needed the box with my gear to improve my odds of survival.

"Please," I said. "Direct me to the street where Lord Edward's house is located. He may have left some clues behind that will assist me."

"I only know that his house is somewhere near Saint Giles in the Fields church." Lady G's flash of anger had passed. "We always met here at my home. It would not have been seemly for me to be seen in that part of London."

Catch 22. Only Bockman knew his home address. But he was locked in an unknown dungeon somewhere in this sprawling city. Crap. Now, I had no choice but to rescue my landlord if I held any hope of returning to San Francisco.

"Just tell me," I said, "exactly where in London Lord Edward is imprisoned."

"London?" She cocked her head in a quizzical pose. "He is not in London."

I clamped my hands on my head. Finding Bockman here in the city was one thing, but tramping off to some far-flung location multiplied the odds against success. Or even worse, invited death. Greed mixed with adventure had justified my initial willingness to time travel, but I was being sucked deeper and deeper into danger.

"He is being held in the old castle keep at Lord Weston's country estate." She chewed on her lower lip. "I will hire a man to guide you. He is a ruffian but will do any task if the price is right. However, I would not tempt him or lay my trust in his honesty. But he does know the way and will keep his mouth closed." She paced back and forth on the garden pathway. "He shall accompany you by coach you until you reach the village. It lies just beyond Hangman's

Forest. For your own safety, it would be best that he knows not your final destination," she said. "Be certain he does not spy after you."

Great. Her grand idea was for me to go by myself into the enemy's lair, led by an unreliable scoundrel, and spring Bockman using only my wits. With every step I took, things were getting worse.

"Got any other great ideas?" I said. "Is there a plan B?"

"Bee plan?" she said. "Elliot of Vail, half the time I don't understand your words. Sometimes I think you arrived from the stars."

"Consider me a lost little boy," I said. "One who asks dumb questions and doesn't yet know his way around."

She rolled her eyes upwards in silent reaction. Lady Greyhurst pursed her lips. I had the feeling she was reconsidering our deal.

"Follow Black Sheep Lane to Lord Weston's home, five miles northeast, in the midst of farmland. His country home perches on a rise from where one can view all of Weston's estate."

"The next thing you'll tell me is that Lord Edward is locked in the castle's dungeon, guarded by mad dogs and a giant jailer."

"Surely," Lady Greyhurst said. "It is only with God's special blessing that you survived your trip from America to England."

She raised her palms and pressed her forehead. Then she lowered her hands, straightened her back and composed herself. My ex had used the same gestures except she never got around to composing herself.

"I know not precisely where he is being held," she said in a calm voice. "He may not be in the castle dungeon. Lord Weston may have secreted Edward in a location where it is less obvious that he is being held captive outside the law. I judge you to be a man of valor. But if this task is beyond your reach, do say so now."

Ah, a challenge to my manhood. Won't work, lady. I've been worked over by experts, like my ex-wife.

"Don't worry," I said. "I'll give it my best shot."

"But where will you secure your flintlock?"

"Never mind," I said. "At least tell me the name of the village where I'm to get off the coach."

"Spindledown."

Lady Greyhurst gave me an odd look. Like I was the village idiot. I was starting to agree with her assessment. Then my dim bulb glowed a bit.

"Lilly's from there," I blurted. "She will help me."

"Perchance, if you are persuasive and do charm her." Lady Greyhurst's face looked doubtful of my ability to pull off that feat. "I advise not mentioning your interest in miniatures."

"But how will I find her?" I was getting frantic. "I don't even know her last name."

"Swinden. Lilly Swinden of Spindledown. Ask anyone, her name and reputation are well known." Lady Greyhurst's enigmatic smile was not reassuring.

ELEVEN

Frenchman's Care

I exchanged my gold bars with Lady Greyhurst for a supply of English coins. She held back several coins to pay for my travel arrangements. Lady G then parked me on a wooden stool in her kitchen, gave me a pitcher of beer, and issued instructions not to blunder off. Her precise words.

She stated in a rather high-handed manner that my presence would only make things more difficult. I chafed a bit at the logic of her argument but blew her a kiss as she waltzed away. She glanced back and playfully stuck out her tongue. Her sense of humor might explain why she found Bockman interesting.

Speaking of Bockman, his London house must be within walking distance of where I now perched. Somewhere, in a room close by, was the Box filled with my handy survival stuff. Most critical was the Particle Enhancement bandoleer. That slime would taste like rare wine if I ever got my hands on it again.

My time-traveling landlord had complained of needing money, so I doubted he would have stabled a horse for his transportation. Hippo had claimed that in old London, instead of carriages or taxicabs, gentlemen were carried around in sedan chairs, enclosed chairs with poles front and rear, carried by two men. Paying two stout Yellow Cabbies to tote him could have been too expensive for Bockman.

No plump cushion protected my buns from the bare wooden kitchen seat. The well-scrubbed plank flooring looked enticing. I stretched out on the kitchen floor while I waited for Lady Greyhurst's return. I fought sleep for a while, then dozed off. The sound of a woman's voice startled me.

"Finding one's partner," Lady Greyhurst said, with one dainty foot planted on my chest, "passed out from drink does not bode well for our venture's success."

"How would you like to be tossed in the fountain?" I grabbed for her ankle, but she eluded my grasp with a laugh.

"Did you make travel arrangements for me?" I asked. "Or have you been shopping?"

"While you were sleeping, I found my proper ruffian." She emphasized the "I" and congratulated herself by positioning open fingers against her chest. "He will see that you get to Spindledown. I have had more than one occasion to use Lame Le Mieux. He carries out tasks best done by a person untroubled by conscience."

"Lame Le Mieux?" I said. "What kind of English name is that?

"He is not English," she corrected. "Rather, a deserter from the French army. Le Mieux was a pikeman badly wounded in the leg during a Lowland battle. He was left on the field to die when his regiment retreated. Then he stole a uniform from a dead English soldier. To disguise his French accent, he wrapped a bloody cloth around his own throat, pretending to be unable to speak."

"Hmmm." I sat up and propped my elbows on my knees. "Proves the man is creative as well as a thief."

"Mistaken as one of our wounded," she continued, "Le Mieux was shipped back to England. He slipped away from hospital and disappeared into London's back streets."

"You seem to be well acquainted with this lowlife," I said. My choice of modern slang perplexed her. "A person without moral character," I clarified.

"You people from the New World are so hard to understand. Lord Edward is also a constant source of confusion," she fussed. "You colonials butcher the proper English language."

"You think my speech is bad," I said, "you should see my handwriting."

Lady Greyhurst was up to her old game. When I asked her a question, she tried to change the subject. I made a "T" with my hands.

"Time out. You didn't answer my question."

I had managed to make her baffled and peeved at the same time. She didn't like being challenged by a New World bumpkin. Get used to it, lady.

"Lame Le Mieux?"

"My awareness of Le Mieux," she answered, "is quite simple. I learned about him from the Queen's chambermaid. He had assisted her in a scandal that involved her sister's husband. Come now, Elliot, we must prepare for your journey."

— — —

Spinster's Close, located in a seedy part of London, was little more than a narrow alley capable of being secured by a heavy iron gate. Inside the diminutive cobblestone lane, shadows rendered the buildings' details into grays and blacks like a charcoal drawing, all colors muted and washed away. Shop fronts evidenced poverty and grime with their dark wooden doorframes and dirty bottle-glass windows. Sagging ropes filled with drying laundry created obstacles to both sight and passage.

My companion, the bent woman wrapped in a tattered shawl

and frayed skirt, bore no resemblance to Lady Greyhurst. Any high-society friends of hers would ignore the tattered wretch. Lady G's disguise took advantage of human nature. A person out of place can be out of sight.

I followed a few steps behind her, staying near the building walls. To disguise my American accent, Lady G had suggested I copy Le Mieux's trick of feigning injury to his voice. A white bandage was wrapped around my neck. The clomping of my boots against the cobblestones echoed in the narrow close.

Halfway down the alley, she stopped in front of an open door. A faded painting of a white swan identified the shop. Vapor drifted out into the lane and curled upwards, accompanied by sounds of female laughter. Through the open door I could see washerwomen bent over a steaming tub.

Lady G motioned me forward. She stood in front of a wide linen sheet that drooped from a clothesline strung across the alley. She reached up, grasped the sheet, and pulled it away, revealing a man in front of us.

"Monsieur Le Mieux." She provided an identity, not a greeting. "He will guide you to Spindledown."

One look at Lame Le Mieux confirmed Lady G's caution. The Frenchman's hairline had receded to the peak of his skull. His long, tangled hair looked like a dirty mop had been plunked on the back of his head. Oily strands draped to his narrow shoulders. The man's threadbare black cloak appeared ready to slide off at any movement. Le Mieux's left foot twisted inward at a forty-five-degree angle, the source of his first name.

"This." She faced the man while giving her hand a flutter in my direction. "This is Mr. Tanner."

I resisted the temptation to turn around to look for the nonexistent Tanner. He was me, at least until I got off the coach in Spindledown. Le Mieux didn't need to know my real name. The less he knew about me, the better.

"Your humble servant, Monsieur Tanner," he said. Thick eyebrows seemed out of place with his pencil-thin moustache that twitched when he tried a smirking smile. "I weel be quick to your commands."

Never had more insincere words been uttered in my direction. Not counting when my new bride had proclaimed, "I do," when she meant, "You will."

Le Mieux held out one soiled hand in front of Lady Greyhurst. She deposited a silver coin in his upturned palm. A second one thunked on top of the first.

"As usual," she said. "Half the money now, and you will gain the other half from Mr. Tanner when he arrives safely at Spindledown. As you can see, he suffers from a throat wound, and the doctor prohibits him from speaking. I'm certain you can attest to that limitation."

"Had zee same problem myself." He curled bony fingers around the silver coins.

"Follow me to zee main road, Monsieur Tanner," Le Mieux said. "I weel take you to zee coach. Zee driver, Monsieur Squarrels, eez an acquaintance. Weel not ask any questions but deliver you proper to Spindledown. Best we hurry."

— — —

Le Mieux shouted a greeting to the coach driver and pulled him aside for a private conversation. The big fellow darted a glance at me. Squarrels had a bull neck, a weathered face, and thick arms that seemed fully capable of controlling the six coach horses. I would have felt better if the driver had smiled and waved instead of scowling.

I joined three fellow passengers, a pear-shaped man and two women, waiting for the stage to depart. Luggage bags were hoisted coach-top amongst crates stowed for the journey. The odor of fresh horse dung permeated the boarding area. Harnessed horses champed. The scene was a blur of activity to my unaccustomed eyes.

The driver donned a long buff-colored coat and pulled leather gloves over his hands. He beckoned the four of us to board the coach. Le Mieux scrambled up into his seat beside the driver. The coach lurched forward, and we were on our way.

The lady travelers were Madame Betcombe and her sister from Normandy. The other male passenger introduced himself as Pontius Cooper. I pointed to my throat bandage and croaked a few sounds, shaking my head from side to side.

The older sister opened a leather-bound book and held it close to her face as a barrier. Her younger sister wrapped herself in silence and brooded out the window, solemn and grey as the clouds that gathered overhead.

Cooper climbed off at the third stop, saying his goodbyes. He had to endure the ignominy of having his luggage thrown at his feet before the coach departed in a swirl of dust. I scrunched down inside my cloak and rested my head against the body of the coach. I tried to keep my teeth from chipping as the coach bounced over rocks and into potholes. I dreamed of pneumatic shock absorbers.

Madame Betcombe and her silent sister departed from the coach at Long Meadow, the last stop before Spindledown. Both women clutched their skirts close before stepping off. Not that their ankles deserved a second look, or a first one, for that matter. Neither had the grace to say, "Have a nice trip," "Goodbye," or even "Excuse me."

Low-hanging clouds had been threatening rain for the past hour. Now the drops fell in sheets slanted by strong gusts. Squarrels appeared outside the far window, water dripping from his hat brim. Without a word of greeting, he untied the outside leather window curtains and rolled them down to cover the coach windows. I suppose he thought he was doing me a favor.

The air inside the coach became dank, rank, and foul. Speaking of fowl, some passenger must have toted a cage of chickens on an earlier trip. A few soggy feathers on the floor provided evidence. I stuck out my boot and nudged a suspicious brindled pile. My nose validated my diagnosis.

With a shout and a whip-snap from the driver, my bumpy ride resumed. The coach slid sideways for a moment before the wooden-spoke wheels gripped the wet road. Rain pelted the curtains, and rivulets dripped onto the coach floor. One curtain came untied and flopped with an irritating noise.

The on-and-off view of the countryside through the flapping side curtain confirmed that evening had arrived and the rain had trailed off. Distant lights flickered here and there from open cottage doors. The steady clop-clopping of the horses' hooves lulled me to sleep.

I awoke as the coach made a sweeping turn to the right. The hoofbeats slowed, then stopped, and the door opened. Lame Le Mieux stuck his head inside.

"Par-dan my intrusion, sire." He doffed his formless hat and favored me with a tight smile that featured yellow-stained teeth. "Monsieur Squarrels, zee driver, invites you to ride with him. The rain eez over and the air eez sweet."

Better than suffocating inside this 1660-model Greyhound bus.

Still, I was wary of any friendly offer from a rogue like Le Mieux. He stood there on darkened road, holding open the carriage door. Britain's most scruffy footman, his wet cloak pulled about him like a shroud, gave a hint of a bow before gesturing toward the top of the coach.

"You sit on zee driver's seat, next to Monsieur Squarrels, and I shall ride on zee rear footman's perch." He ran one hand through the back of his matted hair, lifting it off his dirty collar. "Mind zee mud, lest you soil those fine boots."

Staying inside the coach had a degree of safety that shouldn't be dismissed. Then a slight stirring on the opposite seat drew my attention. Maggots emerged from the tuft of horsehair stuffing poking through a tear in leather seat. A change of scenery would be welcome, a whiff of fresh air a bonus.

"Stand aside, Le Mieux," I said. "Keep both hands where I can see them."

My guide backed away from the open coach door, showing not the slightest trace of annoyance. I gripped the doorframe and stepped down onto the road. I suppose the shifty Frenchman was accustomed to mistrust.

My boot sank up to my ankle in the dark mud. I tried to get my bearings, but the coach-lantern's pale candlelight provided only feeble assistance. Overhead clouds blotted out both stars and moon. My eyes adjusted to the dim light enough to discern close-packed trees and undergrowth flanking the roadway.

"Sir. This be a good spot to relieve yourself." The gruff advice came from above. "We will not halt again until Spindledown."

Mr. Squarrels leaned over the coach's top edge. His turned-up high collar came close to the brim of his leather hat. I could barely make out his face in the lantern light. I didn't want to take Squarrels' advice, but my bladder immediately agreed with him.

"Go into zee woods a bit," Le Mieux urged from the back of the coach. "We will be right here waiting. Take your time doing your business. Some of zee cargo on top has come loose. I must retie zee straps."

Thumping and scraping sounds accompanied his words. The team of horses snorted and shook. This must be the Hangman's Forest that Lady Greyhurst had mentioned.

"Where are we?" I asked. "How far to Spindledown?"

"Hangman's Forest," the driver's hushed voice said. "We will not linger in these parts."

The mental image of a rotting body dangling from a nearby oak limb vetoed any suggestion of my stepping into that foreboding tangle of trees. The roadside ditch would serve my urges. And I wasn't about to turn my back on those two characters either.

I kept Le Mieux and Squarrels in sight and proceeded to fumble with the logistics of wearing tights under my breeches. No wonder women gave up pantyhose. I silently cursed Alice Ho for not providing a front fly in my pants. The waistband twisted when I pulled it down. I almost tripped and had to shuffle around to keep my balance. I looked up. Trees? I shouldn't be seeing trees.

A gleeful chuckle from above and behind me. Then something landed hard on my head. Stars popped in front of my eyes. My knees buckled. I pitched forward and planted my face into the roadside. I couldn't see. Somebody grabbed a handful of my hair and pulled my head upward. My eyes tried to open, but failed. The hard kick that rolled my body over hardly registered.

"He weel not give us any trouble."

"Hurry, Le Mieux," Squarrels' raspy voice ordered. "Get his money. Leave him. Pick up my leather satchel you bounded off his head. Best not tarry. A nasty pair of highwaymen lurk around these woods. Slit your throat as well as mine."

"You weel get your share." Le Mieux spat out the words. "He has more than enough money to pay for delivering him to Spindledown. Something about him eez foreign, a spy or plotter. But there be a caution. He has connections at zee court. Otherwise our Monsieur Tanner, or whatever his name eez, would be a dead man."

Rough hands groped my waist. My sack purse was jerked off my belt. I tasted wet dirt. My last thought was that I needed a beer.

TWELVE

Hangman's Forest

Something was sniffing close to my ear. Leaves crunched. A twig snapped. An animal edged closer to my helpless body. Was it hungry or curious? I willed my eyes to open, but only my left one responded. Get up off your back, I thought, or else be a critter dinner. I sat upright and flung my arms outward.

"Auhhhyeahblah," I yelled.

A nonsense sound. No words. No "who goes there?" Sharp pain rampaged through my head. I fell back to earth, landing in squishing mud. At least I hoped it was mud and not my skull coming apart. The animal scampered off. I turned my face toward the sound. Through my one good eye I caught a glimpse of a retreating red fox.

My sleeve served as a towel to wipe my face. A dim, streaky view of a tree was discernable through my mud-covered right eye. I fingered away the packed gunk. Now I had a matched set of functioning eyes. I rolled onto my stomach, then got up on all fours. A handy position in case I barfed. The head spinning had stopped, so I sat back on my haunches.

The clouds had thinned, allowing stars and a waxing moon to cast their dim light. The road through the forest was a silver "S" that curved in, then out, of my view. The dense woods that lined the roadside resembled the impenetrable walls of a dark fortress built to deter any intruder.

On the backside of my head, my fingers found the spot where Le Mieux's flying object had struck. With a cautious touch I explored the edges of the swelling. Other than being muddy, thirsty, hungry, and hurt, I was okay. Oh yeah, add lost, broke, and honked off to the list. I wasted five minutes cursing the bastard Le Mieux for suckering me, and an additional five upbraiding myself for being stupid.

Uh-oh, my money. My hand darted to my waist where the sack purse had hung. Gone. Then I remembered. Le Mieux had ripped me off. With eager fingers I felt along the jacket lining. Lady Greyhurst had insisted that I hide a few coins. Smart woman. Then I had a nasty thought. Had she expected Le Mieux would rob me?

I'd been sucker punched, once by a Frenchman, and if I counted Lady Greyhurst, maybe twice. I remembered Squarrels' ominous warning about cutthroats lurking in the woods. Time to get my aching body out of Hangman's Forest. On the brighter side, Spindledown village was somewhere along the road. I still had my boots and could walk. I was beginning to think straight.

When I did a more thorough status check of my wound, blood covered my fingers. The blow had gashed my scalp. I unwound the bandage from my phony throat injury and retied it around my oozing head, then trudged down the road. If I had carried a fife, I would have looked like one of those guys from the American Revolution.

I forced one foot in front of the other in a steady cadence. My knees, calves, and thighs protested the miserable night hike by sending time-to-quit messages. As soon as I cleared the woods, I would declare a victory and rest. Perhaps somewhere ahead of me a stream would parallel the road. Fresh water for drinking and cleaning my tired bod sounded so-o-o good.

My thoughts turned inward. What was a San Francisco city-boy comedian doing in a place called Hangman's Forest? I played word games by renaming the woods. Hippo's Grove. Bockman's Beeches. Or maybe Elliot's Oaks.

Sounds of approaching hoofbeats jerked me out of my reverie. Horses galloping towards me. The word "thundering" came to mind. I dove into the nearest space between a pair of trees and tumbled onto the forest floor. I crawled behind a monstrous oak and pressed against the rough bark. My eyes scanned the road for oncoming riders.

Five men astride dark horses rounded the bend. A leader flanked by horsemen on each side. Their capes streamed behind them, exposing breastplate armor. Metal harness trappings flashed as the horses sped through patches of moonlight. Thick clods of dirt arched from behind pounding rear hooves.

The front rider's warhorse appeared to fix bulging red eyes on me. Flecks of foam rimmed its bridle bit. A mass of straining muscles rippled across his chest. The horse's lips pulled back, aiming wicked white teeth at my hiding place. His sharp hooves could slice and dice me. I braced myself for the collision. But the black monster swerved to the side, bolted past me, then faded from my view.

I expected the leader to be some sinuous, dark-eyed, satanic horseman of the apocalypse. But the man that zoomed by me was a handsome, jaw-jutting, wild-haired blond that looked like he had just stepped off a Viking boat, eager to plunder, pillage, and rape. The trailing riders followed him around a sharp turn in the road that lay just beyond my hiding place.

The noise of drumming hooves retreated into the distance. Only to be replaced by a new sound. Men's voices, behind me in the woods, closing fast. Two voices calling to each other like baying hounds coming for the kill. I just knew it, bad guys with sharp knives. My fake throat wound was in danger of becoming real. These thieves knew the woods. No matter which direction I chose, they could run me down.

The road seemed my best chance for escape. Fear pumped a full adrenaline shot into my tired body. The leap from my hiding place to the road landed me three steps behind a man creeping along the edge. He was as startled as I was. Before he could react, I lowered my shoulder and drove my full weight behind the ensuing blow. The impact knocked him sprawling onto the road. I stumbled forward, hurdled over the man's body, and took off running.

"He be on the road." The words were half a curse and half a call for help.

"I will cut him off," another man answered.

The sounds of brush thrashing and running feet mingled with shouts behind me. Somewhere to my right, a figure raced parallel to the road. He disappeared behind the trees, only to reappear seconds later. Was his plan to grab me at a point where our paths intersected?

My lungs burned and my legs wobbled. The road ahead angled sharp right, providing one slim chance to ditch my pursuers. When I thought I was out of sight of the man behind me, I cut left and sprinted across to the opposite side. A rockslide protruded from the bank. I used the fallen boulders as giant steps up to the tree line, where I zigzagged through the forest.

Overhanging branches smacked my face. Roots tripped me. I fell in a patch of nettles. At one point I spooked a rabbit, and we ran together for several yards before he veered off. If I hadn't been looking at him, I might not have fallen over the stream's embankment. I was no Daniel Boone.

I cartwheeled down the slope into the streambed, splashed into the water and flailed my way into a dense thicket lining the water's edge. I tunneled into the brush, my body totally spent. My naked knee stuck out from a tear in my tights. Damn, my best pair, my only pair, ruined. I passed out.

— — —

I awakened to the protest of my aching muscles and throbbing head. I crawled forward in the darkness, guided by the sound of the flowing stream. My groping hand found the rocky edge. I leaned over, splashed my face, then slurped the cool water. I squatted on the ground and listened. The woods seemed normal.

I may be a city boy, but I knew enough to be aware of animal noises. If the critters were going about their nocturnal routines, they felt safe from human intrusion. My pursuers must have given up. I was lost, wet, and cold. But being alive evened the score.

Cold settled into my clothes, my skin, and even into my bones. No matter how tightly I hugged myself, I couldn't generate any internal BTUs for warmth. Building a fire wasn't going to happen. My butane lighter was stashed in Bockman's Box. If I had tucked any matches in my jacket, they would be water-soaked and useless. Rubbing two sticks together was a scouting myth.

I knew I had to escape while it was still dark and distance myself from the guys who had chased me. I tried to figure out which direction to walk. The coach had traveled north. What side of trees was moss supposed to grow on? I couldn't remember. When I had veered off the road to escape my pursuers, I had run left. So somewhere to the right was the road. Maybe. Might as well follow the streambed as it meandered through the forest. Fresh water attracted people. People lived together in houses or huts and built fires.

"Water. People. Warm," I repeated.

Damn you, Bockman. Why hadn't you time traveled back to someplace where I could buy cheap land? Miami or Hawaii. Oil leases or gold mines?

My foot hit something hard and stopped, the rest of my body continued forward. I toppled to the ground and was attacked by flying bugs that wanted a piece of me. I hobbled away from them. Something was different. The moon was now bright in the night sky. I stood in a clearing. I tramped around in a wide circle and found a narrow path. Made by man, deer, or cows? A shortcut between neighboring farms? Didn't matter. Easy walking.

The woods thinned. Trees were now far apart. I stood knee deep among orderly rows of grain. I smelled wood smoke, a siren call of warmth. A farmhouse had to be around somewhere. I couldn't control my body's shivering. Walk, Vail, walk.

I heard grunts. What domestic animals grunted? Pigs and men. Pigs yielded ham, bacon, ham hocks, chitlins. Got to love an animal that gives so much. Big grunt just in front of me. I reached out and grasped a rough wooden railing. A fat sow stood next to the fence. She raised her head and twitched her nose.

"Here, piggy, piggy," I said. "Move over, Babe. I need a bed for the night." I willed my right foot to lift onto the lower fence rail. My boot stayed on the ground. I ordered my other boot into action. Nothing. Ah, the hell with it. I slumped to the dirt, my back to the pen. A wet snout nuzzled my neck.

"Goodnight, dear," I muttered.

THIRTEEN

Bockman's Bonnie Lass

My nose tickled. I rubbed under my nostrils to thwart a sneeze. Another tickle came. I let go a man-sized blast of air, loud enough to wake me from my dream of being chased by a red-eyed horse.

"If you did not sleep with pigs," a lilting feminine voice teased, "you would not get so filthy."

I eased my eyes open. My tormentor sat cross-legged in the grass in front of me. The last time I had seen her was in Lady Greyhurst's garden. I had taken the coach to Spindledown to search for Lady G's maidservant. And here she was. Lilly Swinden. Yesterday's bad luck had turned around.

I lay spread out on the ground, my head next to a pigpen. The sun had risen above a thin layer of clouds lining the horizon. Lilly waved a thick branch of heather in lazy circles above my face.

"Is that how you wake guests here in the countryside?" I raised myself onto my elbows. "Aren't cocks supposed to crow at first dawn?"

"The cock did crow," she said. "But you did not stir. I first thought you were dead, but your snorting lips did assure me you were alive." An amused smile tugged at the corners of her mouth. "I could have thrown a bucket of cold water on you."

"What time is it?" I sat upright and knuckled my eyes.

"'Tis morn." She rapped my hands with the heather stem, like a nun chastising a sleepy student. "Do you not see the rising sun?"

"I mean, what is the exact hour and minute?" I demanded. Then I realized, only the wealthy had clocks.

"It matters not," Lilly said. "The day doth march forward until nightfall. What manner of trouble brings you, Elliot of Vail, to bed among my father's pigs?"

My kneecap protruded from a rip in my tights. Mud covered every article of my clothing. I smelled like the animals grunting in the pen behind me. I was a sorry sight.

"Strictly speaking," I said, "I am propped outside their pen. Wait a minute, your father's pigs?"

"My parents work this farm. I have come to visit as is my custom when Lady Greyhurst grants permission."

"I came all the way from London just to see you," I said and smiled.

Her response was a dismissive puff from her lips. So far, my charm had made no impression on her.

— — —

Lilly's arms were tanned and well muscled from physical work. She looked capable of throwing my bummed-out body off the family farm. I was in desperate need of her help. I had to risk spilling my story to her. Edited version, of course.

"If you give me something to eat," I said, "I will tell you a most wondrous story." I raised my palm like I was taking an oath. "All of which is true."

"I believe it is true you are of muddled mind."

Lilly extended her legs and smoothed her skirt over them. She folded her arms under her ample breasts, pushed them up as if they were plump pillows. They settled back down with a jiggle. Then she picked up the heather branch again and pointed its twig end toward me.

"I know that you are here to rescue Lord Edward." Lilly tapped my forehead with her stick. "I overheard you talking to Lady Greyhurst when you first invaded her garden."

I stuck my legs out too and pressed the soles of my boots against the bottom of her clog shoes. She pushed back. In our little contest, she held me to a tie. The woman was strong-legged as well as stubborn.

"You were thrown off the Spindledown stage." She touched the branch against the tip of my nose. "Robbed and chased by two men lurking in Hangman's Forest. Escaped. Then somehow stumbled upon my father's farm."

"How do you know about these things?" Even I could hear surprise in my voice. "I almost had my throat cut."

"There be tales whispered." Lilly brushed a wayward strand of dark brown hair from her forehead and tucked it over her ear. "William Squarrels has lost passengers before. And he be a cagey man who stays far from the law."

"Who were the two men who chased me through the forest?" Not that I wanted an introduction, just my assailants' names in case we met again.

"Your pursuers were the Watkins, two dirt-poor brothers, landless men who have no honest labor to provide food for their wives and children. So on occasion they drink too much beer and become highwaymen." Lilly gave me a little nod of satisfaction to show she had answered my question. "They waylay travelers foolish enough to be caught in Hangman's Forest. They are more to be pitied than cursed."

"Excuse me for not feeling sorry for them," I said. "I'm quite willing to curse them."

Before she could make her next point by poking the heather in my face, I snatched the branch from her hand. She grabbed my wrist with both hands. We had a tug-of-war, the heather jigging and jagging between us. A determined Lilly would not yield, nor did she smile.

"Are you going to help me free Lord Edward or not?" I scolded.

"Are you going to let me clean your bleeding head wound so it won't fester?" she said.

She released my wrist, stood up, and extended her hand to me. I looked at it with suspicion. Now what?

"Come inside, Elliot of Vail, distant traveler from afar." Lilly smoothed her skirt. "I offer you bread."

"Any chance of getting washed up?" I lifted one arm and sniffed my armpit to demonstrate my serious need for soap and water.

"If you are indeed so careless of your health, I will stoke the fire and draw some well water for the tub. You can bathe. Dry your clothing by the fire. Same as Bockman did. Perhaps you only know him as Lord Edward."

"Bockman?" I thought I was the only one who called him by his last name.

She smiled, sweetly implying she had a close personal relationship. We clasped hands and she pulled me upright. Lilly playing games with my landlord? Good or bad news for me?

— — —

I had carried buckets of well water into the kitchen, bemoaning the lack of inside plumbing. When the water level in the high-sided tub reached six inches or so, Lilly added a kettle of hot water. I stripped down and handed my clothes to Lilly. She had a farm girl's practical nature, making no big thing of a naked man.

I scrunched inside the tub, my arms resting on the rim. I'm a shower person, but the soak in the warm water felt great on my sore muscles. I lathered up the bar of soap and set to work scrubbing off the grime. Some sense of normalcy was returning to my body. Lilly stood beside me and poured warm water over my outstretched hands. I splashed handfuls on my face and over my head.

Lilly went outside for a few minutes and returned with my outfit, mud rinsed off and roughly cleaned. She chatted away while hanging my clothes to dry by the fireplace. If she found the modern fabric strange, she neither commented nor asked questions. Good thing Alice Ho had removed all the elastic.

"I first met Bockman," Lilly said, "when he appeared in our haystack. He was oddly dressed. And wore a feather in his cap. He asked my name. I told him it was Lilly, like the Lily of the Field flower. He said Lilly was a bonnie name and I should call him Lord Edward."

She adjusted the sleeves on her red-trimmed blouse, the same top she had worn in Lady Greyhurst's garden. I struggled to keep from staring at her boobs.

"Did Bockman explain how he ended up at your farm?" I asked as she went over to the fireplace.

"Lord Edward told me that he had traveled far and had become lost. He claimed he was aiming for London." Lilly protected her hand with one edge of her apron and lifted the water kettle from its hook over the fire. "I told him that his aim was poor, being the city was two days' journey to the south."

My head wound had healed enough that I could do without the bandage. I inspected the rest of my body. No major bruises or bumps. I grinned a welcome to Lilly. The water in the tub had cooled. The steam rising from the kettle she held promised hot water.

"Pull your feet back lest I scald them."

She laughed at the way I scooted backward and hugged my knees to protect sensitive parts.

"Smell better, feel better." I rubbed a hand over my stubble. "I feel a beard coming on unless you have a razor blade handy."

"Think you that I am a barber?" She gave me an exasperated look. "Lord Edward also held strong views about cleanliness. Strange ideas. I tried to tell him that bathing more than twice a year was exposing oneself to disease and evil vapors."

I recalled the first items Bockman had asked me to send in the box. I had always assumed they were for Lady Greyhurst. But just maybe—

"Did Lord Edward give you this scented soap?" I held out the soap bar. "And something to put on your hair?"

Lilly looked startled. Her brown eyes scrutinized my face. She crossed her arms and stepped back from me.

"How did you learn our secret?" she said. "He made me promise to tell no one."

"We shared a room." I tightened my lips and resisted the urge to add the words "in Chinatown," "San Francisco," and "California."

"Then you know that he is a magician." Lilly cast nervous glances around the room. She went to the door and peered outside. "If people around here knew, he would be taken from the dungeon and burned at the stake for witchcraft."

"What trick did he do to make you say such foolishness?" I asked.

It wasn't yet time for show-and-tell. I needed her assistance without disturbing her mind with twenty-first-century technology. Lilly seemed a very bright woman, but I doubted she had much formal education.

"He made a box disappear and come back again. Filled with wondrous items," Lilly said.

Surprise, surprise. Buddy Box and Lilly were old friends. And my whole scheme to free Bockman, round up a collection of royal paintings, and return to modern times would be worthless if I couldn't locate the box.

"Show me where he did this trick."

I started to stand up, but she pushed me back down into the tub. She seemed a bit frightened by my reaction. I had better tread carefully if I wanted her help.

"I plan to free Lord Edward," I said. "But I'm without money, save for a few small coins hidden in my jacket lining. All the items I need for his rescue are stored in his magic box. But I don't know where to find it."

"'Tis, I suppose, back in his London house," Lilly said in a matter-of-fact tone. "I last saw it there."

My screwball landlord had made several roundtrips back in time, the box too. The return launch site must be in Bockman's London house. My hypothesis damn well better be valid, or I was trapped in the year 1665. With or without Bockman, I had to find his London house. Lilly could take me to the exact location.

"Where are your parents?" I hadn't seen or heard anyone but Lilly around the farm.

"My father and Mum have gone to work the far fields with Sara and Tom Smyth. They stay the night and return on the morrow. The Spindledown faire is less than a fortnight away. Everyone is anxious to get all the work done."

"Perchance I could rent a horse from your father." What was the going rate for rent-a-nag around here? Wait a minute. I didn't have but a few coins, and Visa wasn't taking applications.

"We have but one horse, and he is old and weary. As is my father."

She sighed as she returned the kettle to the fireplace. Then she turned to me. When Lilly saw my downcast look, she came over to me and took my head between her hands.

"We are but poor farmers," she said. "Father does not own the land. We work the plot for Lord Weston. That high-and-mighty man keeps a fine estate not far from Spindledown. His hired mercenaries keep him safe. He is a powerful man well entangled in royal politics.

"How do I get to London?" With Lilly's help I might have a fighting chance.

"Same as I do," she said. "On the back end of a bumpy cart. The neighboring farmers take milled grain to the bakers in London. I must return again for my servitude to Lady Greyhurst."

"May I ride too?" I said.

Lilly reached down into the bath water, reached between my legs and grabbed a handful of me. Pulled me upright.

"I suppose," she said, "you could persuade me to let you ride."

I laid a hand along her cheek. Her brown eyes smoldering, parted lips tempting. Ah, Bockman, the things I did to save your scrawny ass.

FOURTEEN

Army of Two

The rope latticework that served as bed springs had survived our bouncing around. Our efforts had also smoothed the lumps in the straw-filled mattress. The down-filled pillow was a surprising luxury. But then this was a farm, and there were ducks and geese honking around.

Lilly hummed an upbeat tune that I had no hope of identifying since it wasn't "Greensleeves." She sat on the edge of her bed and fussed with her hair, combing it with her fingers. I lay beside her on my back, resting my head on clasped hands, and admired the repair job Lilly had done to the leg of my torn tights. Almost as good as new. The only comment she made about my costume was something to the effect that Bockman and I favored the same tailor.

Lilly's tiny bedroom held little more than the basic comforts. A narrow wooden bed, a lidded chest, and a plain chair sufficed for furniture. The rest of the farmhouse was equally plain. A spindle beside the fireplace reminded me that mass-produced clothing was still in the future.

"This is delightful, Lilly," I said. "I can rest and recuperate before we return to London. Once there, you can show me Lord Edward's house, and I can retrieve the box. Then I'll be equipped to rescue him."

Lilly lay down beside me, propped her head on one hand and

toyed with my cleft chin. I had made a fine start of a sporty beard. Maybe I'd let my hair grow and wear it in a ponytail with a dashing ribbon.

"Elliot, I must disturb your restful but lazy thoughts," she said. "Hear me out. Your plan does not confront the true nature of the challenge. Why would you travel from here to London and back again to free Lord Edward? 'Tis a waste of time, and I fear he suffers most grievously in captivity."

"My dear Lilly." I leaned over the edge of her bed, retrieved my boots, and tugged them on. "Your ardor for freeing Bockman ignores three problems."

I stood up to make my points. She took umbrage at my towering above her and rose out of bed, confronting me with both hands on her hips. It was hard to one-up this woman.

"One." I waved a finger under her nose. "Except for a couple of measly coins, I have no money. Nothing to barter. No one to borrow from. Nothing to sell. Therefore, I can't bribe the jailer to release Lord Edward."

Lilly batted my finger away. She walked out of the bedroom into the kitchen. I followed her.

"Two." I hunched my shoulders like a Mafioso in a tight suit. "I'm alone in a strange land, a one-man army without weapons. So I can't fight my way into the dungeon. I rest my logical case."

"Have you a number three?" she flared. "Or are your first two protests only a disguise for lack of courage?"

She kicked my shin. This peasant woman was more prone to action than reason. I grabbed my ankle and hopped about.

"Ow," I cried and moved my legs a safe distance from her foot. "Three. I don't even know for sure where he's being held."

I backed over towards the fireplace in case she decided to throw something at me. She gave me a hard stare.

"We will not," Lilly said, "solve any problems if I neglect my labors. The farm does not keep itself. We have already spent too much time in pleasure. Earn your bread."

Then Lilly joined me by the fire. She smiled and gave me a peck on my cheek, her flash of anger gone.

"I believe," she cooed, "I can resolve all three of your protests."

Darn if I didn't think she could.

— — —

I did the Old English farmhand version of slopping the hogs, raking the hay, and gathering eggs while Lilly busied herself with household chores. Thankfully, I didn't have to milk the cow. I demurred on the udder squeezing-and-pulling routine.

Chores finished, Lilly prepared a warm meal for us and directed me to ready the table. I looked around the kitchen for a table, but in vain. She gave me an exasperated look and pointed to a sturdy oak chair against the wall. The chair had a hinged back that held a round wooden tabletop. I tugged the chair-table to the center of the kitchen and tilted the top over the arms to make a table, a clever furniture design that did double duty.

I wolfed down every morsel of food Lilly had placed in front of me—bread, cheese, and a stew full of barley, peas, and chicken. I scraped clean the shallow wooden dinner plate. Lilly called me a fine trencherman. She tidied the kitchen, then sat down on a backless bench across the table from me. I polished off the tankard of warm home-brewed beer, a fine ending to the meal.

"Money," she said.

"My few coins are chump change," I said. "Lame Le Mieux mugged me on Hangman Forest road. Took my shekels. I suspect your purse is bare, and banks around here require collateral."

"I find your language hard to understand." She mimicked a juggler tossing balls in the air. "You throw out words that are not connected. Somewhere in your reply there must be something you are trying to tell me."

My reservoir of natural humor was about dry. My face must have reflected my dour mood. Lilly reached across the scarred tabletop and laid her hands over mine. At least she didn't pat them like a mother soothing her kid.

"Do not despair, dear Elliot," she said. "First, I can solve the money problem for you. I have a simple plan to restore your funds."

"I'm listening." I cupped my hands behind my ears.

"We will go to Spindledown, find Squarrels and the Frenchman you call Le Mieux. Demand they return your money."

"Or what?" I protested. "The last thing I want is to call the constables or the guards. Le Mieux and Squarrels are hard-hearted scoundrels. They would just laugh at us. Maybe beat me up while they were at it."

"True." Lilly favored me with a wide smile that revealed her deep dimples. "However, they will not laugh at Grundle."

"Grundle?" I said. "What or who might that be?"

"Well, if you must know," Lilly stammered. "He is my swain. We have . . ." She cleared her throat. "Grundle is also . . . the local hangman."

I leaped up and made three rapid circles around the kitchen table like a dog chasing its tail. All I wanted to do was to rescue Bockman and make a small fortune by selling miniature portraits. Now, in order to get my money back, I had to make nice with Lilly's executioner boyfriend. What was I supposed to do to help a hangman? Hold his hood while he fought? Spring the trapdoor?

"Lilly, you aren't serious," I said. "Please tell me you are not pulling my leg."

"Nor am I pushing your leg," she said. Her face clouded in confusion, then brightened in understanding. "I jest not."

Lilly intercepted my pacing by grabbing my sleeve and pulling me to the bench alongside her. She said nothing as I moped. Did I have a better plan? My resources had been stripped away. My ability to talk my way out of bad situations, my best weapon, was like damp gunpowder—prone to misfire. I held my hands up in surrender. Lilly's boyfriend, Grundle, could come in handy for getting my money back. People tended not to argue with a hangman.

What an odd first date that must have been. Let me explain the mask and noose, my dear, a bit of S&M. Bloodstains on my jacket? Tomato sauce. I don't have a lot of friends. Must be because I'm shy. Hey, I had just created a new routine—the hangman's first date—for my comedy act.

"Having provided a Grundle solution to your number one objection," Lilly said, "let me deal with your third protest."

"What happened to my number two?" By now, I had learned not to wave fingers in her face. "I'm a one-man army without a weapon. Got a solution?"

"Yes," she said. "To solve your second concern, I will assist you in freeing Bockman."

"Great. Now we're an army of two."

"Your number three is the most challenging," Lilly admitted. "Finding Lord Edward's exact location is difficult. Lord Weston shuttles his prisoner from the old Garwaye Castle dungeon, which he retained when he built his country estate on the castle ruins, to an isolated cottage at the edge of Hangman's Forest."

"Why would he move Bockman around?"

"Some whisper that Lord Weston believes Lord Edward is an alchemist. Weston has filled the forest house with foul chemicals and devices. 'Tis at this remote house, away from prying eyes, where he forces Edward to labor."

"Alchemy," I said. "You mean turning base metal into gold?"

If the idea hadn't been so ridiculous I would have laughed. But there was a kind of lopsided logic. To stave off being killed, Bockman might have convinced Weston that he was the reincarnation of King Arthur's Merlin. My self-styled genius landlord could dole out just enough modern information to stave off the thumbscrew.

"No," Lilly said. "Something more important than gold . . . youth. The elixir of longevity."

"It would be just like Bockman to cook up a batch of wrinkle cream," I wisecracked.

"Do not laugh at my words. You know that Lord Edward holds secret knowledge which he hides from the world."

"Yes, but without his special equipment and compounds, he is powerless." Bockman needed electricity, computer chips, plastic, a chemical catalog, UPS and a few other modern miracles.

"Do you want to hear my solution or not?" Lilly refused to be ignored.

"I suppose," I said. "Your great plan is to walk up to Lord Weston's castle, knock on the front door and say, 'Hi, it's me' like he would be expecting you."

"Yes."

"Yes? What do you mean, yes?" I said. "Can't be yes."

"'Tis."

"Lilly, let me be blunt," I said. "To Lord Weston, you are nothing but a peasant, beneath his station. I seriously doubt he considers you within his social circle. I don't mean to be unkind, but you would be lucky if he didn't set the dogs on you."

"How do you know I do not have something he wants?" Lilly extended one leg, pulled up her skirt and flashed a thigh.

"Sorry to deflate your ego," I said. "As alluring as your charms are, I'm sure he has his choice of rich, pretty, and available ladies. You hold nothing of interest for him."

"Wrong as usual, Elliot of Vail." She slid one hand inside the top of her blouse, and pulled out a folded paper between her thumb and forefinger.

"Here. I hold a message from Lady Greyhurst." Lilly waved the letter under my nose. A trace of perfume lingered. "Why do you think the great lady is so generous of heart that she would allow her servant to return to her father's farm so often?" Lilly said. "You are the one deceived."

"Just a farm girl" had been Lady Greyhurst's dismissive remark to me in her garden. I had fallen for her deception. Face it. Lilly made the perfect courier, passing secret notes between Lady G and Lord Weston. Dumb me. I had believed they were enemies.

"What does the note say?" I had a hunch that Lady Greyhurst's little business adventure had a lot to do with Weston and very little to do with me. Hippo had been right when he warned me to avoid royal politics. In Lady G's chess game, I was a pawn.

"I do not dare break the seal and open it," Lilly said. "I would not wish Grundle to apply his trade to my neck."

She stood and walked over to a gray woolen cloak hanging on a wall peg. She draped it over her shoulders. Then she fashioned a caplike white hat on her head, tying the ribbons snug under her chin.

"Come, Elliot," Lilly said. "We walk to Spindledown to arrive before dark. It is time to test your manhood by convincing Grundle to help us."

"Not me," I said. "Remember, he's your . . . shall we say, close friend. I doubt if I would get a welcoming hug."

"True." She leaned her head against mine and spoke softly into my ear like she was sharing a secret. "Be guarded with your words and actions. Grundle suffers from heated jealousy when other men seek to know me." Lilly's face turned red. Then she brushed past me and walked out into the yard. "He can become mean-tempered on such suspicions."

That didn't sound good.

FIFTEEN

Trouble Brews

Lilly and I arrived at early dusk. The Spindledown Village shops were preparing to close. The cloudless sky promised to compensate for a lack of streetlights. Lilly led me to the local tavern, the Wobbly Duck, where the evening's action assembled. And where Grundle should be.

I stood outside the entrance, peered through the open door and eyeballed the interior. A tavern wench fed kindling into a large fireplace, nurturing a growing flame. A host of bright candles promised a friendly welcome. Wooden trestle tables, long backless benches, worn beams—all looked rough-hewn and soot-stained. Lilly urged me to enter.

A noisy din assaulted my ears as I poked my head through the open doorway. Boisterous shouts from unruly patrons were an odd mixture of anger and hearty laughter. I smelled stale ale, unwashed bodies, and rank smoke. The odors wafting through the doorway signified this English pub specialized in sensory overload.

Two farmers brushed past me, greeting friends while trailing pungent manure footprints across the rough plank floor. The tavern, all in all, was a stinking den of drunken vice that was an affront to proper citizens. My kind of place.

I offered my open hand to Lilly. The few coins I had hidden from Le Mieux rested in my palm.

"This is my total fortune," I confessed. "Is it enough to buy a few tankards of ale?"

She rested her hand over mine and added several small coins. She gave me a sad smile.

"These copper farthings be my poor contribution to your effort," she said.

"Lilly," I interrupted before she could say any more. "I can only guess how dear these coins are to you. I intend to invest this entire sum on beer. If this does not please you, take your money back."

"I know of no better man to free my Lord Edward." Her puckered lips sent me a distant, modest air kiss.

My ego hoped she was referring to me and not to her hulking hangman. Lilly used both hands to close my fingers around our paltry stake. Her skin was rough, but her touch was gentle.

"Grundle will be in the wee alcove along the back wall," she said. "You must proceed alone. If Grundle sees me with another man, he would fight first and listen afterwards."

Lilly had just refused to accompany me into the tavern. That wasn't part of our deal. Where was it written that I had to tackle this foolhardy adventure without fifty percent of my army of two? And how was I supposed to pick him out of the sea of people packed into the village's version of a redneck cowboy bar?

"At least," I said, "tell me what Grundle looks like."

"He is tall as a tree," Lilly said, "thick as an oak plank, and strong as a bull."

"Why would a woman as decent as you choose to consort with this knave?" None of my business, but if I had any hope of convincing Grundle to help me, I had to know the lay of the land . . . so to speak. I hadn't quite got my mind around being in competition with another man for Lilly's charms. "You can do better."

"The local lads are sturdy but boring." Lilly gave an impromptu pelvic thrust. "Once in a while, a bit of nasty adds spice." Then she pushed me hard in the back, sending me stumbling into the tavern. "Besides, Grundle be not just a hangman. His sister is married to Lord Edward's jailer."

Lilly kept pulling surprises on me. Maybe she enjoyed seeing the incredulous look on my face. What else was she keeping from me?

— — —

I sidestepped between two locals, only to collide with a chin-whiskered young rake who glared at me just because I sloshed his beer. He slid one hand inside his jacket. Was he fingering a hidden weapon? I gave him a mumbled apology and deferential bow.

A serving girl lugged a couple tankards of ale while navigating through the crowd of patrons. She adroitly swiveled her hips to dodge pats and pinches. Her maneuver reminded me of the What's Up? Comedy Club waitresses. I related to these hard-working gals with their low pay and all the crap they had to endure from drunken customers. Some things hadn't changed with time.

I caught the serving girl's eye and smiled my friendly best. She raised her eyebrows in silent acknowledgment.

"Grundle?" I mouthed.

"Over there. In back." She turned her head over her left shoulder.

No polite smile. Nothing sparkled. Just efficient communication. The kind of basic you-asked-I-told shorthand of a hustling worker.

I aimed for the tavern's back wall and plowed my way through the throng of rowdy customers. The Wobbly Duck's atmosphere had a tactile quality. You could almost grab a handful of air, give it a squeeze, and your fingers would be covered with grime.

In a dark alcove dead ahead, I could make out a man's form sitting alone at a small table. No window, candle nor lantern to provide light. I might as well have been peering into a dark closet. In fact, his sinister shape reminded me of the monster that I was once convinced lived in my grandmother's closet.

I stopped a respectful three feet from Grundle's table until my eyes adjusted to the dim light. He was hunched over, his face obscured by a hooded monk's cowl. His hands surrounded a tankard, oversized mitts, to be sure, but not pudgy. Long fingers that any football wide receiver would envy.

What career path does a man pursue to become the local hangman? Must be a weird apprenticeship. Was there a school? Did your diploma have a tiny ink drawing of a gallows? What kind of social misfit becomes an executioner? Images of all the old Hollywood B-movie dungeon keepers flooded my mind: oversized giant, shaved head, beady eyes, a nasty disposition, and a thick leather belt dangling a ring of cell keys.

There was no crowd around Grundle. I mulled over how best to open a conversation with him. Know any rope tricks? How are they hanging? I decided not to use any comedy lines. My strategy was to appeal to our shared interest. I forced a swallow to clear my throat so I could speak.

"Beer?" My voice croaked like a frog.

Grundle raised his head. The covering slid from around his face to reveal thick red hair cut in pageboy style. Steel-grey eyes were deeply set in his beardless face. Emotionless eyes reflected either a cold heart or dull mind.

"That be a good beginning." Grundle's voice rumbled like distant thunder from deep within his throat. "Ale quenches thirst, but evil deeds require money."

He stood, tilted his head forward to avoid hitting the low ceiling beam. The man was at least six feet ten. Other than his towering presence, the rest of his body seemed well-proportioned. No oversized features of my imaginary giant.

"Three beers," I said. "Two for you, one for me."

"You are a stranger to Spindledown," Grundle said. He massaged his chin while he mulled over my offer. "Local peasants never offer me beer."

Scrutiny was the last thing I needed. I flagged down a waitress and gave her my beer order. Grundle pointed me to the empty bench across from where he had been sitting. I scooted forward and rested my elbows on the scarred tabletop. He had apparently decided I was harmless.

"I'm Elliot." I knew better than to offer a handshake.

"Like I said, 'tis a start." Grundle resumed his seat. "I am Grundle. People hire me to settle scores. Who do you want hanged?"

"Nobody," I squeaked. I coughed and forced my voice lower. "No one."

"Want me to threaten them with being drawn and quartered?"

"Nope," I said as the beers arrived. The waitress picked the proper coins from the scattering I tossed on the table. She didn't linger. I didn't blame her.

"Hot poker in the eye?" Grundle asked. "Tongue cut out?"

I didn't trust myself to talk, so I simply shook my head.

"Whipped? Burned at the stake?" the hangman asked. "I have a wide range of skills. My fees are reasonable too. I will give you the Spindledown fee. Cheaper than London."

"I need your services to right a wrong." Sweat beads were glistening on my forehead. I licked my dry lips.

"I care not about right or wrong." He drained the tankard without it ever leaving his lips.

"Lilly," I said. "Lilly—"

Grundle whacked the tankard on the table so hard it cracked the wooden top. The din in the Wobbly Duck paused at the sound, then resumed. The hangman reached one open hand toward my throat. I shoved a beer into it. Grundle's arm reversed and then tilted the tankard toward his mouth.

"Some men have done her an injustice." I was talking fast, gathering my legs under me in case I needed to run like hell. "Will you help me help her?"

"I will kill them for free," Grundle snarled. His face was now as red as his hair. Beer drooled from the corners of his mouth. "Kill you too. If you be lying."

"Lilly works for Lady Greyhurst." I decided to keep things simple. Short sentences such as . . . see Spot run. Grundle was already halfway though his second beer. I interpreted his gurgle and head nod as general agreement or at least comprehension.

"Lady Greyhurst sent me to Spindledown," I elaborated.

Grundle was looking around for more suds. I pushed my beer across the table toward him, a major sacrifice. He picked up my beer with one hand while setting his empty tankard down with the other. Ah, an ambidextrous executioner.

"Lady Greyhurst entrusted me with money for Lilly." It was my money, but I had decided to give Lilly a share as a reward for helping me get it back. For my own safety, Grundle didn't need to know the details.

"Why?"

Nuts, he wanted an explanation. My mind tossed out suggestions, and I rejected them just as fast. Which emotion should I play on? Greed, envy, love, sympathy, tenderness . . . forget the last one.

"Good question, Grundle," I said. "Yes, why?"

I scratched my head. His face was impassive or frozen. His arm reached out toward me, index finger aiming for my nose. Was he going to break my schnoz? His threatening hand stopped no more than six inches from my face.

"Why?" he said. "Not . . . have another beer?"

He exposed a mouthful of teeth along with gleeful laughter. It was an unexpected high-pitched *hee-hee*. Like the laugh from a little boy who had just played a joke on his older sister. Grundle slapped the table with such force the empty tankards jumped an inch above the table. The coins scattered in all directions.

"Great idea." I tried to collect the coins before they fell off the tabletop. Two escaped my grasp. They hit the floor and rolled. I started to reach after them.

"Do not bother. Nell will pick them up. More beer," he bellowed at the passing tavern maid. She scuttled away.

I think half the men in the Wobbly Duck would have instantly given Grundle their beers if he would go away. In short order, Nell put four foaming tankards in front of us, scooped up the remaining money from the table, and squatted to retrieve the fallen coins.

"Squarrels and Lame Le Mieux stole my money."

"So?" Grundle shrugged like he couldn't care less. The man was not good at connecting the dots.

"So, I can't give Lilly her money," I said.

He mulled that fact over, nursing his beer for what seemed like a few seconds short of eternity. Maybe a few hints would move the discussion along.

"Lady Greyhurst. Elliot. Money. Lilly," I said. "Le Mieux robbed Elliot. No money. Lilly."

"I understand, Elliot," he said. "I be a skilled hangman." His lazy eye meandered off to one side. He finger-walked his way to the tankard like a cat stalking a mouse. He pounced on the nearest beer. "Not an idiot."

He could have fooled me.

"Nobody appreciates me," Grundle said. A little spark of indignation flashed in his eyes. The hangman propped his chin on the knuckles of one hand and brooded into his tankard. "How would you like mothers scaring their wee ones by using your name?"

I had never fretted over that scenario. I had to steer his focus back to retrieving my money from Le Mieux. With his index finger, Grundle traced spiraling circles in the pool of spilled beer.

"If we get the money back from the robbers, I could buy more beer," I said. Grundle flipped me off with a wave of his hand.

"The village folk call me names behind my back," he said. "All because of one little mistake. I was young."

Well, we all make rookie mistakes. I once built a whole comic routine around a make-believe frigid girlfriend I named Zelda. Found out after I was fired that it was the name of the club owner's mother.

"They call me Two Chop." Grundle's knuckles whitened as he gripped the table edge.

"And that would be because . . . ?"

"I forgot to remove the prisoner's neck collar." Grundle turned one hand palm up and struck it twice with the open edge of his other hand. "Had to hack him twice with my axe before his head came off." He chugged the remainder of his beer and wiped his mouth with the back of his hand. "People remember me as Two Chop. I think that tiny error is what has kept me stuck here in the countryside. Not working in London be an embarrassment to a master craftsman like me."

"Two Chop," I said. "Well, that explains the very words I heard Le Mieux and Squarrels say about you."

I rubbed the back of my skull where the Frenchman had whacked me. The spot was still sore. I didn't need any more justification for my little deception.

Grundle cleared the table with one swipe of his arm. Tankards clattered to the floor. He stood, grabbed my jacket collar, and lifted me off the chair with minimum effort. My boot heels rose several inches off the floor. I dangled in front of him. I forced my mouth into a silly grin.

"Let's go get Le Mieux." He gave a schoolyard bully's laugh of delight and set my feet back on the floor.

"Don't forget my, er, Lilly's money," I said. "I'll buy dinner. Invite your sister too. Understand her husband is in the same line of work. Keeps the jail secure. Making the village safe from troublemakers."

"Oh, you do not want to meet my brother-in-law," Grundle said. "He be the mean one in the family. Not nice like me."

He pulled the dark cowl over his head, then tramped across the tavern room towards the doorway. The crowd parted like waves in front of a speedboat. I followed behind him as close as I dared without being overly friendly.

"Black," he said over his shoulder. "The one thing I hate about this work is always having to wear black clothes. I'm sick of black. I want to wear clothes like yours."

Grundle's mind had wiring all its own.

"I'll give you my seamstress's name," I said. "Alice Ho. Hard to reach, though."

A wave of silence accompanied Grundle and my exit. Tavern patrons hushed when he came near. The bar noises welled back up once he had passed. I nodded and said my goodbyes to the confused customers like I had known them for years. In my line of work, you always need a good closing routine.

SIXTEEN

The Simple Solution

Grundle had a full head of steam by the time he burst through the tavern doors out onto the dirt street. The hangman turned sharp left as if certain of his destination. I jogged to keep up with his long strides.

I had expected Lilly to be standing outside the Wobbly Duck to cheer us while we retrieved my money from Squarrels and Le Mieux. She was nowhere in sight. Had she feared that Grundle might pitch me out the tavern door? Maybe she was just playing it safe, knowing that when Grundle was in a rage, he didn't really care who he hit.

"Grundle," I said as I huffed and puffed behind his broad back. "Does our mad dash indicate you know where the rogues are hiding? Aren't we supposed to have a strategy session first?"

"Penn." He flung the word over his shoulder.

"What pen?" Then I tried several words. "Pigpen? Fountain pen? Pennsylvania?" He ignored my questions. For all I knew, we could be headed to the village penitentiary.

A pool of water filled a depression in the road. I expected the hangman to leap over the puddle. Instead, Grundle put both feet together and hop-stomped like a wayward boy. Muddy water splashed in every direction. His laugh was more gleeful than sinister. I detoured around the pothole and caught up with him. He slowed his pace enough for us to stride side by side.

"Old man. Price Penn." Grundle's short sentences were his speaking style. "Runs the coach station. And stable. Horses kept there."

"I would prefer finding Le Mieux to a horse," I said. Although riding a horse to London would be better than a rustic cart behind a horse, as Lilly had offered.

Ahead of us in the gathering gloom a split log fence enclosed a patch of bare dirt. Inside the enclosure two sturdy dun-colored horses stood head-to-head as if they were engaged in intimate conversation. In front of the corral stood a separate substantial structure, its steeply pitched roof accented by a massive chimney. The two-story, half-timbered Tudor building with its small glass windows looked like a place where Shakespeare could have lived.

We angled toward the building's front entrance, where a carved wooden sign dangled from a protruding iron bracket above the door. A handful of people milled around a small courtyard, waiting to board a stagecoach that was parked roadside. I figured out where we were headed—the Spindledown coach station. This building had been my planned destination when Lady Greyhurst dispatched me from London. But I had never arrived, my journey rudely interrupted in Hangman's Forest when Le Mieux robbed and left me as prey for the Watkins brothers.

"Penn keeps two small hidden rooms. In the back of the building," Grundle said. "For travelers who want to stay out of sight."

"That would appeal to Le Mieux," I said. "That rat would only come out at night."

Without warning Grundle accelerated from hurried walk to fast run. The big guy could really move. The waiting coach seemed to be his target. I sprinted after him, trying to keep up. The black cowl slipped off Grundle's head again, revealing his thick red hair. It added a fiery accent to his arrival.

I realized Grundle intended to position himself in front of the standing coach. Its team of six horses stood placid in their harness. A driver, clad in a long buff-colored overcoat and brimmed black leather hat, stood alongside adjusting the gear. I recognized that outfit.

"Squarrels, you crook" I yelled, "give me back my money."

"Quiet," Grundle ordered.

Oops. My anger would warn Squarrels. Waiting passengers scattered as Grundle and I dashed toward them. I'm certain I heard "Two Chop." Followed by a shouted warning—"Run."

Squarrels turned to see what was causing the uproar. His eyes widened from squint to full open. His head recoiled in surprise at the sight of Grundle. He leapt up onto the driver's seat and snatched a whip from its mounting. In a frenzy of motion, he lashed the horses' hindquarters over and over.

The startled team bolted and jerked the coach into motion. A portly passenger sporting a wide-brimmed hat festooned with black feathers had been caught with one foot perched on the coach's step. The man fell backwards, sprawling on the road. The coach doors flopped as the stage gathered speed.

Grundle stood in front of the coach with his arms extended in a classic halt pose. The charging horses had no intention of obeying the hangman's order. His face reddened with anger. Thudding hooves assaulted my ears. The lead horses' nostrils flared. Their heads lifted. Necks arched. Grundle blinked. A look of surprise lit his face. His mouth formed an "O." The stupid jerk was going to be trampled along with my best chance of getting my money back.

I did a dumb thing. I charged full speed into Grundle, hitting him on his right shoulder. The impact sent both of us flying sideways. A passing horse delivered a glancing blow on my back. The force sent me tumbling over Grundle onto the roadside. I rolled to cushion my fall, then sprang to my feet just as the coach passed. Squarrels leaned over from his high perch on the driver's seat. His hat was missing, hair in disarray. His eyes gaped with fear. He raised his hand and threw something at me.

"Take it," he cried. "Tell Grundle I returned my share."

The coach sped away, leaving the hangman and me by the side of the road. Grundle sat with his elbows on his knees, watching the fleeing Squarrels. He seemed unfazed by our near calamity.

I picked up the handkerchief-sized bundle Squarrels had tossed at my feet. I teased open the drawstring. Inside was half my stolen money. Grundle's face appeared over my shoulder to stare at the collection of coins.

"Which ones are Lilly's?" he asked.

I guess executioners are not into saying, "Thanks for saving my life." So I made a show of examining both heads and tails on each coin.

"None of these," I said. "Le Mieux must still have her portion."

"Old Penn," Grundle said, "will take us to Le Mieux."

The chaotic scene in front of the station had calmed some. People huddled on the other side of the road in nervous conversation. The man who had fallen from the coach sat on the roadside. A pained expression twisted his face as he cradled his right arm. Luggage had scattered where passengers had dropped their bags in haste to avoid Grundle's charge. One woman, wearing a velvet dress, whispered something in her companion's ear while pointing at Grundle.

"Those horses got my blood up." Grundle dusted himself off, cracked his knuckles. "Fun too."

He clapped me on the back, nearly knocking me to my knees.

Was that my thanks? Did that mean we were now buddies? My new friend tromped off toward the station.

Dusty traces left by the vamoosed coach lingered in the air. As I turned to follow Grundle, I thought I caught a glimpse of a figure standing in the dark shadow between two thatched cottages. A woman. She wore a close-fitting bonnet, a cloak draped around her strong shoulders. I looked again. No one was there.

Grundle was already across the road and taking aim at the station entrance. He was on the hunt for Lame Le Mieux and I didn't want to miss the action. I stuffed Squarrels' money purse inside my shirt and hastened to join the hangman. If that was Lilly, I'd find her later.

SEVENTEEN

Grundle's Fumble

Side by side we barged into the station's spacious waiting room and stopped. Rows of backless benches provided serviceable seating for travelers waiting for their coaches. Four sturdy, slat-back chairs had been pulled close to a massive stone fireplace that graced one wall. Flames licked up from neatly stacked kindling, igniting logs to warm the night air.

Grundle gave the room a cursory examination, then headed into the tavern area. A few feet beyond the dining area was a solid door with no identification sign on it. Maybe it led to the stationmaster's office or perhaps to an outside privy. Grundle never slowed his pace nor tested to see if the door was locked. He head-butted the door and it burst open. A moment later I heard a man's loud protests, each accompanied by several thumps.

If a fight were in progress, Grundle wouldn't need my assistance. I strolled into the room, taking my time. I was right. The big bruiser held a man's thin ankle, the only part of Grundle's quarry that had not escaped out an open window.

The man kicked the wood framing with his free foot and shouted a string of curses. They alternated between pleas to be let go and assertions regarding the character traits of Grundle's mother. The hangman reached one of his long arms out the window and returned with a slight little man held secure in his grasp. One hand encircled the man's scrawny neck while the other firmly held the man's ankle.

Grundle raised his captive for display like a fisherman with a prized catch. He released his grip on the man's neck, then turned him upside down. Grundle's fingers gripped tight around the thin ankle. Grundle kept the puny little guy's head six inches above the floor. Wisps of gray hair stuck out in every direction from a balding head.

"Elliot, meet Master Price Penn." Grundle faced the man forward. "Old Penn wants to say hello."

Penn stopped struggling. He raised a liver-spotted hand a couple of inches and wiggled his fingers at me.

"Pleased." He grimaced beneath an oversized nose that called undue attention to an otherwise plain face. His ears stuck out like Alfred E. Neuman in the What, Me Worry? poster. Grundle had the satisfied smile of a kid holding a balloon.

"We are looking for the rogue Lame Le Mieux," I said. "If you tell us where he is, Grundle will release you."

"Don't believe . . . I know the gentleman," Penn protested.

I wasn't convinced my assurances to Old Penn were worth anything. Apparently, Penn didn't think so either. By now his face had turned beet red. He twisted and turned his body in a futile effort to free himself.

Grundle gave Penn an up-and-down shake, like you would a champagne bottle when you wanted to spray your buddies at a bachelor's wedding party.

"Oh, the Frenchman," Penn sputtered. "I'll be pleased to escort your lordships to his lodgings." He waved his arm in the general direction of a side door.

Grundle gathered a handful of Old Penn's shirt, pulled him upright, and released his ankle hold. Penn tottered on unsure feet, then tucked his shirttail inside the waistline of his breeches. Grundle waved a finger under his captive's large nose as a cautionary warning not to try anything.

"Le Mieux is always trouble," Penn complained. He rubbed his ankle and tugged his worn stocking up his skinny calf. He ran a finger under his wet nose and glared at Grundle.

"I will fetch my lantern," Penn said.

We stepped out the side door into a narrow pathway that hugged the building, then walked single file along the building's outer wall. A row of rampant rosebushes screened our movement from any casual observer passing by in the moonlit night. Penn stopped when we reached the building's back corner. He grabbed the far end of the Tudor's dark framing, then pulled the siding towards him. The section swung open, revealing a secret narrow passageway.

Grundle grasped Penn's collar, jerked him backwards, then muscled his way around the startled stationmaster. I caught the old man under the armpits to keep him from falling. His muttered thank you arrived on bad breath. He would have turned tail had I not blocked his retreat. I rescued the lantern from his trembling hand.

"Has Le Mieux paid for his room?" I figured the stationmaster-turned-innkeeper would see the logic of his situation.

"Aye." Penn raised both palms upward and nodded in a what-can-I-do? gesture.

"I believe Le Mieux to be a vile scoundrel who would rob his own mother," I said, "or betray his best friend."

"Aye," Penn agreed. "You do know the man."

He turned on his heel and followed Grundle while I brought up the rear. The corridor led past mortared stonework that must have been the backside of the waiting room's fireplace. I tugged Penn's sleeve and pointed to the stone.

"The station building," Penn said, "is full of hidden passages and cubbyholes. See this iron bolt? A spy-hole."

I held the lantern close to where Penn pointed at the back of a red brick between two stones.

"During Cromwell's time," Penn said, "Catholic priests hid in fear of their lives. A Quaker or two were also my guests, when they were considered rebels. Room's been unused since King Charles II took back the throne."

"Except," I quipped, "to hide a thief who has the proper coins."

"Aye. It be a profitable trade."

A shout of alarm echoed down the passageway, followed by silence.

"I do believe Grundle has found the Frenchman," Penn said and ducked his head under a low beam that served as the lintel over a small door.

I followed suit and emerged in a gloomy room lit by a single squat candle. Moonlight showed through a two-foot-square opening in the roof. A slate slab that served as a plug for the ceiling hole dangled from a chain. A convenient cover that could be inserted or removed at the dweller's option.

A three-legged stool lay tipped over on the floor. On the top of a well-worn gate leg table was a torn chunk of bread in a pool of beer apparently spilled from a chipped earthen cup. We had interrupted Le Mieux's dinner.

Grundle guarded a quivering Le Mieux, who had backed into a corner of the room. He pulled every appendage inwards away from the hangman. The Frenchman's tattered cloak, wrapped tightly around him, resembled folded bat wings. I was glad to see that Grundle wasn't beating the tar out of Lame Le Mieux, although the hangman did have his game-face on and looked mean enough to bite Le Mieux's head off.

"Greetings, Monsieur Le Mieux," I said. "Lady Greyhurst says bonjour."

Le Mieux tilted his head sideways to peer past Grundle's frame. Frantic eyes fixed on me.

"Ah, Monsieur Tanner," he said. "Pleased to see you once again." The man was shoeless. One of his stockings had come loose from his breeches to reveal a knee crisscrossed with scars. He rolled his fists in oily supplication. "Sorry to hear about your accident in Hangman's Forest."

The guy had balls. I'd give him that.

"Return the money you stole from me," I said. "Then perchance Grundle will not kill you."

"Pray that I could restore your money," Le Mieux said, "but I have given it all to Price Penn in payment for my room and substance."

Penn's shaky hand appeared over my shoulder and jabbed the air. I looked around to find Penn standing on tiptoe directly behind me. The stationmaster gripped his other hand on my shoulder.

"Liar." Penn spat out the word. "Liar. He keeps his coins in a sack around his neck." The old man waved his arm like an overeager student to garner Grundle's attention. "From the pureness of my heart, I shall refund any money due Elliot."

"I, too, will restore the borrowed funds," Le Mieux said. "How-some-ever, the coins hide under the bed in a hole I dug in the floor. Here, let me get them for you." Body trembling, he edged past Grundle and stood beside the soiled straw mattress covering the bed. "Grundle, I am too weak to pull the heavy bed aside. Take hold the footboard and move it for me."

Grundle bent over, placed his hands under the frame and lifted the bed off the floor with ease. I smelled a rat.

"Wait, Grundle," I commanded.

Too late. Le Mieux vaulted from the floor to the bed and bounced upward. His outstretched hands latched on to the framed opening in the ceiling.

I leapt after him. Managed to get my arms around his cloak, hung on, then reached my hand up to grab his throat. My fingers clutched something, but Le Mieux twisted away and kicked me in the groin. The bottoms of Le Mieux's cruddy stockings were all I saw as I fell to the floor. He pulled himself skyward in one swift motion and disappeared through the roof opening.

Grundle stood gap-mouthed beneath the opening, still holding the bed off the floor. Penn was motionless, hands in a praying position, afraid to move.

"I'm sorry," Grundle said. His face reddened in embarrassment, his lower lip protruded, and he buried his chin on his chest. A hangman, hanging his own head in shame.

I stretched myself full length on the floor for dramatic effect. When I had Grundle and Penn's attention, I raised my arm ninety degrees in a victory salute. Grasped in my hand was Le Mieux's money sack. I had torn it from his neck as I fell.

"Gooooal." I imitated my favorite soccer announcer.

"Which coins are Lilly's?" Grundle leaned over me, hands clasped behind his back, like a hiker studying an interesting bug on a trail.

"First we have to find her," I stalled.

The last thing I needed was Grundle monitoring my payment to Lilly. It wouldn't surprise me if her lover lug wanted me to give it all to her. Now, where did he get the idea that it was her money? Oh, yeah, from me.

Grundle stared about Le Mieux's room. The hangman had a dejected slump in both face and posture as if the only thing that would cheer him up would be to hammer some unlucky soul. Old

Penn must have had the same thought because he quickly reiterated his eagerness to cough up the money the Frenchman had paid him for room, board and hideout.

"Le Mieux will be far gone into the night," Penn said. "The Frenchman is well practiced in evading pursuers."

The hangman knit his brows as if he hated coming to the same conclusion. He scowled at the hole in the ceiling, as it had been responsible for letting Le Mieux escape. Then he picked up the empty bed and threw the piece of furniture across the room. The frame hit the wall and splintered into pieces. His anger vented, Grundle looked in my direction with a quizzical expression.

"What do we do now?" the hangman asked.

"Let's call it a day," I said.

None of us in the room felt like chasing after Le Mieux. Penn had nothing to gain, Grundle was dispirited, and I no longer cared. Thanks to Grundle's confrontation with Squarrels and Le Mieux, I had retrieved nearly all my money.

"I must go soothe my paying passengers," Penn said. "Thanks to your confrontation with Squarrels in the courtyard, you frightened the coach horses into bolting." He directed his barb at the hangman, who made no comment.

"Elliot," Grundle said. "I shall see you later."

Grundle seemed to think the whole escapade unworthy of his concern. He pulled his monk's cowl over his head and stalked past me. He growled at the old stationmaster, who cringed in response.

"I need a cheap room for several nights." My bones were tired, my stomach ready for ale and food.

"One just opened up." Penn held the broken headboard in his hands. "Although the bed might need a wee bit of repair."

"I recall that you were anxious to return my money," I reminded him.

The geriatric gave me a forced smile, as if it hurt every tooth that remained in his mouth. After he turned the three-legged stool to its upright position, he cleared the remains of Le Mieux's interrupted meal from the table.

"I suppose you want fresh straw in the mattress?" He pulled the coarse ticking off the bed. Penn's question implied that I was a fussy guest.

"Yeah," I said. "Who knows what Le Mieux left behind?"

Old Penn backed out of the tiny room, dragging the soiled mattress into the passageway. The stale bread and chipped cup rode piggyback on the top covering. He promised to return with fresh bedding.

Spindledown was a small village. Somewhere nearby Lilly was spending the night. In a comfortable bed, I hoped.

"Alone," I said to the ceiling.

EIGHTEEN

Triple Play

Penn woke me with a knock on my bedroom door, greeted me with a smiling face, and offered a jug of clean water for the washbowl. He stood by while I washed up in the basin. Handed me a towel to demonstrate he was at my service. If nothing else, Old Penn knew his duties as an innkeeper.

"A fine day welcomes you," Penn said.

He gave a cheery weather report. I had the feeling Penn would have said the same thing if there were a downpour outside. But then, after recovering my money, I'd slept well.

"Stay here," I said. "We need to talk."

I had my cash back from Squarrels and Le Mieux. The only missing coins were those the Frenchman had paid to Old Penn for room and board. But I still needed information about Bockman.

"Best we talk outside." Penn led the way through the secret passage and out the hidden door. He looked about, to make certain we were alone. "Grundle is around the station somewhere. I did see him lurking about earlier this morn."

Chirping of birds and the heady fragrance of the old-fashioned cabbage roses lent a note of tranquility to the scene. Penn made an effort to set a pleasant tone between us.

"Planted the roses myself," Penn said. "Are they not a beautiful magenta color? A visiting Dutchman brought the rootstock to me before the war."

"Money, Mister Penn. Return my money." I didn't intend to get off the subject. "Take me to your office. Now."

All of a sudden, I was ordering people around. This wasn't my usual self. A comedian's role is to make fun of bosses' behavior, not engage in it. I smiled to let him know I wasn't angry.

"I take you to be an honest man, Mister Elliot." Penn tented his fingers in a halfhearted plea. "I pray you be gracious and allow me to keep a small sum for my service of revealing the thief, Le Mieux."

Like he had had a choice. I had a hard time staying mad at the old geezer. He was a small businessman trying to survive in a backwater village. Besides, he could be an asset to me. A stationmaster would hear lots of inside information from travelers coming and going to Spindledown.

"How about we trade?" I said. "I'll let you keep a third of the money Le Mieux paid you. I get the room."

"Since the Frenchman won't be using the room," Old Penn said, "I might, with great regret, agree to your request." He made his chin quiver to demonstrate how harsh my terms were.

"You must have an ear for the local gossip," I said.

"Aye." Penn perked up. He hitched his trousers and fiddled with his rolled sleeves. "Idle chatter and rumors pass through my station. Patrons from the Wobbly Duck spoke of your boldness in seeking out Grundle. They said you are a stranger who appeared in Spindledown from nowhere."

Actually, I had come from California in bits and pieces of particles beamed in by a computer named Blue. I could explain, but he wouldn't understand. Sometimes I was not sure I did either, but here I was in Spindledown.

"Tell me," I said, "the exact location where Lord Weston has imprisoned Edward of Bockman."

Penn looked at me for the longest time. He massaged his wrinkled forehead as if sorting his thoughts. Then Penn worried his hands over his response.

"Revealing such information," Penn said, "is not worth my life."

"You are already too old," I retorted. "You could die tomorrow. I may even sic Grundle on you today. What if I let you keep more of the money Le Mieux paid you? Perhaps then you could recall the exact location."

"I have neither daughter nor son to care for me in my infirmity." Penn coughed, beat his chest, and rasped, "My health has been poorly. When cold weather returns, all sorts of aches will be visited upon me."

"Would keeping half the money Le Mieux paid you be stronger medicine than the one given by a physician?"

"I feel better already," Old Penn said. He offered his hand to seal our deal. "I give my oath to assist you."

I gave his bony hand a perfunctory shake, then waited to hear what he had to say, alert for any evasion. He didn't avert his eyes or hold back. He revealed his inside information with glee, like my ex talking to her girlfriends about me.

"Lord Edward's location changes during the month." Penn lowered his voice. "Most likely, on the first fortnight you will find him in old Garwaye Castle's dungeon. When Lord Weston built his new country estate upon the ruins of the keep, he preserved the underground dungeon. On the later portion of the month, the jailer ties Lord Edward behind his horse and trots them both off to a cottage in Hangman's Forest."

Poor Bockman. Being pulled behind a horse could ruin a person's day. Not to mention the effects of being cooped up in a dungeon for two weeks.

"A caution." Penn added a disclaimer. "Such are the rumors, I can not vouch for the truth of such gossip."

"Where, precisely, is the cottage?" I asked. "The forest covers a lot of land."

"Hard to give directions to a stranger," Penn said. "Best be shown the way. I could guide you—for a fee."

"I could wring your neck," I said, "for free."

Grundle appeared through the outside doorway. Ignoring the two of us, he gathered a handful of the globular rose blooms. Thorns jabbed his hands, but no pain registered on the hangman's face.

"What in God's name are you doing?" I asked the giant.

"Lilly sits in the waiting room." Grundle was as eager as a kid showing off a new baby sister. "Come and meet her."

"First, Penn and I must settle our business," I said.

Penn and I convened at his office desk while Grundle waited in the corner, his nose buried in the bouquet he had picked. Penn placed a cautioning finger to his mouth. I nodded in silent agreement. Grundle didn't need to overhear our talk about Bockman or money.

The stationmaster produced a key and opened the fold-down top of his upright desk. I had seen enough television antique shows to know, most likely, Penn's piece of furniture had numerous hidden compartments. The handcrafted walnut secretarial piece could be sold for big bucks in San Francisco.

"Too bad your desk won't fit into my box," I said.

Penn looked perplexed, but I didn't bother to explain. He shielded his action from me by knocking a sheaf of papers to the floor. He stooped to gather them. Magically, money appeared in his hand. Per our deal, he gave me half the stash. I added the coins to the money sack Squarrels had thrown at me.

"You two done talking?" Grundle pulled back his hood, licked his palm and patted down wayward hairs protruding from his page-cut.

"We be good to go, man." I raised Le Mieux's money sack in one hand and Squarrels' sack in the other. Both Penn and Grundle looked at me like I couldn't speak the King's English.

The door into the waiting room dangled from one hinge, thanks to Grundle's unconventional entrance. When we filed in to greet Lilly, I had to be careful. One misstep and my new buddy, Grundle, could stomp on me for frolicking with his filly. How would Lilly handle two swains, boyfriends, whatever, in the same room?

Lilly sat on a backless oak bench in the passenger waiting area. She wore the same tight-fitting white bonnet and grey cloak. Her knees were together, feet flat on the floor, and her back erect. She graciously thanked Grundle when he presented the roses, never a hint of displeasure that he had just handed her prickly thorns among purplish-red flowers. All prim and proper, something I didn't expect from her.

"Greetings, Mistress Swinden," Old Penn said. He bowed as much as his aged back permitted. "I pray you would grant me pardon to see to my overnight guests. They be anxious as to when they can complete their journeys."

"Of course, Mister Penn," Lilly said. "I will see you before I leave."

Her words held a hint of warning to Penn. Did the stationmaster know that Lilly and I had been together outside the Wobbly Duck? Old Penn treated her with deference. Then it dawned on me. Villagers knew this servant girl made regular visits to Lord

Weston's home and was received at the front door. Good insurance to stop loose tongues.

"Elliot." Grundle introduced me to Lilly by jabbing a thumb in my direction.

Lilly remained seated. She didn't offer her hand or leap into my arms. Her dark brown eyes gave me a hard stare even though her smile was polite.

"I helped Elliot get something for you," Grundle said. He urged me forward. "Show her. Show her the shillings we took from Le Mieux."

Excitement animated his face. His protruding lips reminded me of an exuberant chimpanzee minus the grunts. There was no use stalling. I had to surrender the money Le Mieux robbed from me to Lilly. I wouldn't risk Grundle getting suspicious.

"The money is safe," I said. "Thanks to Grundle's power of persuasion. I'll explain later."

I started a wink for her to play along, but Grundle chose that moment to give me a friendly slap on the back. The blow caused both my eyes to pop wide open.

"My brave heroes," she said. "Pray tell me more, Lord Elliot."

Lilly held the rose bouquet over her heart and leaned forward. She was so enjoying my discomfort.

"You remember," I said, "the coins that Le Mieux stole from me while I rode coach from London, er, to bring them to you, from Lady Greyhurst, for payment, for services . . . ah, forget it. Here." I handed her Le Mieux's money sack.

"We got money back from Squarrels too," Grundle bragged. "But none of those coins were yours. Sorry."

He turned his head away. Lilly looked at me and almost smiled when I rolled my eyes.

"I shall examine this purse," Lilly said, "and tease out those that belong to me when no thief may spy upon me."

She slipped Le Mieux's purse into her skirt pocket. Grundle stood awkward for a while in front of her, then excused himself and retreated out the back door. Penn returned from his public-relations mission, shepherding three unhappy travelers while uttering promises to set things right.

"Cannot explain Squarrels' odd behavior." Old Penn escorted the trio of travelers to the bar with the usual reassuring BS management spreads when things go wrong for customers. "Yes, it is disturbing. I will personally make new arrangements."

Suddenly, the front door was thrown open with such force that it bounced off the wall with a loud wham. Everyone in the room turned toward the sound. In the entrance stood a coffee-colored man dressed in fine silk livery: canary-yellow waistcoat, matching breeches, and a green sash. He held an oversized walking stick embellished with a silver bell.

"Stationmaster Penn." The black man's powerful baritone voice demanded attention. "Your services are required."

No one in Spindledown, save perhaps Lord Weston, could afford to dress his servants in so fine a uniform. Penn smelled money and high society. The stationmaster made haste to abandon his old customers for these new ones. Penn had natural management potential.

"My full skills and facilities are at your master's command." Penn hurried to the front, wiping his hands on his shirt. "Horses stabled, coaches repaired, and food prepared."

"Lady Greyhurst arrives," the servant intoned.

He struck his staff on the floor three times. The silver bell *clanged clanged clanged*. Lilly and I exchanged puzzled glances. Lady Greyhurst? What was she doing here in Spindledown?

NINETEEN

The Gaggle of Nobility

Lilly stood by my side as the lords and ladies of Whitehall Palace filed into Spindledown Station. She provided me with a running commentary on the new arrivals. A petite, raven-haired woman with eyes the color of coal entered. Her languid walk stood out in sharp contrast to the busy scene.

"See her hint of fine peach-colored stockings displayed upon slender ankle," Lilly whispered in my ear. "Those legs belong to Anne deLongue, Maid of Honor. She is a distant cousin of King Louis of France." She jabbed me in the ribs. "She is estranged from her English husband because she kept those shapely legs too wide apart while he was across the channel fighting Lowland battles."

A willowy blond in a mulberry silk dress strutted through the doorway, her hand upon a dumpy middle-aged man's arm. She wore pearl earrings and a matching necklace. A lace-trimmed shawl draped over her tapered shoulders.

Her male companion wore a somber shirt, plain black breeches, and unadorned dark shoes. They made an unlikely pair, like teaming a thoroughbred with a plow horse. Behind the couple, a fop in his long curled periwig pranced through the doorway, his steps called attention to his high-heeled shoes with silver buckles. A black star-shaped beauty patch adorned his right cheek.

"Look, Elliot, at his curious attire," Lilly said. "Methinks people with money are prone to daft behavior."

"That guy would be right at home in my neighborhood," I said. "Do you know who he is?"

"That be the Honorable Jemain, bastard son of potty John Burgess, who is a Member of Parliament," she said. "His father keeps a tight fist on the King's purse strings. His Majesty does fume and fuss at John Burgess for being parsimonious with money needed to fight the Dutch. The King grants title and privilege to Jemain in a vain attempt to influence the father."

"We have a similar political situation back in the Colonies," I said. "We call it Congress, pork, and earmarks."

"What have sexual favors and pigs' ears to do with governance?" She threw one hip into mine to accent her question.

"Later," I said. Her perplexed facial features coaxed a smile from me. "Where do you suppose Grundle disappeared to? What is he up to?"

"I know not." Lilly twitched her nose like the actress in *Bewitched* and tilted her hands upwards. "Grundle's moods are prone to hop one way, then the other."

"Should I be worried?" I asked.

"With Grundle," she cautioned, "it is always wise to worry."

Lady Greyhurst made her grand entrance into the waiting room. She looked luscious in her long grape-colored traveling cloak. Underneath the opened garment, a high-waist bodice with a delicate lace collar accented her long neck. The cutout fan she fluttered in front of her face produced dancing shadows across her eyes. The woman was sexy, even though she seemed hot, bothered, and weary. No mean feat for any female traveler.

Lady G turned and spoke to the bell ringer. He nodded his head several times, his placid expression remaining unchanged. He raised his wooden staff in salute and scurried to carry out his errands.

"Elliot of Vail?" Lady Greyhurst seemed surprised to find me standing beside Lilly. She favored me with a warm smile. Even to a cynic like me, her response seemed genuine. She beckoned us forward.

Lilly curtsied while I only managed a stiff bow. Questions raced through my mind. Did Lady G know Lame Le Mieux had dumped me in Hangman's Forest? What were she and her London entourage doing in Spindledown?

"Lady Greyhurst," I said. "Your attire does do justice to your beauty—this time," The last time we had been together in Spinster's Close, she had worn a tattered shawl to disguise her looks.

"And your wardrobe," she bantered, "would benefit from more variety."

"Spindledown is not noted for its tailors," I answered.

I still wore the only outfit I owned. My costume was starting to show the wear from constant use.

"Lilly," Lady Greyhurst said, "do assist in making our traveling party comfortable. Speak to the stationmaster to see what food and drink can be placed before us. Our journey from London has been arduous."

"Yes, madam," Lilly said. "I shall convey your orders to Mr. Penn."

"Make sure you have delivered my message?" Lady Greyhurst said.

Lady Greyhurst raised a cautioning finger to Lilly and stressed her last three words to ask a question rather than to make a statement.

"I was on my way," Lilly muttered, "when you arrived without notice."

Lilly gave Lady G a perfunctory curtsy and headed off to find Penn. She left me standing there in front of Lady G. I was tempted to casually mention to Lady Greyhurst that her secret message to

Weston was still tucked into Lilly's blouse. Let her stew on how I knew. But I controlled my natural bent for mischief. No sense bringing trouble on Lilly.

The black majordomo approached the two of us. Tucked under one arm was a silver-trimmed wooden case about the size of a loaf of bread. His trim body was accented by the close-fitting garments he wore with unassuming grace. He belonged in fine clothes. But not me. I always had trouble finding a pair of blue jeans that fit.

"Robert," Lady Greyhurst said. She fluttered her fan in impatient sweeps. "What news do you bring?"

"Stationmaster Penn states that the loose carriage wheel will be repaired in an hour," Robert said. "Time permits a light repast to be served. Your servant, Lilly, believes she will be able to provide bread, soup, roasted chicken, and strawberries from the station's meager kitchen."

"The fare is limited," Lady G said, "but should suffice until such time as we banquet at Lord Weston's estate. Give me the chest." She folded her fan and let it dangle from its thin strap around her wrist.

He handed her the elegant case. Lady Greyhurst dismissed him with a curt nod. Robert took his leave with a graceful bow and pivoted as if he were the member of a dance team.

"Useful lad," I said. "Expensive clothes. Does Robert work for you?"

"He is in the service of Viscount Overton," she said, "by whose kind grace we have come from London in his two fine carriages," she said. "That titled gentleman has mooned over my attentions for several years to no avail. Though, methinks, he would make a suitable husband for a woman past her prime."

"Overton must be dull and ugly." I offered my unsolicited opinion and tilted my head to add a question mark.

"On the contrary," Lady Greyhurst said, "his qualities are most appealing." She arched one eyebrow and hinted at a smile. "He is rich, tolerant, and undemanding in bed."

Lady G's fellow travelers had filled the waiting room. The elegant gaggle milled about, chatting and laughing.

"Is there a private place for us?" Lady Greyhurst asked. "Somewhere from prying eyes and ears?"

"Will you be missed?" I had in mind taking her to Le Mieux's hidden room. But would someone notice her absence and come looking for her? Or wonder who I was to be with her?

"'Tis a comfort stop," she said. "Until everyone has relieved himself or herself, my absence shall not be noticed. But we must hurry."

Lady G and I slipped through the broken door to Penn's office, then along the outside wall and into the hidden room. Sunlight beamed through the ceiling opening and illuminated floating dust particles.

"Don't waste time asking questions." Lady Greyhurst tapped the side of her head with the folded fan, as if urging her thoughts to hurry. "Just listen to what I say."

Lady G was brisk. I folded my arms across my chest and waited for her report. My so-called partner was all business.

"Twelve miniature paintings are here in this case." She leaned forward and handed the paintings to me. "Good to excellent in quality. The bills of sale show the amount plus the commission you owe me. As soon as you pay me, our private venture will be concluded." Her earnest voice demanded my attention. "'Tis best that Lord Weston does not find these paintings in my possession. He wants a piece of every pie."

"No time to look at them now," I said. "I trust your artistic taste." I didn't have a choice but to trust her. I surprised myself because it didn't bother me.

"And I must trust you to discharge your debt to me." Lady Greyhurst said. "Send me word by Lilly when you are ready to settle our account. She will be running errands between Lord Weston's estate and Spindledown merchants. You can count on her to deliver the money to me."

Lady G would have been shocked to know that Lilly already had half my money tucked in her skirt pocket.

"Have you located Lord Edward?" Lady Greyhurst asked, almost as an afterthought.

"Not yet." I needed to ask her one tough question. "What the hell is going on between you and Lord Weston?"

Lady Greyhurst shushed me by placing a delicate finger on my lips. My mouth tingled, either the result of her hot-wired feelings or from static electricity. I reached out to her. Would she have another kiss in her heart for me? The prior garden smooch had seemed like a promising sample. No way. She placed both palms on my chest and pushed me away.

"All of us from London," Lady Greyhurst said, "are staying at Lord Weston's estate, which lies north of Spindledown. The generous man has offered lodging to our Whitehall party until the trouble ceases."

"What trouble?" I said.

"Don't you know?" Lady Greyhurst said. "Is Spindledown Village so far from the news? The whole of London city lives in fear. The King has taken refuge in Salisbury. Those who are able flee to the safety of remote villages."

"What is the problem? I said. "Has the Dutch fleet sailed up the River Thames to bombard the city again?"

"No, you fool," she said. "The black plague has broken out in London. Thousands are dying. Regardless of status, no one is safe from the disease. No one dares return."

No one? As in, I can't get back to Bockman's house? I can't retrieve Buddy Box? Hippo had mentioned the 1665 London plague during his briefing, but I hadn't paid much attention. I thought the disease an obscure risk, not a personal death threat. Or grounds for being trapped in 1665 England.

"No one knows what has caused the outbreak," Lady Greyhurst said. "The court physician believes miasma, poisonous air, infects all who inhale it. Others say it is God's punishment for man's sin. The viscount gathered together his intimate friends and arranged for us to travel to safety in the countryside."

I grabbed my head and stomped around in three tight circles in total frustration. Lady G ignored my histrionics. My problems weren't hers.

"I must rejoin my party," Lady Greyhurst said. "It would not be wise for me to be missed."

She hurried through the hidden passage. I followed her out to the open path that ran alongside the building. As we approached the back doorway to Penn's office, Lady G abruptly whirled around. She enveloped me with both arms. With one hand behind my neck, she arched her back and pulled me over her in a classic, super-amorous pose. Her lips pressed onto mine. I was fully enjoying the feeling until I heard the rustle of a skirt. I opened one eye to see Lady deLongue observing us from the open doorway.

"Oh, there you are, Lady Greyhurst. I was wondering where you had gone." She smirked. "Do finish promptly."

The raven-haired beauty gave me a full-body scan with her eyes, sniffed, then retreated through the office entrance. Lady Greyhurst broke her hold, brushed her fingers across her lips.

"Better to be accused of stealing a kiss than thwarting a King." She hurried into the station without a backward glance.

Lady G, what dark deeds are you mixed up in? Hippo had

counseled me to avoid seventeenth-century politics. But what if dangerous plots had come looking for me? I felt a step behind this beautiful, complex lady.

"You," I admonished out loud, "are definitely dangerous to my health."

— — —

The clique of nobility and their Whitehall sycophants polished off the meal while downing copious quantities of ale. They stuffed their mouths and drank their fill, grousing all the while about the taste of the food, sourness of the wine, and slowness of Lilly's service. I avoided most of that pretentious scene by remaining in the kitchen and chatting up the cook.

She sweated over her cooking fires and struggled to cope with the unexpected guests. I pitched in to keep the poor woman from coming undone. I did nothing that required any culinary skills, just added an extra hand. My real contribution was to coax a laugh from her sour face by acting out an improv skit mocking the upper-crust visitors' snobbish airs.

Bench legs scraping against the floor, accompanied by upwelling voices, indicated that the group was preparing to leave. The cook recited a raunchy limerick to me that had something to do with the Pope, then bid me Godspeed.

I ambled into the waiting room to determine how Lilly and Penn were holding up under the strain. The room was now nearly empty. Lilly bused the tables, stacking dishes and platters. Penn was nowhere to be seen.

"Where's Old Penn?" I asked. She ignored my question and appeared peeved with me. "As a gentleman, it wouldn't be proper to offer you assistance."

"Did you enjoy yourself with Lady Greyhurst?" Lilly's question dripped acid tones. "I overheard Lady deLongue making snide remarks about your romantic tryst. You behaved like a cad, pressing yourself upon my lady."

Holding dirty dishes in each hand, she brushed past me, taking care to plant a greasy chicken stain upon my jacket sleeve.

"Lilly, I was an innocent victim," I protested. "Kind of . . . "

Time for me to go outside. I didn't need any more questions from Lilly. True or false, my answers would only make her mad.

In the courtyard, two teams of four matched horses were waiting for the viscount's party to board their assigned carriages. The animals were majestic in their trappings. Bright-colored ribbons had been woven into their manes. Grooms held bridles and soothed horses belonging to palace travelers who had ridden their own mounts. Robert barked orders like a drill sergeant to scurrying servants. Clustered in separate circles, the lords talked to lords, the ladies with ladies. What a privileged world they dallied in.

Penn kowtowed to the man who had paid the bill. The gentleman was elegantly dressed but not flamboyant. An aquiline nose, erect posture, and dark hair graying at the temples gave him a distinguished look. His demeanor signaled he was in charge. That must be Viscount Overton, the kind spirit who had enabled Lady Greyhurst to flee in style from the ravages of London's plague.

Lady Greyhurst gathered her skirt together to board the lead carriage. Robert was about to offer Lady Greyhurst a helping arm when they both froze at the great clamor of hoof beats. I had heard that sound before.

A troop of mounted men galloped into Spindledown, their red capes swirling behind them. They were the same mystery riders who had nearly trampled me in Hangman's Forest. Their leader, with his blond Viking looks, slowed his black warhorse to a trot in front of the coach station. He had an unsmiling face and a hard edge. The man didn't need his uniform. His whole demeanor declared military.

"I am Captain McAllen, in the service of Lord Weston," he shouted to the waiting travelers. "I seek Lady Greyhurst. I have a message."

Lady G stepped forward. McAllen reared his horse in front of her. The big animal pawed the air before settling back. Lady Greyhurst held her ground, neither blinking nor cringing. I had to admire her haughty stance and outward calm.

"My good lord sends you greetings," the Captain said. "He charged me to escort your party to his estate."

"We give thanks to Lord Weston," Lady Greyhurst said. "And take comfort in the safety he has provided. Is there more to your message?"

"My lord states that he would be most grateful if you would bring your servant, Lilly Swinden, with you to assist the lady guests. Also a manservant, if one is available, to serve the other lords. The estate's staff of servants will be sorely stressed to offer the proper care to so many people."

Lady Greyhurst nodded, then ordered Old Penn to come to her. The other members of royalty were quite willing to leave the decisions to Lady G. Except Viscount Overton. He watched the action from the sidelines, the corners of his mouth lifted in the satisfied smile of a mentor.

"Mister Penn, pray find Lilly and instruct her to approach quickly. I need her services."

I edged my way to the rear of the courtyard to melt into the small crowd of villagers who were observing the high society show-and-tell. They whispered to each other about ribbon-bedecked gowns, identified individuals, and gawked at gold jewelry. The royal court held both fascination and envy for the common folks, kind of a seventeenth-century version of Hollywood celebrities.

Captain McAllen took charge of the procession. He ordered a brace of mounted guardsmen in front and back of each carriage. Other soldiers took up flanking positions and mixed among the individual members of the procession who had ridden their own mounts. Satisfied that all was in order, the captain directed his second in command to proceed. The carriages drove off with their cargo of nobility.

Captain McAllen watched them depart, then trotted his warhorse over to the courtyard. The few remaining Spindledown citizens drifted away. The stallion stared his bloodshot eyes at me. I had the eerie feeling the captain's ebony warhorse recognized my fearful face from our previous encounter. I wished him Godspeed to the glue factory.

Lilly exited through the doorway without acknowledging my presence. She affected as much arrogance as her farm-girl upbringing permitted. She handed McAllen a tied bundle about the size of a school backpack that must have contained personal items. The Captain secured it in front of the saddle.

Leaning over, he grasped Lilly's arm and swung her up behind his saddle. She straddled the horse's flanks and wrapped her arms around the Captain's waist. Was I just going to let Lilly go away?

"Wait, sir." I stepped forward and stood next to the horse. "I understand there is a request for a manservant to assist Lord Weston's servants. I offer my services."

The warhorse turned his head toward me, bared his teeth, and tried to nip my face. I ducked away. Captain McAllen turned his head and spoke to Lilly.

"Do you recommend this oaf?"

"He vexes me at times," Lilly said.

"Be gone," the Captain ordered.

With a dig of spurs, the great horse leaped forward into a gallop. I scrambled out of the way to the taunt of McAllen's laughter.

Lilly turned around to see if I was watching. I had seen that "I'll-show-you" look before. It was the same one my ex-wife had given me when she accepted a ride on the back of a throaty Harley, hanging on to my no-good leather-pants neighbor.

I waved and blew Lilly a kiss. I knew where she was going and how to find her. Clarity of thought was a rare event for me. But I had a flash of certain knowledge. With all those royal guests, Weston would have to move Bockman to the hidden cottage in Hangman's Forest.

TWENTY

Fair Exchange

I sauntered into Old Penn's office. He sat at his desk, stacking into neat little columns the coins he had collected from Viscount Overton. The stationmaster's look of annoyance showed that he took my interruption as an intrusion on his privacy.

"Do not you know to knock?" Penn said.

"Since Grundle removed your door, I didn't see the necessity," I said. "Where does Two Chop Grundle hang out when he wants to be alone?"

"Do not know," Penn said. "Do not care." He secured the desk with a key attached to a small braided-leather thong. Penn twirled the loop around his index finger, probably deciding if he wanted to reveal any more information. "Best we leave that mad dog lie," he said at last. "The hangman can cause more harm than good."

I pulled a chair close to Penn, straddled it, and rested my arms on its crest. All this rescue scheming was exasperating. I just wanted to free Bockman and get the hell back to San Francisco. Of course, with my valuable miniature paintings in tow.

"Would the fact that Lord Edward's jailer is Grundle's brother-in-law have something to do with your reluctance?" I asked.

"Indeed," Old Penn said. "While there be no love between them, Grundle would not knowingly help you free Lord Edward."

"The word 'knowingly' leaves me some room for maneuvering

with Grundle," I said. "More to my immediate concern, you promised to lead me to Lord Weston's forest cottage."

"A moment of moral weakness on my part."

Penn drummed his fingers on the desktop, then rubbed his chin stubble. He wore an ankle-length leather apron that, like Penn, had seen better days. Viscount Overton's payment had made the innkeeper more hesitant to assist me.

"Join me while I clean the dining area and tavern," Penn said. "We can decide what is best."

— — —

I sat at the long community table that dominated the center of the dining room and enjoyed a tankard of warm ale while the old stationmaster did his chores. To put him in an amiable mood, I paid for my brewski. The price was only pennies, so I refilled my tankard from the beer supply behind the unassuming wood-plank bar.

"To put a fine line on my prior oath," Penn said, "I will take you close to the cottage's location. Exactly where it rests is unknown to me. Captain McAllen's guardsmen stand watch. Be forewarned, my weary body cannot stress itself to help you free Lord Edward."

He wheezed, coughed, and moaned, adding sound effects to his reluctance. He slumped in his chair to make himself appear smaller. He added a tremor to his hands.

"True," I admitted. "I have meager resources. My sad state is the result of Grundle's forcing me to surrender half my money to Lilly, who then proceeded to ride off to Weston's estate. On the ass-end of the Captain's warhorse."

"Lilly Swinden is a free spirit." Penn swept the floor with a worn witch's broom that shed bits of straw in its trail. "A mixture of tenderness and toughness."

"She's a handful," I agreed.

"That too," Penn said with a sly smile. He opened the front door and swept the collected dirt onto the courtyard. He banged the broom on the side of the doorway, dislodging any resident dust. "I trust the wind to remove the trash."

Penn untied his apron, hung it on a wall peg, and shuffled into the kitchen. When he reappeared, his jaws clutched a stubby clay pipe. He sat down across from me and proceeded to light his pipe with a glowing ember filched from the kitchen fire.

"Here is my advice," Penn said. "Go to France. Secure a private audience with King Louie, raise money for an army." Penn pointed the stem of his pipe at me. "Come back, start a revolt, take over the throne, and then set free any imprisoned supporters."

"Not exactly the strategy I had in mind." Elbow on the table, I rested my chin on my palm.

"Well, that is how Charles II got back his throne." Penn favored me with a gap-toothed smile, then raised a cautionary hand. "I would not listen to any plot to overthrow our good King."

He made his declaration in an overly loud voice to make certain any eavesdropper would hear the proper words. I recalled Lady Greyhurst's cryptic remark when she had broken away from our kiss. Better to be caught stealing a kiss than thwarting a king. Plus, her mysterious messages sent to Lord Weston via Lilly, AKA UPS—United Peasant Services—hinted of a furtive plot. I had no designs on the English monarchy. Charlie Deuce made a fine King as far as I knew.

"So, you have a plan to rescue Lord Edward?" Old Penn hunched over the table and lowered his voice. The pungent pipe smoke assaulted my nose. Spare-The-Air day hadn't yet arrived in Spindledown.

"More or less." I hedged. "My scheme is teeming with danger."

Lilly's abrupt departure had reduced my army to a single soldier—me. I had to find some local toughs to join my cause, or Bockman would never be sprung from his prison. A vague idea surfaced as I emptied the second tankard.

"First, I need to find some strong-backed men, handy with their fists, skilled with sword or dagger. Ruffians familiar with the pathways in Hangman's Forest, willing to do anything for money. Stupid oafs who could be convinced to follow me, a bad Robin Hood, to rob the rich and keep the money."

Penn dug his little finger into his ear, rooted around for a while just to make sure he had heard me correctly.

"Do all Carolina colonists have such outlandish thoughts?" Penn said. "If so, I fear for England's future."

"Yes, all of us from the New World are born rebels," I said. "But right now I need desperate men, capable of being goaded to attack a guarded cottage. Dirty rotten brigands who would join me in a foolhardy adventure."

"Spindledown's citizens are honest farmers, servants and tradesmen," Penn said. He worried the bowl of his clay pipe between his thumb and index finger. "None in this shire fit your nasty descriptions."

"Except?" I prompted.

"Le Mieux and Squarrels have run away." Penn, ever the innkeeper, used his sleeve to sop up a small beer spill on the table. "Grundle is mean enough but prefers to work alone."

"So that leaves . . . " I pantomimed a drum roll and rim shot.

"God's grace." Old Penn tilted his head upward and puffed a cloud of reeking tobacco smoke toward the ceiling. "You would not be foolish enough to be thinking about enlisting two local cutthroats?"

"Yes, I am. What do you think of Elliot's new gang—the Watkins brothers?"

"The word 'disaster' comes to mind," Penn said. "You might also be castrated if Lord Weston captures you."

"But you will lead me to the Watkins brothers' lair, and I will reward you," I leaned toward him.

"Why would I agree to help you?" Penn said.

"Because you will need all the funds you can gather," I said. "The deadly plague drives people from London. Your coach line falters. People who live in the city are eager to leave, but not to return. Your drivers refuse to go into London. As we say in the Colonies, your business model now sucks."

"New words I have not heard before," Penn said. "However the image doth form in my mind." He tamped the pipe bowl, huffed and puffed to fire up the tobacco, and gazed around the dining room. "This modest coach station is my sole source of income. I do not see a bright future until the plague passes."

"If the plague is as deadly as reported," I said. "Even after it passes, the number of potential passengers for your coach service will be drastically cut."

Talk about doing business in a declining market. I needed to convince Penn to honor his promise to lead me to Weston's hidden cottage, find Bockman, then get us out of this seventeenth-century quagmire.

"Granted. I am in dire need of money," Penn said. He worried a nervous hand around his chin. "But 'tis dangerous to show you the way to the Watkins. They shun locals and hate strangers."

"Come on, Penn, you are not getting any younger."

"True, but I would like to get older." Penn pushed back his chair, then walked behind the bar. "Since you insist on holding me to my word."

His head dipped below the bar top. Clinking bottle sounds mixed with his reedy voice. Penn was singing one of those old drinking songs with countless verses. Often sung by groups: drunken Germans at Oktoberfest, Scottish Highland Fling celebrations, or Englishmen at their soccer beer gatherings.

"Found it." Penn's shiny bald head rose over the bar like the morning sun over a hill. He held a reddish, fired-clay bottle. "Here is the gunpowder you will need to talk to the Watkins."

"Thanks, but I don't happen to own a gun."

"Drinking this liquid will blow their heads off." Penn's chuckle made his clay pipe bob up and down as his lips moved. "Dutch Courage. A strong drink favored by soldiers what come back from fighting abroad. Cures stiff joints, gout, and other such maladies."

Penn padded back to the table. He gave the bottle a farewell kiss. Then surrendered his prize to me.

"I have a physician friend who doth prescribe a dram or two of this tonic," he said. "We share a toss during damp winter nights while we warm ourselves in front of the station fireplace. He calls this strong potion Genever."

The bottle contents gave off the fragrance of juniper. I took a sip, swished it around in my mouth, then spit the remainder out. Gin. Primitive gin. Instant headache. Exactly what I needed to tame the wild Watkins brothers.

TWENTY-ONE

Bravely to the Woods

We hiked from Spindledown to Hangman's Forest before the afternoon heat rose. Penn had equipped himself with a stout walking stick to steady his gait and defend us from wild beasties, his word for critters. I had tucked the Genever bottle inside my jacket for safekeeping. A leather pouch filled with hard cheese, apples, and fruit tarts augured well for a decent lunch.

The forest trees grew close together. Their tops hunched over as if they guarded lost secrets. The dense canopy strangled the light, cloaking the forest floor in somber tones. Thick undergrowth provided cover for animals and outlaws alike. A sentinel crow decided we were intruding on his territory and cawed a warning to the rest of his flock.

"What was that sound?" Penn pirouetted on one foot while holding his walking stick chest-high in a defensive pose. "Did you hear that? Over there, no, over there. Behind the yew tree."

The only thing I saw was another tree, and even more trees on both sides of the narrow pathway. The crow took wing, chastising us for trespassing into his realm.

Old Penn, jumpy as a hare, was a reluctant guide. He panicked at the slightest noise. I couldn't decide if he did it for my benefit or if his fright was genuine. I stepped on a fallen branch, causing a snapping sound.

"Hear that? Must be a bear," Penn said. "A vicious wild boar stalks us. Perchance, a fearsome stag will attack. No, I was right the first time. A mother bear must lurk nearby to defend her cub. The animal is warning us to tread no closer."

The birds were singing their songs, no animal was growling or snarling at us. I was no woodsman or survival freak. But even for a rookie like me, I wasn't concerned.

Penn found a fallen tree next to the trail and sat on the weathered trunk. I stood in front of him with arms crossed. He insisted on this rest stop. Our third in the short time we had been in the forest. I glared at the dawdling stationmaster and turned the corners of my mouth down to show my annoyance.

"Sorry, Lord Elliot," Penn said. "My heart races. My breath is labored. I must rest, then we should flee while we still have the spirit to save ourselves."

"Penn," I said. "Did you hear an anguished cry of a man in pain?"

He placed fingers behind one ear and cocked his head. With his other hand he tugged his collar away from his sweating neck. His brow furrowed in concentration.

"No," he said.

"Well, you are about to," I said. "If you don't shut up, I will kick your scrawny arse down the trail." Good grief, I was starting to talk like the locals. "And when you fall down, I'll drag you by your heels. Your pledge was that you would lead me forthwith to the Watkins brothers' hideout. They do know the woods and can locate Lord Weston's hidden cottage."

Old Penn uttered a groan and toppled backwards. His arms spread wide on the ground among low-growing ferns. His legs rested over the log, both feet sticking up in the air. Eyes closed, mouth agape, and tongue protruding.

"Do you care that a vile viper is poised to strike your head?" I said.

The words were scarcely out of my mouth before Penn scrambled upright and stood before me. Penn was proving more trouble than he was worth.

"I should never have revealed that I knew the way to the Watkins brothers," Penn fussed. "Any man who works with Grundle has a black heart."

"That's me," I agreed.

The old man would be useless in a fight. Then, too, I had to consider the consequences for Penn if Lord Weston found out the innkeeper had helped me free Bockman. If only the old fossil were more energetic. I wanted to arrive at the Watkins' camp before dark. Bottom line, I only needed the stationmaster to point me in the right direction to find the cutthroats' den.

"Best we stop for our repast," Penn announced. "My tired body needs sustenance to continue our arduous task."

Crap. Another delay. What could I do but go along? Penn and I sat cross-legged among vibrant green grass in a small clearing. Penn retrieved a short-bladed knife from within the pouch and set to work quartering the apple and cutting slices from the chunk of whitish-yellow cheese. Before long the old innkeeper had laid out a modest but tasty meal.

"'Tis fine Bolster cheese," Penn bragged. "A local farmer supplies my station's eatery. Popular with travelers to take along on lengthy coach rides. I turn a modest profit on each sale."

The robust taste of farm cheese paired well with the crisp apples. We munched on the strawberry tarts while negotiating a new deal. I stayed away from the powerful gin.

"Set me on the right path to the Watkins brothers' hideout," I said. "I'll not hold you to your oath of helping me find Bockman."

"Aye, the Watkins know the pathways and concealed nooks in Hangman's Forest," Penn agreed. "If they do not first kill you."

A base of operations in the village was more beneficial than having Penn accompany me. The old man would be valuable back in Spindledown Station. The hidden passages and secret rooms would provide a vital refuge after I sprung Bockman.

"But you owe me a favor for keeping Grundle from doing serious harm to that rickety body of yours," I added.

While he was contemplating my words, I commandeered the remainder of the Bolster cheese. Who knew what I would find to eat in the forest? Gnawing on roots or roasting grubs lacked culinary appeal to a city boy like me.

"'Tis modest praise, but I will not deny I prefer you to the hangman," Penn admitted. "If you return alive from your mad adventure, I will provide refuge for you and Lord Edward of Bockman. God's truth, you must realize Lord Weston will send Captain McAllen and his guardsmen hunting for you."

"Penn, I take this action with great reluctance." I removed Squarrels' money sack from around my neck. It was all the money I had. "Take my shillings for safekeeping. I trust you to guard them until I return. The Watkins tried to rob me once before in Hangman's Forest. Better I have no money to tempt them."

Old Penn took the coins. He tugged a soiled linen cloth from his sleeve and blew his bulbous nose with a resounding honk, loud enough to scare away his imaginary bear. He stuffed the handkerchief back into his sleeve.

"I am taken aback that a stranger such as you would place your faith in me," Penn said. "Money is very important to me. Some would call me a sharp-nosed miser. But in truth, each coin I have earned in my life has come at a dear price in labor and sweat. Here, this is my gift to you. Not much of a weapon, I fear." He offered his little knife to me handle first. "But perchance it be of use."

I wasn't sure what benefit a puny three-inch blade would be in a fight, but I appreciated Penn's gesture.

"Penn, there is one thing more," I said. "In my room, there is a small chest of miniature paintings. Keep them safe until I return. If I don't come back, they are yours. Sell them when you are in dire need of money."

Old Penn bit his lips as he struggled to contain his emotions. He looked at me with watery eyes. Then he placed his hand over his heart for a moment. Embarrassed, he jumped to his feet.

"We had best tidy up and set afoot," he said.

Penn now set a brisk pace along the path as it snaked through Hangman's Forest, as if he had some firm destination in mind and wanted to get there without further delay.

Tree branches crowded each other, pressed closer and closer together like bar patrons on Saturday night at the What's Up? Comedy Club. The weeds became taller and vines thicker beside the trail, drooping over the pathway until it seemed to disappear. I stumbled over hidden rocks and shied away from spider webs that decorated the waist-high bushes.

The ground sloped downward, and before long, the smell of rotten vegetation invaded my nose. The soles of my boots squished through stagnant water. We were paralleling a pond. Reeds defined the water's edge. A small toad with a yellow stripe down its back chased a hopping insect. If I had been paying more attention to my feet than the flora and fauna, I wouldn't have bumped into Penn, who stood poised in front of a fork in the path.

"'Tis here we part," Penn said. "You go right. I go left back to Spindledown station. Mark this point well in your mind. Getting lost in Hangman's Forest is all too easy for the unwary."

Tell me about it. My panicked dash through the woods to escape the Watkins brothers had been without direction. I just ran like hell until I nosedived into the stream. Then I stumbled along until I happened upon Lilly's farm.

"Keep a lit candle in the window for me," I said.

"You are not worth the cost of beeswax." Penn gave me his best silly smile and wished me Godspeed before he hurried off as fast as his bandy legs could carry him.

I tried to mark the trail's junction in a way that I would recognize if I passed the spot again. I cut a double notch in the trunk using my little knife. I searched my memory for any Boy Scout or Wild West Indian tricks. Twigs bent in the correct direction coupled with a loose knot tied in the stalk of the tallest weed was the best I could do.

Bad times called for bad gin. I pried out the cork of the Genever bottle and swigged a mouthful of Dutch Courage. Made me wish for the familiar taste of Particle Enhancement slime. Well, almost. But it did remind me of Hippo. He would had spouted a host of comic one-liners about how bad the gin tasted.

I did my good-luck routine of throwing right and left jabs in the general direction of the pathway. Then I commanded my right foot to advance one full step, followed by a high knee, left foot one pace forward, mimicking the British soldiers in old war movies. I clicked my heels and marched forward.

About one hundred yards down the path I encountered a massive tree trunk blocking my passage, its thick base splintered by lightning in a long-past thunderstorm. Missing patches of bark, like old sores, disfigured the trunk. Moss, the color of rotten spinach, covered the trunk's upper surface.

The ground dipped sharply under Mother Nature's barricade. The dirt appeared to have been dug out by someone or something.

If I doubled over, I could squeeze under the overhanging trunk. To steady my nerves, I sucked in air, held the breath for a count of ten. Then I ducked my head and wiggled my way through the opening.

Beyond the fallen tree, a clearing surrounded a massive grandfather oak. Big sucker. It was an ancient specimen that had stood regal in Hangman's Forest for several hundred years. About ten feet up the trunk, the oak forked, each branch thicker than a wine barrel. The tree's dark limbs had grown twisted like condemned men in agony. The uppermost branches rose above the forest crown.

A rope, thin as Old Penn's wrist, was fastened to a thick limb. The rope dangled to a frayed end that stopped halfway to the ground. Time and weather had turned the strands grey-black. I could handle that unnerving sight, but not the pile of bleached bones scattered below. The skull's empty eye sockets reproached me. So this was why they called it Hangman's Forest.

I have never believed animal instincts were a human trait. But when the hairs on my neck stood up, I paid attention. Was I just spooked by images of past violence or something more? Yes, someone's eyes were watching me.

I slid my hand along my waistband, making no sudden moves, until I found my knife. I palmed it and pretended to wipe sweat from my brow, all the while looking around me for a hidden foe. I found him standing on the path in front of me.

No more than twenty feet away. Just standing, hands down along his side. A short bit of a boy. No wonder I had not seen him right away. A mass of curly hair, an undernourished frame, and large round eyes set deep into sockets. Clothing consisted of nothing more than an oversized shirt. Barefooted. A child four or five years old.

"Don't be afraid," I said. "Are you lost?"

He answered me with a side-to-side shake of his head.

"Come here. I won't harm you."

The lad hesitated, then came forward, keeping his eyes on me. Unsmiling, wary, ready to bolt at the slightest danger. I offered the waif an open hand, palm up. Grime seemed a permanent part of his skin. He placed his small hand in mine. His skin felt cold. I crouched to his level and smiled.

"Let's go find your mother," I said. "She will be worried."

He gave me that "no" shake of his head again.

"My name is Elliot," I said. Cheerful like, so as not to scare him. "What's your name?"

"Lit'le Tom." His voice almost inaudible. His mouth barely moved in his solemn face.

"Nice to meet you, Little Tom," I said. "What is your last name?"

"Wat-kins."

TWENTY-TWO

Bolster Cheese

Little Tom licked the chunk of Bolster cheese as if it were a lol-lypop. I had expected him to wolf it down when he accepted the modest leftover from my forest picnic. The kid had yet to smile. From the looks of him, life hadn't given him much to smile about.

"Can you take me to your mother?" I said. He did that "no" headshake again. "How about to your sister?"

He took the cheese from his mouth and nodded agreement. He gripped one of my fingers and tugged me forward. In his other grimy fist he clutched the Bolster.

We tromped along the path as it meandered through the thick forest. I gave up trying to evoke a response from Little Tom. Either he ignored me or didn't know the answer to my questions. Then he let loose my hand, ran ahead a dozen yards, and with a beckoning hand urged me to follow.

The path he chose seemed almost nonexistent at times. Little Tom would, without warning, veer off right or left where there didn't appear to be a pathway. After a few yards, the trail would reappear. We maneuvered a maze of trees, bushes, and undergrowth.

I lost sight of the little rascal when he detoured around a huge ball of upended tree roots. I hurried to catch up with him. The tyke waited for me on the other side.

He stood with a young girl. I judged her to be nine or ten. A full head taller than the boy, she held Little Tom in front of her. Both arms were wrapped around him in a protective embrace.

"Elliot," Little Tom said and pointed at me.

"Is this your sister?" I asked.

He gave me an affirmative nod. The boy wasn't big on words. She hadn't said anything either. But I had the feeling her mind was sorting things out.

His sister wore a shapeless shift of faded colors. Her long brown hair, parted in the middle, hung straight and loose to her shoulders. Unfettered by ribbon, braid or tie. She, like her little brother, was barefoot. Her skinny arms and legs sticking out from her dress were far cleaner than Little Tom's.

"Who are you?" the girl asked, suspicion clouding every word. "Why are you with my brother?"

"I was lost in the woods," I said. "And your brother rescued me."

Not exactly true, but I wanted the lad to get full credit for a good deed. In case he was in trouble for wandering off.

Little Tom presented his sister with his well-licked piece of cheese. He had saved his treat to share with her. The boy had class. She took the cheese, broke it in half and returned a piece to him. The morsels went into their mouths at the same time. They both chewed and chewed as if they were following an unwritten food command to extract every trace of flavor.

"You are not very smart coming here," the girl said.

"I am looking for Little Tom's father," I said.

I rested my back against a copper beech tree, propped one foot onto the trunk and waited for them to finish. The *thunk* sounded as I felt the hair on the top of my head being pinned to the tree. I tried to duck, but something held me fast. I raised my hand over my forehead and gingerly felt the hilt of a dagger.

"You found him." The deep, nasty voice came from the front of me. A knavish-looking man stepped from the woods.

"Dada," Little Tom said.

Little Tom's Dada had a tangle of thick dark hair that merged into a shaggy beard. He matched me in height but was twenty pounds or so lighter. Little Tom ran to him with open arms, only to be scooped up and plunked into his sister's care.

"Are you big Tom Tom?" I stuttered his name as he approached.

Hostility clouded his face. I didn't mean to sound sarcastic. He just took it that way. His hand pushed the base of my neck against the tree trunk. He kept me pinned while he pulled his dagger free. I decided against a smart remark, like thanks for the haircut. How much do I owe you?

"Do not hurt him," Sister protested. "His name is Elliot." Little Tom squirmed in his sister's tight hold. "Little Tom said Elliot saved him from falling into the pond."

I hadn't saved the little bugger from anything, but I appreciated her white lie on my behalf. Little Tom's Dada gripped a fistful of my shirt while he considered what to do with me.

"I have no money, not a single copper farthing," I said. "But I know where to find lots of gold."

"I do too," he snorted. "The king of Spain gets ships full of gold and silver from New Hispania. But it does me no good." He spit onto the ground.

"He gave us wonderful cheese to eat," Sister said. "We were so hungry and Elliot did not keep any for himself."

The kids' dad released his grip and stepped back. I ran a hand over my head to reassure myself that my scalp was intact, then straightened my shirt and adjusted the sleeves on my doublet.

He pondered my fate for what seemed like hours on my emotional clock but only a minute according to my rational mind.

"My father's name is Tom too," Sister volunteered.

"Tom Major," he stated in flat voice.

"I thought your name was Tom Watkins," I said. Was he reluctant to identify his real name?

"Watkins be me family name. My grandfather was named Tom Senior Watkins. My father was Tom Junior. So, when I came along, he called me Tom Major."

While I tried to sort out the Watkins lineage, a second man, shorter than Tom Major, appeared at the edge of the clearing. He had similar facial features but much thicker shoulders and girth. His rat's-nest beard surrounded a mouth that seemed frozen in a sneer. The handle of a wicked-looking knife protruded from a sheath fixed to his belt.

"Greetings, older brother," the man said. He kept one hand out of sight. "Who did you catch trespassing in our woods?"

"He calls himself Elliot," Tom Major said. "Sister claims he saved Little Tom from harm."

"This is my uncle, Tom Minor," the girl piped up from the sidelines in my direction.

Minor's only response was to bare his teeth like a vicious dog.

"You have any luck poaching?" Tom Major asked while he tried to see what his sibling held behind his back.

"Enough to feed us, my Meg, my brats and yours too." He displayed a dead rabbit by its hind legs. A splotch of red stained the light-gray fur.

Minor scrutinized me without saying a word. I did my best to act nonchalant. Studied my fingernails while trying to keep my knees from shaking.

"Methinks I have seen you before," Minor leaned forward and poked my chest hard enough to hurt. Not exactly a friendly gesture.

"I just got off a sailing ship from the Carolinas a week ago," I said. "Came to visit my friend Grundle, the hangman. Family. Distant cousin."

Tom Minor turned from me. He held the dead animal out to Sister.

"Here," he ordered. "Take this rabbit. Run ahead home and give it to Meg. Tell her skin it, clean it, and make stew for tonight. And find one more plate. Seems we have another gaping mouth to feed."

I reached into my jacket, took out the gin bottle, and displayed it as if I were a sommelier.

Minor pulled back from me, dagger drawn. He tapped the knife tip against the bottle of gin. "What is that?"

"I brought wine for dinner," I said. "Should go well with hasenpfeffer."

TWENTY-THREE

The Hovel Home

The kids dashed off to deliver the rabbit to some woman named Meg. Based on Tom Minor's terse remarks, I assumed Meg was his wife. The brats were their children, cousins of Sister and Little Tom.

The Watkins brothers demonstrated their suspicious nature by keeping me between them as we walked single file along the trail. Minor led the way, I was the middle, and Tom Major brought up the rear. I slowed my steps to bring him closer.

"I offered to return Little Tom to his mother," I said over my shoulder. "But he kept saying no."

"She be dead." Tom Major spoke in a matter-of-fact voice. "Died a-borning Little Tom. I know you are thinking the lad misses his mother. But 'taint true. He never knew her."

"His sister tries to watch over him." I said. She had vouched for me so I wanted to give Sister a boost in her father's eyes.

"Little Tom takes care of himself most times," he said. "His sister works to earn her keep around here."

The path broadened, allowing us to walk side by side. He waved off any further conversation. Then the path forked. Minor took the right branch of the fork at the same time Sister appeared, walking towards us from the left branch. I followed Minor while Sister ran to her father. He bent over to listen to her.

I only heard a phrase or two. Cook him right up. Hurt her knee. The status report completed, she fell into step beside him. He tousled her hair eliciting a smile.

The path opened into a clearing. I realized it looped around the Watkins' place. That explained how Sister showed up coming the other way.

A broken wagon wheel leaned against a tilted fence post. A wooden bucket with two missing staves lay abandoned in the weeds. The Watkins brothers must have a rule that when an item was thrown away, moving it was against the law. A pair of men's pants and an often-mended shirt had been spread over a thick patch of raspberry bushes. A treadle-powered sharpening wheel, mounted on a wooden frame, rested under a silvery ash tree.

A freestanding sagging porch roof shaded the dwelling's front entrance. Bent poles held up the four corners. None seemed equal to their task. My impression was that leaning too hard against any post could cause the overhead structure to collapse.

Windowless walls of caulked stacked stones formed the exterior of the building. The stone structure supported a sloping slate roof, rough-patched here and there with mud-packed branches. From the front yard I saw the broken remnant of a blackened chimney. In fact, every wall showed damage from fire or force. The Watkins family squatted in that shell of an old house.

"What happened to the original building?" I asked.

"Ruined during Cromwell's civil war," Tom Major said. "Owners all killed, so we moved into the abandoned house."

But the remains were not a house, a cottage or even a shack. A gracious person would call the place a hovel. I called it a dump. The Watkins clan called it home.

Outside the open front doorway a hatchet-faced woman stood behind a stone grinder. Her right eyelid drooped halfway over the iris, like she was winking at the world. If she was curious about me, she kept it to herself. This had to be Minor's wife, Meg.

Meg wore a dirty white apron tied around her waist. Her long-sleeved black dress was faded and torn. A close-fitting bonnet kept her unkempt hair off her forehead. Her lined face mirrored a lifetime of poverty.

"About time you showed." Meg directed her ire at Little Tom's sister. "Get over here. Grind the barley,"

The girl scrunched up her nose in protest but complied.

"Here," Meg said. "Take the handle of this here quern. Keep turning the stone round and round. No slacking or I'll box your ears."

The grinder consisted of two stones, the bottom one concave, the top one convex. Sister wrapped both hands around the upright handle and rotated the top.

A squealing pigtailed girl ran around the corner of the house, chased by her identical playmate—twin girls on the verge of being teens. Meg grabbed a braid from each head as the twins darted past her.

"You're supposed to be watching the stew and getting the food ready." Meg pulled them inside the doorway like she was leading two frisky colts to pasture.

"Those brats give me nothing but problems," Minor complained as he leaned into the open doorway. "Meg, bring us some bannocks and a pitcher of ale. My reward for catching a rabbit and risking the wrath of Lord Weston's gamekeeper."

Tom Major and I stood in the yard beside a wattle fence. Inside the enclosure, four runty chickens were occupied with scratching the barren ground in hopes of finding something to eat. One poked his head through a small opening in the fence's intertwined twigs and branches, pecked my boot a few times, and retreated.

"Weston won't miss one rabbit," Minor declared. "He has more land than he needs. Why should my family go hungry?" He directed the angry question in my direction. "Just because the high-and-mighty lord wants to keep all the game to himself?"

"Fine by me," I said. The only illegal poaching I had encountered in San Francisco had been Hippo Hyman's propensity to steal my breakfast doughnuts.

Tom Major pulled three chairs into a semicircle around a low table on the porch. Identifying the object as a table was being kind. The table, two X frames holding a split log, served as a convenient place for the Watkins brothers to prop their feet. The brothers sat on squat slatted wood chairs. I parked myself on a gimpy-legged, cane-backed chair that was more holes than support.

"What are you doing alone in our Hangman's Forest?" Tom Major asked. "Do you not value your life?"

"Who sent you here to spy on us?" Minor demanded. "We do not trust strangers. And from your clothes and speech, you are a very strange stranger."

Various eye twitches, nose sniffles, and mouth twists accompanied each of his statements. Mistrust of his fellow man had probably kept Minor out of jail or from feeling Grundle's noose around his neck. Before I was forced to answer, the twins arrived. One carried a fat, salt-glazed pitcher of homemade ale, the other a large round oatcake cut into quarters.

"Farls," Tom Major said. "Me favorite."

The two Toms smacked each other's hand whenever one and then the other reached for the griddlecake. A roughhouse game they had no doubt played since childhood. Tom Major managed to snatch a wedge in his hand, declaring himself the winner.

"Damn brats never do anything right." Minor stood and went into the house. "You expect me to drink from my hands?" he yelled.

He returned with three greenish, thick-walled glasses carried between his fingers. "I found these fancies in the bottom of the water well where the previous owners had hid them."

He blew into each glass to clean them. I would have preferred the dust to his breath. We settled back into our chairs, mumbled toasts to each other, and drained the first beer. Time for my sales pitch.

"I hear tales whispered of Lord Weston's prisoner," I said. "People say he keeps a wizard skilled in alchemy."

Neither of the brothers reacted. They seemed content to munch their oatcakes.

"Magic," I said. "Does that word ring a bell?"

"We seen magic tricks at the village Harvest Faire," Tom Major said. "The magician made cards and balls disappear from his naked hand. One time a farmer showed a two-headed calf."

"And a woman so fat," Minor said, "they had to move her in a cart pulled by oxen."

He folded his arms and raised his chin to demonstrate he was a man of the world. A thought knocked on my brain. Neither of these rogues knew the meaning of the word alchemy. I needed to get back to basics.

"Weston's prisoner can turn lead into gold," I said. "Where do you think the high lord gets the money to buy his vast estates, to build his big house? Think of all the servants he has. The fine horses and his troop of guardsmen."

Both sat upright and leaned toward me. The chance of finding gold in Weston's forest cottage was almost nonexistent. I would have two very angry Watkins brothers to deal with. But what choice did I have other than to make up an enticing story? Nothing else would tempt these thieves. Gold was their maximum motivator. And now I had their attention.

I poured another round of ale, then reached for a bannock. No one slapped my hand away from the oatcake, which I took as good evidence they were thinking about my questions.

"You lie," Minor stated with heated conviction in his voice.

"How do you know this be true?" Tom Major's voice remained calm.

"The wizard is a man from my homeland, far away, across the ocean. He is famous for his stimulating elixirs," I said. Particle Enhancement Liquid had none of the redeeming qualities of a good drink, but the slime qualified as magic in my book.

"Have you actually seen him make gold?" the younger Watkins brother persisted. His father should have named him Doubting Thomas.

"I have seen him take worthless pieces of paper," I said, "and turn them into money sufficient to create a successful merchant venture worth great sums for himself. He calls the magic process OPM."

The initials translated as Other Peoples' Money. That's the story of many an entrepreneur's start-up company. The magic paper was called stock certificates. I hadn't really lied.

"So, the prisoner makes OPM," Tom Major said. "I have heard of such a substance. In the meanest London taverns desperate men smoke OPM sold by the Chinese. I've been told physicians ease pain with an OPM tincture."

"That elixir is called laudanum," I said. "Weston sells his wizard's OPM for gold."

I struggled to keep a straight face. The Watkins brothers nodded in agreement. The fact that they accepted my story as logical spoke volumes as to their ability to reason.

"I know Lord Weston has moved the prisoner," I said, "from the Garwaye castle dungeon to a cottage somewhere in

Hangman's Forest. Join me in a raid on the house. Together, we can overcome the guard, free the wizard, and take the gold."

I put on my best aluminum-siding-salesman's smile and waited for their response. Tom Major mulled over my story. Minor crossed his arms and leaned away from me.

"I know the hidden cottage you speak of," Tom Major said.

"But we stay clear away," Minor said, "lest the guardsmen come after us like hounds chasing down a fox. No sense buying trouble. One time we—."

"Husband, luv," Meg interrupted as she walked out the doorway. "Build a fire outside to warm us all. It be getting dark soon." She looked as uncharming as a woman could be. "Stew be ready soon. The twins are hungry and so am I."

The men needed no urging, they picked up the glasses and stood up, ready to eat. Meg's promise of hot food trumped my sales pitch. Maybe a full belly would improve the Watkins brothers' mood.

— — —

Dinner was over, the mismatched plates cleared. The three of us men sat by the fire, taking in its warmth. In a circle beyond us, Meg and the rest of the Watkins family gathered. It was easy to forget they lolled behind us in the darkness. They kept quiet except for a giggle or two, followed by shushes from Meg. Once, when the fire flared, I could see Little Tom with his head in his sister's lap, sound asleep. She stroked his head and sang softly to him.

I rationed the gin, making certain the Watkins brothers got the lion's share. I had a mental image of Bockman rattling his chains at me. Urging me to do something, and soon. The prospect of getting the two Toms to join my wild scheme was looking up, but my booze supply was draining down. Tom Major and I debated various tactics for attacking the cottage. Minor sat silent and brooding as if chasing an elusive thought.

"Now I recall where I know you from," Minor snarled. He was on his feet and looking mean. "You be the man who jumped me from behind. Then ran away." He turned to his brother. "Remember? When we tried to ambush the Spindledown coach?"

"So, he be the one who escaped us." Tom Major shrugged his shoulder. The older brother didn't seem too troubled about what had happened. "It does not matter now."

"I won't throw in with a man who attacked me," Minor declared. "I have me pride." His boast was accented by obnoxious sounds erupting from his top and bottom. "Cannot forget that you bowled me over. Hit me from the back when I wasn't expecting."

"You were trying to rob me," I said, and offered him another tot of Genever.

"A small thing." Minor dismissed my protest. "A trifle."

"'Tis true, Elliot," Tom Major explained, acting as mediator between his brother and me. He poked at the fire while he mulled over the problem. "We do not count robbery as a serious crime. Sometimes people get hurt."

The wheels had come off my grand plan. I had gone from being almost accepted by the Watkins to being their enemy—at the least, Minor's foe.

"We will take a vote," Tom Major decided. "All in favor of helping Elliot, say . . . raise your hand."

Major and I raised our right hands. Minor kept his over the pummel of his dagger. Victory. I had a majority.

"Tie," Minor said. An arrogant smile lit his face.

"Two to one, how can it be a tie vote?" My incredulous voice brought a scowl from both brothers.

"'Cuz you can't vote," the older brother explained. "You are not family."

"Not fair," I said. "How are ties resolved?"

"Mostly we fight. Hitting, biting and kicking until one gives up," Minor said.

Tom Major handed me the gin bottle to help me deal with the bad news. I took a big gulp. The gin burned my throat all the way to my stomach. My style of fighting used words, not fists. A put-down counted more than a knockdown in my line of work.

I needed to find a weapon that kept Minor from using his knife skills to carve my hide. Something different. Otherwise, Robin Hood-Bockman would spend the rest of his days as a prisoner, and I would be mincemeat. Too bad I wasn't back in King Richard's time when differences were settled with lances and charging horses dueling it out in a tournament. Come to think of it, a long lance would help keep Minor's knife away from me. Make it hard for him to kick and bite too.

I staggered to my feet. Minor shook a fist at me from across the fire. I waved the bottle at him in a gesture of defiance. Big brother Tom Major pried the gin bottle from my hand and took a swig.

"Thomas Minor of Watkins," I said. "Do you descend from a long line of Englishmen?"

"Far back as I know," he admitted with great reluctance. He was not eager to agree to anything I put forward.

"Free men, stout men who fought with honor."

"Aye," Minor boasted, thumping his chest.

"Pig's eye." Meg's derisive snort intruded from beyond the fire.

"I challenge you, Sir Thomas Watkins, to a duel," I said. "Like the chivalrous heroic, your ancestors, did do combat." My tongue tripped over the exact wording, but he got the general idea. "If I win, you will join me in stealing the gold from Lord Weston and freeing Edward of Bockman."

"Agreed. Choose your weapon," Minor shouted. "Knives or bare fists?"

"Neither. We fight like knights of old. Lances, we charge each other in full battle armor mounted on fast steeds."

"Pardon, Elliot." Tom Major tugged at my sleeve. "We don't own horses."

"Any armor?" I asked. "Two swords?"

"Sorry. We be poor men with barely naught to call our own."

"How about lances?" I insisted on my choice of weapons.

"Well, I suppose I could cut each of you a tall sapling, strip the bark, and sharpen one end to a point," Tom Major offered, trying to be helpful.

"Done." Minor snatched the bottle back from his brother and drained the last drop of gin. "We fight at noon on the morrow."

"Promise me," Meg shouted from beyond the bonfire, "after you run him clean through with your lance, I get his boots."

"Your feet are too big," I joked.

Tom Major laughed. Minor glared at me and drew an index finger across his throat. I should learn when to shut up.

TWENTY-FOUR

Tournament of Fools

My attempt to cajole the Watkins brothers into helping me had degenerated into a deadly contest with Minor, the ill-tempered younger brother. Now, we had agreed to settle our differences via a jousting tournament. I could be dead by noon tomorrow. Bockman would stay in jail, Lilly would never get to know the real me. Penn would inherit my paintings.

"Bedtime," Tom Major announced. "Everyone go inside the house, including Elliot. Not that I don't trust him." He gave me a cynical smile.

A wave of cold air rolled through the forest. All around me the Watkins clan stirred into motion. Little Tom had fallen asleep with both arms around his sister's neck. I offered to carry the lad, but Minor stepped between us and blocked my way.

Meg woke Little Tom, then shooed all the children toward the house, ignoring their pleas to stay up late. She threw water on the embers. The fire hissed, steamed, smoked, then gave up and died. Minor kept me outside their hovel until Meg and the kids were settled in for the night. He couldn't resist threatening me.

"When you see my lance coming at your heart, it be the last for you," he said. He brought both fists down, hunched his shoulders as if he were in a bodybuilding competition for Mr. USA. "I am strong, you be soft."

"Of course," I said. "We will follow the tournament rules as laid down by King Henry VIII himself." Never mind that monarch had died over one hundred years earlier. I had no idea about jousting protocol, but I figured Minor didn't either. "Unless you intend to cheat."

"If I don't know the rules," Minor sneered, "how can I cheat?"

"Both of you listen to me." Tom Major said. He had stepped outside to join us on the porch. His shirttail hung out as a signal he was ready for bed. "I'm the eldest, so I will set the way of the fighting. I've never seen a real tournament," Tom Major admitted, "but I been thinking on how you two can joust. I guess you need a field. Some weapons."

He hesitated, looking to me for guidance.

"Most important," I said, "a knight must have a squire and page to shine the shield, bring beer and lead the cheers."

Tom Major raised his index finger as if he had discovered a novel idea.

"The brats can be Minor's squire and page." He ran a hand through his messy hair, then yawned and stretched, as if making decisions drained him of his energy.

"Then," I said, "I claim Little Tom and his sister as my assistants."

I was negotiating with Tom Major and keeping Minor quiet. Pretty good, considering my circumstances.

"Too young to be much help," Tom Major said. I thought their father would object, but he shrugged like it didn't matter. "But they be on your side if you want."

"My brats will do me proud," Minor said. "Though might take some yelling on my part to convince them." He rubbed his back against the doorframe like a sullen bear. "How do I ready myself for the fight?"

"First thing in the morning," Tom Major said, "I will chop

down two saplings, cut off the side branches and make lances. Each of you will make your own armor and shield. No limits. No rules."

I didn't like the sound of that. A contest without rules played to the Watkins' strength. Both brothers had a lifetime of experience with breaking laws. My only run-ins with the law were two DUIs.

"You will face each other on the morrow when the sun is directly overhead." Tom Major raised his arm and pointed skyward like an old-time revival preacher talking to heaven. "If you are not ready by then, the fight will—ah—be later." He gave a curt nod as affirmation. "You two will keep battling until one yields or dies."

The three of us shook hands to seal our deal. Minor tried to crush my hand in his grip, but I extracted it before any bones broke.

"You better win," Tom Major warned his younger brother, "I'm not of a mind to take care of your wife."

"Meg's a fine woman," Minor protested.

"You be half right, she be a woman," Tom Major said. "Now, both of you come inside and go to sleep." He shoved his younger brother in his back to hurry him along. "Make sure Elliot does not escape."

— — —

I sleep alone, excluding those rare occasions when I convince a San Francisco lady to join me for an overnight romp in my Chinatown apartment—but not here and not tonight. All seven members of the Watkins clan, plus myself wedged into the hovel they called home.

Under most circumstances a rope tied around my ankle would not have kept me from sleeping. Except that three yards away the other end of the rope was fastened to Minor's ankle. Every time he turned over, I felt a tug. Which, when added to his snoring, snorting, and lip slurping, made a good night's rest impossible. Then a scuffing sound ended my hopes for even a fitful sleep.

The night darkness was dissolving into morning's grey. The noise had come from Meg. She busied herself shoving kindling into a makeshift stove. I suppose you could classify stacked bricks without a stovepipe as a stove. She fanned her apron to flame the ash-coated embers into life.

The humble stove, surrounded by a bed of small round stones, occupied the center of the living area. No oven, no grill. An iron chain ending in a hook dangled from a ceiling timber high above the stove. The empty stewpot from last night's dinner sat on the floor. Meg had attached a kettle by its metal handle and heated the water.

"I take my coffee black," I said.

Startled, Meg jerked her head and looked around. We were the only ones awake. She put her finger to her lips warning me to speak softly. If I hadn't known about her drooping eyelid, I would have sworn she winked at me. My guess is that she didn't want to wake her husband any more than I did.

"We have no coffee, nor black tea either," she whispered. "This be a morning drink I make from wild herbs. In the eventide, I brew chamomile to help in sleeping."

Meg used the corner of her apron to lift the kettle from the hook. Wisps of steam rose from the spout. She rested her metal teapot on a low wooden bench, removed the lid, and added a handful of flowers and plant leaves, then returned to her makeshift stove.

I raised myself on my elbows to watch her. Meg lifted the folding handle of a flat metal plate and attached it to the iron hook. She adjusted the dangling griddle to hang horizontal over the fire. Then she rubbed a chunk of fat across the griddle and spooned a thick batter over the hot surface. She was making bannocks for breakfast. The smell of the oatcake batter browning roused her husband. Minor lumbered to his feet, rubbed his eyes, and headed outside.

"Minor, remember—" I wanted to remind him that our ankles were tethered together, but he cut me off with a dismissive hand wave.

I grabbed my leg and braced myself. A yard from the front door Minor's foot jerked backwards. He tumbled over, his forehead hitting the floor. He managed to sit upright. Then he rubbed the rising bump on his head and flung a stream of curses at me.

The commotion awakened the entire Watkins clan. Alarms and questions filled the air as various individuals woke up. With fury in his eyes, Minor fumbled for his dagger, found it, and drew it free.

"Now, now, younger brother," Tom Major said. "Save your anger for the tournament."

He stepped on Minor's hand, pressing it against the floor. Minor struggled for a moment before relaxing his grip on the dagger's hilt. Minor untied the rope, stumbled to his feet and stormed out the door. Thank God Tom Major had intervened.

"Don't fight on an empty stomach," Meg yelled after her husband. "I'll bring you a cup of mugwort tea. Warm bannocks will temper your mood." She busied herself with the kettle, filling several cups with hot liquid.

"Elliot," Tom Major said. "I hope you are a smarter fighter than house guest." He picked up a cup from the bench and handed it to me. "Drink this. Then you best spend the morning getting ready for the tournament."

I sipped the tangy herbal tea. The hot liquid was a welcome wake-up. Nothing like mugwort in the morning.

— — —

In San Francisco I had made my living doing stand-up comedy skits, evidence that I had a talent for improvisation, making up things as I went along, being resourceful. Give me a box of spare parts. I'd create something useful.

First thing I needed was a helmet. And of course a sturdy shield to deflect Minor's lance. I explained my objective to Sister and Little Tom and sent them scrounging to see what raw materials they could find.

Tom Major had designated one side of a grassy area in front of the Watkins home as the tournament site. I had staked out my position on the far side of the field. Midmorning he delivered my battle lance and an apology at the same time. Ten feet long and four inches thick, the wooden pole tapered to a quirky bent end.

"'Tis not as straight as I liked," he said. "Was the only one I could find." He mumbled the lame excuse as he walked away.

Oh, that's wonderful. I got a lance with a crooked end. A host of young trees grew around the Watkins house. But Tom Major had made my lance from the only sapling in all of Hangman's Forest that wasn't straight.

Sister and Little Tom came trooping up to where I stood. Sister's hands were spread wide apart as an improvised means of measurement. The little guy held his hands in a circle, fingers and thumbs touching.

"What's the matter, kids?" I could see their grim faces.

"This much longer." Sister had spaced her hands apart by three feet. She urged her brother to hold up his circled hands. "And this much thicker. Father made Uncle Minor's pole bigger."

They lowered their arms and waited for my response. Little Tom's face was more solemn than usual. Sister put a comforting arm around his shoulder.

"I suppose your uncle's lance is straight," I said. They nodded in agreement.

"And he took his big knife," Sister said. "Sharpened the end of the lance into a point to better stick you with."

Little Tom bobbed his head to confirm his sister's warning. I fought back the fear that rose in my throat. The Watkins brothers had stacked the deck against me.

I considered running away, but they would hunt me down. I couldn't abandon the kids and risk Minor's retribution against them for aiding my escape. My only choice was to stay and fight. Underdogs do win sometimes, though not often enough to give me any comfort.

Tom Major, the elder brother, might be a rascal, but I believed he would hold to his word. He would help me rescue Bockman and keep his younger brother under control. If—big if—I somehow managed to win the duel.

"Sister and Little Tom, thanks for warning me," I said. "Don't worry. I have a sure plan for beating your mean uncle."

Relief brightened their eager young faces making me determined to win. They didn't deserve to see me skewered on a bloody lance. Some crafty tactic would occur to me. It had better.

I sat on the ground and laid the ten-foot-long pole across my knees. The improvised lance proved cumbersome in my untrained hands. I used my little knife to carve crosshatching three feet from the thick end. My hope was that it would keep my grip from slipping.

Not only was my weapon bent at one end, but also too heavy for me to keep steady. I practiced aiming the point chest high, but the bent tip ended up pointing skyward or plowing the ground. I tried different hand positions. First with the lance end tucked under my armpit, with my right hand gripping the shaft. That didn't work. Then I tried a two-hands position, like holding a fire hose. But the end result looked like a bad golfer putting.

I even mimicked a bayoneted rifle charge, taking aim at the knothole in a distant tree. I sprinted across the clearing, shouting a rebel yell. The lance point didn't hit the hole. Hell, I missed the entire trunk. I threw the lance down in disgust.

Little Tom took my hand in his and tugged me to come along. His eyes had a bright sparkle, but he still didn't smile. He was as excited as I had ever seen him. The little shaver guided me to where the broken bucket I saw on arriving lay nestled in the weeds. He pulled it free from the ground and put it over his head. The upside-down edge rested on his narrow shoulders. He peeked out at me from the gap created by the two missing staves. I peered in the opening.

"Boo," I said and was rewarded with the first tiny laugh I had ever heard the ragamuffin utter, a genuine, happy sound. I lifted the broken bucket from his head.

"Little Tom, you have found me a knight's helmet. For that service, I will make you my official page." I took a thin stick off the ground, tapped him on each shoulder, then on his noggin. "I, Elliot of Vail, Knight of California, dub thee my number one page boy."

Little Tom jumped up and down to demonstrate acceptance of his new status. I turned to our next task. With a fist-sized rock I knocked out another slat to widen the opening. The iron loops securing the top and bottom ends gave the old bucket strength.

Sister joined us, hiding something behind her. Hesitant and a bit shy, she presented me with a long white feather lost by some bird somewhere. I wasn't sure if she found it in the forest, or her aunt Meg's rooster was missing part of his tail. She wedged the feather under my helmet's top iron band. Now I had a royal plume, a sporting touch.

"Come with me, Sister. I know where to find a shield," I said. "I need your help in making it strong."

She giggled and did a little skip step. The kids were enjoying the task of making my equipment. It was a game for them but a deadly quest for me.

I found the broken wagon wheel still leaning against the old fence post. The castoff had one redeeming quality for me—its iron rim. I hefted the wheel over my head and smashed the center against the top of the post, knocking out the spokes and hub. I held the now empty iron rim in front of my face like a big, round picture frame.

"Sister, we are going to make a strong shield," I said. "Go break off small oak branches, lots of them. And bring me vines to tie them to the rim."

Sister understood. She clapped her hands in glee and scampered off. Before long, she returned with an armful of branches and a fat necklace of vines around her neck. We stripped off the side branches and broke the wood into various lengths to fit the diameter of the iron wheel rim. I used the vine to tie wood sticks to the rim, first a layer in one direction, then a second layer at ninety degrees. The end result was a double covering of wood stakes around the rim edge. Thanks to the branch stubs and twig ends, my shield looked like a super-sized porcupine.

My homemade shield was far too heavy to hold in front of me for very long. But it didn't matter. My strategy was to take the first thrust of Minor's sharp lance on my shield's center. As soon as his lance point penetrated the wood covering, I would throw the heavy shield aside. The weight of the falling iron rim should tear the lance from Minor's hand. If all went well, I would then strike him with my shorter lance before he could recover.

The key to my hopes lay in the twisted vine handle I fashioned on the backside of the shield. I attached it to the rim's top rather than the middle. Minor would assume a blow to the shield's center would cause maximum damage. As an added enticement for his aim, I tied a bunch of white wildflowers in the shield's center.

— — —

The sun shone directly overhead. My forehead and hands were already sweating from the heat and from anxiety. I gathered my loyal force—Sister, Little Tom and me—onto our end of the clearing. Forty feet or so across from us, Minor's team waited for his appearance on the field. His older brother was there along with the twins, but I didn't see Meg or Minor.

The twins had woven green ivy and bright flowers into crowns for their hair. Meg had provided strips of colored cloth for the brats to wave, so Tom Minor would have his own cheering section. I plucked two dandelions from the grass, tucked one yellow flower into Sister's hair and the other over Little Tom's ear. My team might be outmanned but not outclassed.

Tom Major, the empty gin bottle in his hand, approached and greeted us with forced pleasantness. I was glad he didn't ask where I wanted my body buried or if I had next of kin to notify, things that might upset the kids. He used the neck of the bottle to draw a line in the dirt.

"This be your starting line," he said. "Stand behind it until I give the signal from the middle of the field. When I drop the bottle, start fighting."

"Does Elliot have to die?" Sister asked, getting to the heart of the matter as youngsters often do.

"No," her father said. "Either he or Uncle Tom can give up. The winner then decides whether to kill him or let him live."

Neither Sister nor I found that remark reassuring. Little Tom returned to his solemn demeanor. I peeled off my doublet. The fresh air felt good on my skin, a small thing to savor before battle. Besides, it would only hamper my arm movement during the fight.

"Here, Little Tom," I said. "You can wear my jacket while I fight. A page's clothes do honor his knight."

I put his skinny arms through the doublet's sleeve holes. My jacket hung almost to the ground on the tyke's little body. He looked like a man cut in half, yet still able to walk around. The scene reminded me of an old Monty Python scene.

"Whee." Little Tom ran around in circle eights, eluding Sister's attempts to capture him.

A racket from the house attracted everyone's attention. Angry words were delivered in loud and scolding shouts like those that can erupt between a husband and wife. The sharp point of a lance emerged from the doorway, followed by more lance. Then still more lance. My foe, Thomas Minor Watkins, Knight of Nasty Knaves, stepped out into the sunshine, clad in metal armor. Well, sort of.

Over his head he wore Meg's upended stewpot, the handle under his chin. Minor had cushioned the pot's inside rim with a red cloth, the loose end dangling over his right ear. Had he wrapped the cloth into a turban? My opponent brandished the metal bannock griddle as his shield. A homemade throwing spear, his secret weapon, protruded from his belt. If a dagger tied to a stick could qualify as a javelin.

"I hope you lose," Meg shrieked at her husband.

She wielded a long-handled wooden spoon, beating her utensil-stealing husband on his back, all the while berating him. The twins waved their pompoms and cheered.

TWENTY-FIVE

Gripping Battle

I watched Meg spoon-whack her husband's stewpot helmet one final time before she retreated to the sidelines. She scolded her twins for some minor infraction, then fanned herself with her open hand.

My armor-clad opponent toed his designated starting line across the field. In addition to protecting himself with a metal helmet and shield, he had padded his shirt with straw. He resembled an over-stuffed scarecrow.

Minor struggled to hold his lance steady. It slipped from his grasp. The sharp end bumped off the ground.

"You played a dirty trick on me," Minor shouted, red-faced. "You greased the handle of my lance."

What was the man talking about? I had not been near his lance. Was he trying to trick me into lowering my guard?

"Don't blame us," I yelled. "We are innocent." I shook my fist at him, then turned to the kids, who stood a short distance from me. "Aren't we?" I asked.

Little Tom, covered from neck to feet by my jacket, did a slow side-to-side headshake. As was his habit, the lad neither smiled nor changed expression. Sister, head down, stared at her clasped hands. Her lips were pressed tight.

I knelt to speak to her face-to-face. She pursed her lips and softly whistled a tune while her eyes roamed about, studying the treetops as though watching birds in flight. There are times when you are wiser not to ask a kid for details.

"Okay," I said. "We are good to go."

"Ho-kay, Ho-kay," Sister and Little Tom chanted in unison as they hoisted my lance from the ground and presented it to me.

I put on my bucket helmet, centering the opening for the best view of the battlefield, and raised the tip of my bent lance skyward. Thanks to the crosshatched groves I had whittled, my lance stayed steady in my grip. I reached for my iron-rimmed wooden shield and wrapped my fingers tight around its twisted-vine handle. I would raise its heavy weight the moment my opponent started his charge.

Minor rubbed his palms with dirt to boost his grip, dusted them, and gave me an evil smile. Then he leveled his lance and aimed it at my heart.

In the center of the field, Tom Major extended an arm holding the empty gin bottle horizontal to the ground. The moment it hit the dirt, the fight would begin. He teased the two of us by pretending to drop it. I couldn't keep my eyes off the bottle. Come on, come on, I wanted to get this charade over with. Tom Major darted a glance at his younger brother to alert him and then opened his grasp. The bottle seemed to fall in slow motion, end over end like it had been dropped in water.

"Death to Watkins' enemies," Minor bellowed as he charged.

"For Bockman, gold and glory." I yelled my defiant response. I lifted my metal-rimmed shield to my chest, grunted from its weight. Then I lowered the lance tip and ran towards my enemy.

Minor's contorted face loomed larger and larger. His jaws opened wide. He mouthed some insult I couldn't understand. His eyes were fixated on the center of my shield. He tucked the flat metal griddle close to his chest. The iron pot on his head bounced up and down with each of his long strides. The loose end of the red turban cloth rippled backwards from his head. The sharp point of his lance held steady and true on its target.

The space between us evaporated. My heavy shield tugged against my hand, smacking my forearm. My bicep muscle ached from the weight. But I had to keep my shield high to prevent Minor's lance point from striking over its top rim.

"Are you sure the twins are yours?" I taunted Minor.

A moment of doubt filled his eyes, followed by blind fury at my insult to his droopy-eyed wife. He lunged forward, lance point aimed at the white flowers fastened to the center of my shield.

I skidded to a stop and braced myself for the lance's impact. The initial shock drove me back on my heels. The sharp tip smashed through my shield, splintering the wood. Minor had pierced my defense.

Wait. Wait. The deadly point emerged and drove toward my chest. I threw my heavy shield to the ground. Minor's lance was ripped from his hands, snared by the crisscrossed wooden cover. His lance point embedded itself into the dirt. The shaft bowed, then whipped over and cartwheeled, carrying my skewered shield on its shaft like a shish kebab.

I aimed my lance's bent end at Minor's chest and tensed for the impact. His eyes were flicking from side to side, trying to locate my lance point. His momentum sent him rushing right past me. I missed his entire body.

I dropped my lance, grabbed the loose end of his turban. The red cloth filled my clenched fist. I held the flowing material with both hands, setting my heels into the dirt like a rodeo cowboy throwing a calf.

Minor spun like a top as his red turban unfurled. The cloth tore free from under his helmet. He careened off a tree, righted himself, and turned to face me. The iron stew pot covered his eyes. He lifted the rim with one hand and tilted his head back for a better view.

"I will stick you like a pig." He pulled his javelin from his belt and ran towards me. Sunlight glinted from its polished dagger tip.

I snatched my lance up off the dirt. I positioned one hand on top of the shaft and the other a shoulder's width below. Holding my lance parallel to the ground, I sprinted toward Minor. As soon as we were within six feet of each other, I jammed the end of the lance into the dirt and kicked my legs upwards. I pole-vaulted up above him just as he drew his arm back to spear me.

At the apex of my vault, I kicked Minor's iron helmet as hard as I could. My feet jammed the stewpot against his skull. Iron thudded against bone. Minor went down like a pole-axed ox.

I fell to the ground, sprung to my feet, then whirled around to face Minor, fists ready to pummel him. But he lay motionless on the grassy field, javelin loose in his hand. I retrieved his spear, drove the knife end into the ground, and leaned on the shaft to steady myself.

My stomach did a couple more flip-flops, then calmed. My adrenaline rush was fading. I removed my wooden helmet and wiped my face.

Little Tom and Sister ran up to me, arms outstretched. I sank to my knees, and we had a hug fest. I wished I had a picture. The bold knight, his faithful squire, and the junior page in their moment of victory.

Meg ran to her fallen husband, who lay sprawled in front of me. She pulled her stew pot off his head and examined her cooking utensil for damage. Satisfied, she pried her iron griddle from his fingers. The twins hung in the background and for once kept quiet. Meg turned to me.

"I guess you get to keep your boots," she said. Maybe she

winked at me or maybe she didn't, hard to tell. "Too small to fit me anyway."

"If my brother isn't dead," Tom Major stomped up to us carrying an expression of grim resignation in his face, "I guess we will help you free the wizard Bockman."

One glare from him sent Meg and the twins scurrying toward the house. He ordered Sister and Little Tom to follow their Aunt Meg. They waved goodbye to me and scampered off.

"I have seen him worse off," Tom Major said and stooped over his fallen brother. He placed his ear against his chest. "He will come around in a bit."

Major dragged his younger brother over to a nearby tree and propped him against the trunk. The older brother seemed relieved, but maybe that was because he wouldn't have to take care of the almost widowed Meg.

"You are a tricky bastard," he said to me. "Lot to admire about that in a man."

"I hope I knocked some sense into him," I said and managed a small smile.

I gathered up both lances and heaved them into the woods. Those weapons wouldn't be of any use in attacking Lord Weston's forest cottage. And now I had an army of three. I was making progress, as long as I overlooked having devious allies motivated by booze and greed. One fight won. If I only knew how many more.

TWENTY-SIX

On the Hunt

Flushed with success after my recent battle, I convened a council of war to plan Operation Wizard. My senior general perched on my right with his elite Special Ops commander next to him. Actually, any cynical observer would note that my army consisted of the Watkins brothers and me. My fantasy took about thirty seconds to evaporate.

Our headquarters occupied a tiny clearing at the edge of the thick forest that surrounded the Watkins' house. Two fallen logs served as our furniture. I lounged on one log with my legs outstretched. Across from me, the elder brother rested his elbows on his knees and leaned forward. He would speak for his younger brother, Minor, my defeated adversary.

Minor had his back to me, ignoring his older brother as well. For the past twenty minutes he had been studying a trail of ants marching along the forest floor. He was in a funk, nursing an egg-sized knot on his cranium, courtesy of Meg's stewpot and my hard kick. Hunched over, he held his aching head between his hands.

"Can we approach Weston's forest cottage unseen?" I asked.

"Yes and no," Tom Major said. "This be the cottage." He dragged a dirty finger along the ground, drawing a square in the dirt. "This be Weston's country estate." He repeated another square drawing a few feet away. "Here be the private road that the guards use." Then he snaked double parallel lines northwest to southeast, connecting the two. "The distance from Lord Weston's estate to the hidden cottage is almost a league. First part is open land. Then about two-thirds the way, Hangman's Forest starts. Close to the cottage, the road narrows to one-horse wide, and it passes under many an over-hanging tree."

Tom Major shook his younger brother's shoulder to get his attention. Minor's dull eyes seemed to have trouble focusing. He lifted his legs in slow motion over the log and faced us.

"The footpath to the hidden cottage," Tom Major said to his brother. "Does it come out in front of the house or to the rear?"

"How did I get this bump on top me head?" Minor asked, pointing to his ear.

"Meg's stewpot," Tom Major said.

His answer was cryptic and his tone soothing. Minor seemed satisfied with his brother's explanation. That also meant my mean muscle man was too befuddled to be of much value.

I had kept Minor's dagger after our fight, untying it from the improvised spear he had fashioned. My rationale had been that any weapon in the hand of Minor was a threat to my well-being. Now I had to take the risk. I pulled Minor's knife from my belt and displayed it in front of his face.

"Here, Minor." I felt like an indulgent owner talking to a dumb dog. "See your pretty knife. Would you like it back?"

Minor nosed close to the blade, corralling his eyeballs long enough to focus on the dagger. The sides of his mouth turned up in recognition. I kept a firm grip on the hilt. Minor licked one finger and slid it along the blade's edge. Blood oozed from the shallow cut. Minor smiled.

"Oh, it's you, Elliot," he said. "What are you doing with me knife?"

"We go to war." I balanced the dagger between uplifted palms to present the weapon to its owner. "I need a mighty fighter to help me free the wizard, Lord Edward of Bockman, from the evil Lord Weston. Will you come to my aid as you pledged in your sacred oath?"

"No," Minor said. "My head hurts. Go find Bockman yourself."

Tom Major guffawed. He took his younger brother's dagger from me and tucked it into his belt alongside his own.

"Remember," I said. "Look at me."

I steadied Minor's chin between my hands. His wiry black beard felt like a metal scrubbing pad.

"Lord Weston," I said, "keeps you from feeding your family. He is wrong to keep you from hunting on his land. Therefore, you and your brother are entitled to take his prisoner from him."

"Let me think." Minor picked his nose while he considered my argument. "I am starting to remember what happened." He draped one arm around his older brother's neck. "Did I happen to lose the fight to this New World stranger?"

"Sad to say, brother, you did," Tom Major said. "Now we are honor-bound to help Elliot free the prisoner Bockman."

Minor stood and beckoned his older brother closer. They put their heads together.

"But we Watkins have no honor," Minor slurred. "I trust him not, nor he us. What am I not thinking clearly about?"

"Gold."

"Ah." Minor patted his older brother on the cheek. "That answer I can grasp."

"Pardon me," I said. "I couldn't help overhearing. The point is that if we don't attack Weston's hidden cottage, you will never know if the money is truly there."

My strategy was worthy of Cortez, the Spanish conquistador,

who promised his followers Aztec riches. After his army was safely ashore, he burned their boats so they could not abandon him. The moral of the story? A smart leader never fully trusts his troops.

My grand scheme had four steps. Lure the Watkins brothers with the promise of gold. Attack the hidden cottage. Free Bockman. Then run like hell to Weston's estate, where the Watkins brothers would not dare follow.

I distinctly recalled that Lord Weston was hiring menservants to care for Lady Greyhurst and her party of high-society refugees. All I had to do was knock on the back door of the servants' quarters and use Lilly as my reference. Lilly would vouch for me if she weren't still smitten with Captain McAllen of the high horse.

"I have an idea," I said. Tom Watkins waited for me to speak. Minor strayed over to the undergrowth.

"My plan is without guile," I said.

Hiding Bockman might be a problem. No, hiding him *would* be a problem. What if I found him injured, sick, or loony tunes? Too many unknowns to deal with right now. I would stash him in the stables or a chicken coop. Squirrel him away somewhere around Weston's estate until we could take off for Spindledown, then on to London.

"We sneak in along the back path," I continued. "Lay in ambush outside the cottage, and overpower the guard when he comes outside to take a piss."

"You call that a plan?" Tom Major protested. "Minor could do better."

He looked to his younger brother for agreement. Minor was ramming a broken branch into a tall bush. He then whacked it over the top.

"In a minute." Minor had a vacant look in his eyes. "I'm finishing off Elliot. I promised Meg his boots."

"Well, Elliot," Tom Major lifted his palms in resignation, "it does seem like your plan is best." He interrupted his bother's assault on the beleaguered shrubbery. "Minor, here's your dagger back. Sorry to spoil your fun, but we have to go rob a cottage."

My army of three now had the effective power of two and a half men. Perhaps Minor's awareness would perk up along the trail. On the other hand, when Bockman and I fled from the Watkins brothers, it wouldn't hurt to have Minor spaced out and angry at bushes.

TWENTY-SEVEN

By Rope and Sword

Like wolves on the hunt, the Watkins brothers set a punishing pace. They loped through the woods as if Hangman's Forest were their playground. Then again, it probably had been since childhood. They kept going on and on without a break, through thick groves of trees, across flower-filled clearings, and over lazy streams. They were following a trail I could never remember.

Were they giving me a subtle message that I was unfit to escape, or were they just testing me? My sides ached and my breath labored. I saw double, sweat stung my eyes, and my throat demanded water. I stumbled to the ground. Got up, ran for another few minutes trying to keep up with the brothers. I fell again. I lay face down, motionless.

"You would not last long in our woods," Tom Major's gruff voice passed judgment on me.

I longed to walk the Watkins brothers up and down my steep San Francisco hills until their legs fell off. I rolled onto my back and forced one eye open. Tom Major towered over me, hands on hips, like an all-pro linebacker after a hard tackle.

"Where's your half-baked younger brother?" I leaned my elbows on my knees while my head cleared. "Off beating up some ferns?"

"Elliot, some day your mouth will get you in serious trouble," he said. "Minor's run ahead to scout the cottage. 'Tis not far away, so best we keep our voices low. Sounds carry in the quiet of our forest."

"Has your brother got his senses back yet?"

"I think so," Tom Major said. "But with Minor it is hard to tell."

"What do we do now?" I should have been answering questions, not asking them. Tom Major squatted on his haunches, feet flat on the ground, arms resting over his knees. If I tried that position, I might never get up again.

"We wait until he returns," Tom Major said. "Here. I made you something."

He lifted an object out of the weeds. A piece of scrap wood, two feet long with a thick knob on the end. He swung it back and forth.

"A weird baseball bat?" I asked, suspicious of any gift from the Watkins brothers.

"A cudgel. Your tiny knife will be of no use when we attack the cottage. But this . . ." he tossed the club to me, "this will knock a man down, sure as can be."

"Thanks." I managed a one-handed catch. "Now we are fully armed. Two daggers, a paring knife and a billy club."

"And rope too." Tom Major pulled up his shirt to show me the rope coiled around his stomach. "I brought plenty to tie up anyone we capture." He cupped an ear. "Shush. "Minor's come back."

A few moments later Minor strode into the clearing and squatted in front of his older brother. Minor tried to ignore me. But I horned in by moving close to Tom Major. Any information gleaned about the cottage, I needed to know too.

"Smoke from chimney, so someone is inside," Minor reported. "A lone horse is tethered on the near side of the house. The jailer's, I think," Minor continued. "Few men know of the trail that comes out behind the cottage. I see no signs of any visitors, but I dared not go around to the front where the road begins for fear someone would see me."

Minor had recovered his wits. Was that good or bad news for me? I took a firm grip on the cudgel.

"How much trouble do you think Bockman's jailer will give us?" I asked. "Will he fight us when he sees we outnumber him three to one?"

"He does his best work when people are helpless," Tom Major said in a dark tone. "The jailer is armed with a sword. He is skilled in its use."

Grim-faced, he folded his arms and looked away. His younger brother didn't seem eager for any more fighting either. In their hearts, the brothers were thieves, not fighters.

I decided to skip the pep talk about money. I didn't want the Watkins brothers to focus solely on finding gold at the cottage. The scene could get very ugly when the truth came out. Besides, something about a sword fight gave me the shivers. The Watkins brothers might be cutthroats, but they were not trained swordsmen. It could be a bloody mess trying to take down an armed jailer. I didn't want anyone killed. Just captured.

"Here's my new plan," I said, making up things as I went along. "We sneak to the back of the cottage from the cover of the footpath. I go around to the front door and provoke Bockman's jailer into chasing me. Then I run around the back corner. As soon as he shows up behind me, you hit him over the head."

Tom Major worked his mouth while he decided if my idea had any merit. Of course Minor rejected my plan. He stood and placed a hand on Tom Major's shoulder.

"I say," Minor said, "we burn the cottage down and knife them as they come out, coughing and blinded by smoke."

No way. Bockman might be chained and unable to move. Collateral damage didn't seem to be a concept that bothered Minor.

"Smoke from the fire would draw too much attention," Tom Major said. "Brother, we do not want Weston's guardsmen galloping down upon us."

Tom Major used the tip of his knife to pick his stained teeth. Minor fingered his dagger's pommel while looking at me from under hooded eyelids. Minor's bad attitude had resurfaced. Next, he could be stabbing me in the back. Literally. I smacked the ground with my new cudgel to get their attention.

"Tom Major, give me the rope," I demanded. "If I find the jailer asleep when I enter the cottage, I can tie him up without a fight."

And that would also squelch any temptation for the brothers to tie me up instead. The older brother hesitated, then surrendered the rope to me. Minor scowled as if I had ruined a secret plan he had been hatching.

— — —

Weston's cottage was straight ahead. The Watkins brothers had positioned themselves in the undergrowth on either side of me. The three of us were hidden along the tree line, close to the back of the house.

My nose twitched and itched. Some pollen-laden weed was determined to make me sneeze. I pinched my nostrils to squelch the urge because the jailer might investigate any strange noises. I started to sneeze anyway.

A hand pushed my face into the ground. A muffled *snert* was all that escaped. The hand withdrew. I raised my head. Tom Major shook a finger at me in reproach.

Weston's meager cottage consisted of a thatched-roof, single-story square building on a small rectangular lot. The building had one side window but no opening in the back. The house was devoid of any charm, not even a flower bed or vegetable patch. No fences or outbuildings. One thing for sure, the place was not a farm. No animals except for one ordinary mare content with switching her tail at flies. No saddle, implying that its owner was not planning to go riding any time soon.

The modest cottage blended into its surroundings, making it hard to find. The unpretentious dwelling appeared better designed for secret meetings or a lusty rendezvous than as a welcoming retreat. This would be the place if you wanted to hide someone from prying eyes. I now understood why Weston stashed Bockman here.

I tied a knot in the rope end, opened a loop, and then coiled the rest of the lasso, ready for action. The tethered brown horse nosed into the scattered hay and uttered an occasional snort. Honeybees scouted for pollen, but that was about all the action. No human voices interrupted the serenity. As they said in the old World War I movie, "All quiet on the western front."

Still, something bothered me. There were no unusual sounds and nothing odd in sight. But a hodgepodge of smells permeated the air. Citrus, musk, rose, molasses, wet cardboard, old sweat socks, and lavender. My nose had olfactory overload. I ran out of odors I could distinguish.

"Do you smell something?" I poked Tom Major in the ribs.

"The whole place stinks," he agreed. "Reminds me of the flower and herb market in London, including the rotten garbage and tossings from chamber pots. Something is wrong. Best we forget the whole thing. No money is worth our lives."

"I smell an alcohol still." Minor raised his head above the tall weeds that concealed the three of us. "I once tried my hand at making French apple brandy." He scratched his head as if to help dredge up memories. "You remember, brother. The Frenchman with the twisted foot said he would show us how, but then he ran off with our pot still and what little drink we had made."

"Le Mieux," I said more to myself than to them.

Minor gave me a confused look like he hadn't heard me right. He inched back in the grass. Uh-oh. The Watkins brothers were about to chicken out and leave me stranded. I had run out of options. Time to free Bockman from his prison.

"Whatever is going on, it doesn't matter," I said. "Follow me to the wizard and the gold."

The Watkins brothers and I crept across the open yard behind the cottage. Each of us held fingers to our lips cautioning the others to tread softly, as if we were three mice tiptoeing past a sleeping cat. When we reached the rear of the house I flattened myself against its wall.

I air-walked two fingers in a line to mimic my going around to the front of the cottage. I rapped my knuckles on an imaginary door. Made a fright face and ran my fingers back around the corner. I simulated banging my cudgel over someone's head to demonstrate the result I wanted.

Tom Major nodded and took the cudgel from me. He pretended to knock his younger brother on the forehead. Minor bared his teeth and put the tip of his knife under his older brother's chin. I guess one concussion was enough for him.

Tom Major brushed the dagger aside as if being threatened by Minor was an everyday event. I cautioned them to stay put. They bobbed their heads in agreement. Time to go. All this time travel, thousands of miles from home, all for this one moment of action. San Francisco seemed an eternity away.

I punched a half-hearted left jab for good luck, much to the confusion of the Watkins brothers. I sidestepped along the cottage wall. The mare raised her head and watched me as I inched my way past her. I must not have impressed her. She returned to her search for interesting grass to munch. To be certain that no one would see me, I crawled under the shuttered window. Once clear, I stood, checked that my lariat was ready, then edged forward to the corner of the cottage.

I needed a beer. A couple of fast headshakes cleared away that stupid idea. Deep breaths steadied my nerves. I moved around the corner.

The cottage door was built to keep people out—solid oak planking, reinforced with iron straps. The huge keyhole in the heavy, black iron lock looked like it would hold a ten-pound key. Good news. There was no peephole in the solid planking. The jailer would need to open the door.

I forced a gulp to free my stuck Adam's apple. I spread the rope's running noose into a wide loop and spun it like a cowboy doing tricks. A modest skill I had learned from a redneck comedian at the What's Up? Club. I raised my fist and hammered on the door, waited a few seconds, then pounded harder.

"Who goes?" A man's gruff voice asked from inside the cottage. Grundle's brother-in-law sounded as nasty as his reputation.

"Me goes," I shouted. "Open up, orders from Cap'n McAllen." Might as well use the boss's name.

I heard a key being inserted into the lock, then the sound of a bolt sliding high on the door, followed by a second sound lower down. The door opened partway to reveal a shirtless, blotchy-faced man with a hairy chest. If he weren't ugly enough, his drawn rapier sword was even uglier.

"Howdy, partner," I said. "I'm here to take the prisoner off your hands. I know he must be a pain in the butt."

"Huh?"

"The wizard has overdue science books at the San Francisco library. I have a warrant for his arrest."

He flicked his sword at me. The movement was more a warning than a stabbing thrust. The jailer was a man of few words.

"Watch it, pig breath," I said.

I whipped the lasso loop over his arm and jerked. I missed. The noose tightened instead around the blade. I yanked hard to pull the weapon from his hand. But he whipped the blade upwards like a fisherman setting his fishhook on a striking bass. We tugged back and forth until the blade's sharp edge sliced through the rope strands.

"Catch you next time." I threw the coiled rope at his head and took off running.

I could hear the swishing of his blade as it slashed through the air behind me. Close behind me. I dashed around the corner and headed toward the back side of the cottage. The Watkins brothers had better be ready to pounce.

My pursuer was right behind me, hurling loud curses. I planted my foot and pivoted ninety-degrees around the far corner. Tom Major held the cudgel overhead, his arm cocked and ready to strike. Minor, in a three-point stance, waited to tackle my follower. I spun around to join the brawl.

Tom Major swung the cudgel at the jailer's head, but his target jerked his head to one side. The man had the reflexes of a cat. The club hit the top of the man's ear before landing on the base of his neck. He grunted in pain, blood streamed from his torn ear, but he kept to his feet, sword in hand.

Minor tackled the jailer's legs. In a swift downward jam, the swordsman drove the hilt against the top of Minor's head, knocking him sprawling. Tom Major leaped forward and swung his cudgel to club the sword from the jailer's hand. The man parried, then slashed his long blade into Major's side. The cudgel dropped from Tom Major's grip as he fell to one knee, hands clutching the bleeding wound.

I jumped on the jailer's back and wrapped my arms around his head. He bucked and twisted to throw me off. Minor had recovered and joined the fray, knife in hand. He stabbed the jailer's arm. With a grunt of pain, the jailer released his grip on the sword handle. We forced the man to the ground. He squirmed like a snake under me.

"Stop or you die." I spat the words into his ear. I straddled the prostrate man, pinning him. Minor reached across my shoulder and pressed his dagger against the man's neck. That stopped his struggles.

"Here, take my knife," Minor said. "Keep him quiet. My brother is cut serious."

"Take me home" Tom Major's face was twisted with pain. "I fear I am bad hurt."

Red stained his hands as he tried to stem the flow from the sword cut. He toppled over onto the ground. My worst fears had come to pass. The attack had turned into a bloody mess.

"Lie still." Minor knelt next to his older brother and eased him onto the grass. "I will tend to you."

"Who the hell are you?" the jailer growled. "Do you not know whom I serve? You are all good as dead."

Minor stood and came to where I sat on the jailer. He held his older brother's dagger in his hand ready to plunge it into the man's back. Minor had murder in his eyes.

"Then I best kill you first," Minor snarled.

"Minor, back off," I said. "Go get the rope so I can tie him up. Get your brother to a doctor. Now."

"We have no money. No physician will care for us," Minor said. The bitterness of his words soured the edges of his mouth. "Meg knows the folk medicine. She will treat him. That is the best I can do."

"Your life will end right now," I lowered my lips to the jailer's ear and whispered, "unless you do as I say. Only I can stop him from taking his vengeance."

The jailer nodded to show he understood.

"Pray you have coins with you," I said. "Give me your purse. Make no false moves."

He fumbled around his waist until I saw his fingers close over a leather thong. He pulled a leather sack purse from inside the band of his trousers and motioned me to take it. I cut the purse loose. I hefted it. To my surprise, it was heavy.

"Looks like we came right after payday." A muffled obscenity affirmed my guess. I tossed the jailer's money over toward Minor.

"Here. Take this."

He made no attempt to catch the sack. It fell at Minor's feet. He still wanted to vent his anger on the jailer. Then he reached down and picked up the money. He glared at me in frustration.

"Take Major and go. I will stay here to make sure no one follows you. Take the jailer's horse."

"Stranger, you know not our laws," Minor said. "Steal a rabbit, get punished. Steal a horse, get hung by Grundle. No, I will take my brother home, staying to our forest trails."

Minor stuffed the purse into his breeches and retrieved the rope. We bound the jailer's wrists behind him. I looped the rope around his neck and coiled the rest so I could hold it like a leash. I returned Minor's dagger. He spat at the jailer but said nothing.

"Help me stand up," Tom Major pleaded.

I gripped his hand and pulled him upright. A moan escaped

from his clenched mouth. Minor put his head under his wounded brother's arm and walked him to the footpath. There were no good-byes. The Watkins brothers faded into the forest without looking back.

If I still dared to free Bockman, I was on my own.

TWENTY-EIGHT

The Wizard Walks

"Take me to Lord Edward," I said. "Behave yourself and I'll fix the wound in your arm."

The jailer rose to his feet and faced the cottage. What would Grundle, the hangman, do if he saw me with his nasty brother-in-law? Knowing Grundle, he would either fall down laughing or decide to kill me. I retrieved the jailer's sword, then prodded him with its tip, just hard enough to get his full attention.

"Giddy-up," I said as I flicked the lasso rope.

I dreaded walking through that cottage door. The last time I had seen my landlord was at the entrance to his room in San Francisco. He had been a sad sight with his torn clothes, unkempt beard and battered body. Most of all, I remembered his haunting eyes, reflecting a man on the verge of ruin. I might find Bockman more dead than alive. His final message to me had been scribbled on a scrap of torn parchment—a plea to rescue him from a dungeon. Now, here I was in seventeenth century England, transported by a computer named Blue. My mission: To find its master and return him to his modern California home.

The jailer looked over his shoulder as I prodded him towards the cottage door. The dark stain of dried blood from his torn ear smeared his neck.

"Lord Weston," he said, "will pay a handsome sum if you free me. I will vouch that you helped me drive off the scoundrels who tried to steal his prisoner."

"Do you take me for a fool?"

The look on his face answered my question, I only wished he wasn't so obvious about his true opinion.

"Halt," I ordered.

He started to argue, then stopped when I pulled him up short just outside the open doorway. I kept a tight grip on the rope while I peered through the entrance. The dim interior of the large room was cloaked in shadows, making it difficult to see. But I could make out some features.

The cottage's interior room had floor-to-ceiling iron bars that separated the big room into two equal parts. A door in the middle of the bars secured the only access to the jail cell. The iron bars were spaced a hand's width apart, close enough to keep a man secure yet allow air to circulate. No movement, no occupant.

Inside the cordoned-off space, a large round object filled the middle of the jail area. The dim light kept me from identifying it. Where was Bockman? Was he still at Weston's country estate? If so, I was screwed.

The jailer's vest and shirt hung from a wall peg. A simple wood-frame bed was pushed against one wall. Beside it, a water jug and washbasin occupied the top of a mirrored nightstand. The only other furniture was a vintage trestle table and two straight-backed chairs. The front area of the room was the jailer's living quarters.

I dragged one of the chairs outside to the front walkway. I tied the jailer to the chair and the chair to the hitching post.

"Where is the prisoner, Lord Edward of Bockman?" I asked.

A shoulder shrug was his only reply.

"You had better tell me." I brandished the sword.

"Nothing you can do to me will surpass my punishment from Captain McAllen for failing in my duty."

The jailer had dared me to test his courage. Crap, I was no good at this bad-guy routine. I would have to find Bockman on my own.

I wrapped my handkerchief around the jailer's injured arm. The stab wound from Minor's knife didn't appear to be too deep. I patted him on the head.

"Stay," I ordered. "Be still." Then I returned to the cottage.

I stepped close to the bars that separated the room and examined Bockman's cell through the iron bars. Instead of the sparse jailhouse furnishings that I had expected, the space behind the cell bars was filled with tall tables, flat boxes and holding bins. Gunnysacks, barrels, crates, and baskets littered the floor. Roots, seeds, peels, dried flowers, leaves, lumps and clumps of herbs spilled from them. Shelves mounted on the sidewalls held jugs, tin boxes, bottles and beakers filled with different colored liquids. The riot of colors and odors was overwhelming.

Candles and hanging iron saucer-shaped oil lamps augmented the light from a high barred window. An assemblage of kettles and pots crammed a fireplace built along the back wall. Some of the cookware hung from chains, others rested on iron grates. Liquid bubbling from one pot dripped and sizzled into the fire below. Bockman's jail appeared more a chemistry lab than cell.

Now I could identify the object in the center of the jail. It was a large bulb-shaped copper pot-still. Pipes curled from the top of the pot condensed the vapors into a five-gallon jug that collected the distilled alcohol. Restoration moonshine.

A shuffle of footsteps sounded from behind the apparatus. Movement caught my eye. The toe of a green slipper appeared. Bockman rounded the edge of the still. In his hand, he held a small cup. My missing landlord had the preoccupied look of an absent-minded professor or a mad scientist. I wasn't sure which description best fit.

"I hope," I said, "you're making a supply of Particle Enhancement Liquid. We could use a new batch to beam us back home."

Bockman raised his head at the sound of my voice. His eyes darted from one side of the cell to the other in confusion. Then he spotted me.

"Vail?" His voice was spacey, either from mental fatigue, alcohol fumes, or distillation overdose. "Elliot Vail? Is that you?"

My missing landlord was attired in a long black dressing gown with a red velvet collar. Oversized cuffs turned back and buttoned to the sleeves. The once-fine fabric of his cambric shirt was stained by a spectrum of spills. Royal-blue ribbons kept the open shirtfront tied together.

"Bockman," I said, looking at his feet. "Don't you think the green satin slippers are a bit much?"

In emotional situations, I tend to retreat into sarcastic remarks to cover my true feelings, a pop-psych analysis once rendered by my ex-wife and verified by a couple of other failed relationships.

"My God, Elliot, I had given up hope you would ever come for me."

Tears streaked Bockman's cheeks. He came to the iron partition and thrust his arms through the bars. His hands trembled as he sought me out.

"I see you've updated your costume," I said. "I kind of miss the Robin Hood feather."

"Castoff clothes from Lord Weston." Bockman clutched my arms. "He made sure I couldn't go anywhere in public without drawing attention to myself. Just as well. Mine were in tatters."

I had expected Bockman to be wearing a long flowing beard befitting a wizard. Instead, he sported a neatly-cropped, pointed beard that reminded me of Sir Walter Raleigh. There were flecks of gray among the sandy hairs.

"I claim lifetime free rent in the San Francisco apartment," I teased. "As my reward for rescuing you."

Bockman hesitated, smiled. He reached out, extended two fingers, and pretended to poke me in the eyes in vintage Three Stooges style.

"Agreed," he said, "but only if you get me out of here right now. The key is the small one on the ring attached to the front-door key."

The big fat key was still inserted in the front door keyhole. The jailer had left the keys there while he chased after me. I detached the small cell key from the large ring.

"Hurry," Bockman urged. "Captain McAllen sends one of his guardsmen to ride over and pick up the elixirs. He arrives at midafternoon today."

I had a hundred questions for Bockman, but now was not the time. I twisted the key in the cell lock, and the heavy iron dungeon door creaked open. Bockman rushed out and threw his arms around me.

I had kept my promise and freed my landlord. A rare accomplishment for me. My ex-wife would never believe me capable of such an upstanding character trait. I even surprised myself.

"Thank God," he said. "I was going crazy being cooped up." He spun on his heels and went back into his jail cell.

"Bockman, what the hell are you doing?" I said. "We've got to get out of here before we get caught."

I heard bottles clink, clink. Then tin boxes scraped as they slid from the shelves and clunked against each other. What was Wizard Bockman doing? He reappeared toting a bulging gunnysack over his shoulder like a freaky Santa Claus.

"I assume," he said, "you don't have much money with you. Remember, it's 1665. Bartering works best." He rested the sack on the floor and fished out a glass bottle that resembled a miniature green bowling pin. "This is better than shillings or even the new gold guineas."

"If that green glass is a bottle of beer," I said, "you are in for a rude awakening. I can get a full tankard at the local tavern for a copper farthing."

Bockman danced an improvised jig around me, hopping on one foot, then another. His eyes twinkled, his mouth opened in merriment. The edge of his gown swished over the floor, stirring up a dusty trail.

"This, Elliot, is why I'm still alive." he played one-handed catch with the bottle. "And doing quite well, thank you. Do I look like skin and bones?" He added, patting his little potbelly. "See what I can do."

He set the bottle on the floor and did a dozen rapid pushups. He sprang to his feet and clicked his heels like some deranged elf. I had to agree that my landlord appeared to be in better physical shape than I had expected.

His mental state was another matter. Bockman had always been a flaky geek. His time in old England hadn't made him any more normal. I might have to drag him out of harm's way.

"This will improve your love life, Elliot," he crowed. "If you have any."

He tantalized me with the small green bottle. I reached for the bottle, but he snatched it back.

"Recall how the Particle Enhancement Liquid made you feel all tingly? This is not the identical stuff but has the same effect."

Bockman bowed as if receiving applause from an admiring audience. The guy was flaking on me. I was tempted to whack him on the side of the head to get him back to normal. If Bockman ever had a normal.

"This magic elixir," he continued, "is King Charles' favorite aphrodisiac. All the high-society lords and ladies buy my potion. He keeps me locked up so no one else can use my services. Lord Weston wouldn't dare kill me."

"Does it work?" I asked.

"Doesn't matter, as long as people believe it does. Lots more effective than warm chocolate with cinnamon and hot pepper, which was all the rage until I took the market away."

"Considering that you were in a dungeon the last time I heard from you," I asked, "how did you manage to pull that off?

Bockman spun around in circles like a whirling dervish, his long dressing gown flaring. He finished with a brief shuffle-step dance routine. He affected a leer and cocked his head to one side.

"My partner, Lady Greyhurst," he said, "put on a grand per-formance to convince Weston that my green liquid was just the thing to spice up their sex life. Three days and three nights of super whoopee made a believer out of him. My elixir was consumer-tested, so to speak."

"She made a pact on your behalf with Lord Weston?" I asked. Bockman's mind must have run off the rails. "To do what?" If Lady G and Weston were in cahoots, then she had faked me out royally.

"To use my skill as a chemist to create powerful new potions, elixirs, and liquors to sell for profit." Bockman extended both arms over his head and spread his fingers into a "V"-for-victory sign. "The agreement was that Weston would keep me fit and also provide all the supplies I required to create the products. I plea-bargained work for him, to escape being skewered on his sword. Kind of a work-furlough arrangement."

"You, Lady Greyhurst and Weston all became business partners?" I wasn't sure whether Bockman's story was real or imaginary.

"You got it, bubba," Bockman said. "She handles sales. Me, manufacturing. Weston puts up the capital. I call our deal the Randy Accord."

"What does the King think of this private venture?"

"Oh, he doesn't know about it. All is secret. Otherwise, his Supreme Studness would take over the business as a royal monopoly. No. We are plotting to expand our market into France, Spain, and the Lowlands. The King would declare us guilty of treason for doing business with England's enemies. Treason equals having your head chopped off."

Bockman grasped my jacket lapels and pulled me close to him. His eyes searched the empty room to make sure no one was listening. Then he directed his attention back to me.

"I have a new five-year business plan." He tapped his forehead. "In here. So they must keep me alive."

"Wizard Bockman." I took hold of Bockman's skinny shoulders and shook him. "I'm glad your entrepreneurial spirit is alive and well, but don't you think it's time we get the hell out of here?"

"But I have a new product." He blinked. That owlish quality again. "A blockbuster. Can't make it fast enough."

"Come on, Bockman, grab your stuff and let's scram."

Enthusiasm drained from his voice. His voice trailed off. Bockman rubbed his hands across his face.

"Yes, of course, Elliot," he said. "Sorry to have gotten carried away. This venture has kept my spirits alive while waiting with feeble hope for you to rescue me."

"It's okay, Bock, you're free." I gave him a brief man-hug before shoving him toward the door. "Now I suggest you and the jailer switch clothes. And bring a bottle of your strongest moonshine."

"I'll have you know I make a very fine variety of liquors," Bockman huffed. Bockman rummaged in his gunnysack and pulled out a clay jug. "Sells under the Wizard's Private Reserve label. We offer a B&B knockoff, absinthe, and this orange-flavored brandy."

Bockman's state of mind bounced between staying and going. Maybe he suffered from Stockholm Syndrome, captives relating to their captors. I took the jug from him and thumbed toward the door. Bockman didn't argue. The reality of our plight had sunk into his addled brain. As we walked outside, I plucked the jailer's shirt and vest off the wall pegs. The tied-up jailer greeted us with an evil eye as we approached.

"You are going to look smashing in your new outfit." I gestured toward Bockman, who was busy peeling off his clothes.

The jailer did his best to scoot his chair away from my proposal. I removed the cork from the jug and held the container to jailer's mouth. He pressed his lips together and shook his head.

"Let me explain." I drew the sword from my belt and stuck the tip into the man's nostril. "In your circumstances, I suggest that refusing a free drink would be bad for your health. Drink, and keep drinking."

"Never has a man felt more reluctance at such a happy prospect," the jailer said.

I tipped the jug and poured the golden liquid into his mouth.

~ TWENTY-NINE ~

The Road to Spindledown

Bockman and I steered the drunken jailer into the cell. I sat the man down next to the pot-still and pulled the dressing gown's red velvet collar high around his neck to help conceal his face. Bockman fished through a bin of assorted bottles and surfaced, holding a smallish amber-tinted one. He poured the contents into a cup, which he filled to the brim with alcohol from the still.

"One of my outstanding products. A best-seller in Scotland," Bockman bragged. "A potent sleep potion I concocted from anise, valerian roots, lemon balm, passion flower, and a couple of other soporific ingredients. Make the jailer drink this cocktail."

By now, the jailer was quite happy to drink whatever liquid he could get his hands on. I locked him inside the cell and tossed the key inside the water jug to delay his release when his buddies found him. Bockman preened himself in the mirror, admiring how he looked in his jailer's clothes.

I took my phony wizard by the scruff of his neck and escorted him out of the cottage to the accompaniment of the jailer's loud singing.

"He pulled out sword and pistol,
And caused them to rattle,
The guardsman sang while in battle

Bring me your daughter
And a thousand pounds of gold
Fa de fa de, fa de fa de
Come diddle with me"

The voice paused, a belch erupted, then his voice trailed off. Then came a snort, followed by ripsaw snoring. Bockman grinned at me, picked up his sack, and started down the road leading from the cottage.

"What about taking the jailer's horse?" I asked. Why walk when we could ride?

"My wizardry does not cover beasts of burden," Bockman said. "I have no idea how to saddle a horse, do you?"

"Well, no," I said. "But how hard can it be?"

I found out. Each time I tried to throw the saddle over the horse's back, the animal shied away. Bockman offered to hold onto the bridle, only to drop the reins when the horse nuzzled its nose against him. I managed to get the saddle on the mare's back once, but before I could cinch the saddle girth, it slid under the horse's belly. Riding upside down wouldn't work. The strap came undone and the saddle fell to the ground.

"Elliot, I have analyzed your problem," Bockman said. "And devised a perfect solution. Unlike my logical mind, yours ignores the obvious."

Bockman had the audacity to lecture me? The guy who had sprung him from prison? But I had made no progress in saddling the nag.

"Okay, genius, enlighten me."

I leaned one elbow on the horse's flank and propped my head against my fist. The gentle mare remained placid. She was amiable in spite of my failed attempts at gearing her for a ride.

"We must take my heavy sack of medicines and elixirs with us to Spindledown," Bockman said. "We need the jailer's mare to be our packhorse. We could walk and lead the horse, but by the time we get to Spindledown, Captain McAllen and his guardsmen would track us down."

Walking to Spindledown with a troop of mounted cavalry hounding us did not sound like a winner.

"We lack the job skills to use this horse in the proper manner," Bock pontificated. "Therefore, we need to find another horse. One that is pre-saddled."

"And just where do I find a pre-saddled horse?" I was getting exasperated with my unstable wizard delaying our escape. "Is there a livery stable rental agency around the corner?"

"No, but the solution is coming to us," Bockman said. "When Lord Weston's guardsman makes a product pickup this afternoon, I propose you capture the rider and take his horse."

"What do you mean, I capture the rider? How about we capture him?

"I'm the planner," Bockman said. "I will act as the decoy. The rough stuff is your department."

He wiggled his fingers at me as if casting a spell. And that is how I ended up perched on an overhanging branch of a tree.

Below me lay the narrow road to the cottage. I held my lariat at the ready to rope the expected rider. Bockman hid behind a thick patch of bushes by the side of the road. One moment there, the next gone from sight. He was supposed to stand in the road to slow down the rider so I could lasso him. My so-called decoy was nowhere in sight. Why had I trusted the unstable flake?

A nearby whinny jolted my musing. The rider was approaching before I was ready. I pulled my legs tight to my chest and tried not to move. The guardsman passed below me headed for the cottage. As he moved through the patches of shade and light, the sun glinted off his helmet.

Uh-oh, Bockman really had disappeared. Had he run away?

— — —

I parted a cluster of branches and craned my neck for a better view of the cottage's front entrance. The guardsman's horse, a sleek chestnut stallion, was tied to the hitching post. The beast stomped the ground with his hooves, pawed at the dirt, and shook his long black mane. The animal was filled with nervous energy.

The guardsman burst back through the open door, his red cape billowing behind him. He snatched his horse's reins and vaulted into the saddle. He jerked the stallion around and raked the animal's sides with his spurs. The horse leapt forward.

The mounted rider would pass right under my overhanging branch. I stood and braced myself against a protruding limb, my feet balanced on the thick branch where I had been sitting. I glanced up the road. Where the hell was Bockman?

The rider galloped closer and closer to my hiding place. I opened the running noose, aimed at the guardsman's torso as horse and rider thundered toward me. The man looked up just as I threw the loop. His eyes locked into mine and widened in surprise. His leather-gloved hand jerked the reins.

The stallion's long neck arched backwards. I watched in horror as my noose dropped over the horse's head and onto his muscular neck. The horse's forward motion stretched my rope taut. I shot off my overhead perch like a cork from a champagne bottle.

Everything was a blur. My mouth opened wide. A scream erupted. I hit the ground. My breath was knocked from my chest. Hooves sliced past my face. I tried to let go of the rope, but I was ensnared. I bounced off the dirt, landed, and bounced back again.

The galloping horse dragged me. My body flipped on my back, then to my stomach. I grabbed the rope with my other hand and held on.

A blinding flash. Then an explosion ahead of me. The horse reared as the rider struggled to bring him under control. The rope slackened. I pulled my hands free and slid to a halt. The stallion fell to the ground, his rider thrown onto the roadside. The horse stood and shook himself.

The guardsman made a half-hearted attempt to rise, then collapsed onto the ground and rolled onto his back, arm covering his face. I stumbled to where he lay. Bockman, holding the fallen rider's sword, stood triumphant over the prostrate figure. I wanted to punch Bockman, but I was too battered to lift my fists.

"As I predicted," Bockman waved a hand in the direction of the horse, "our pre-saddled transportation has arrived. See? That wasn't so hard. A little chemistry, a little imagination."

He stabbed the sword into the dirt. The handle wobbled back and forth. I wanted to kick him in the ass.

"What the hell did you do? What was the explosion?"

"A little homemade flash-bang grenade." Bockman did that beckoning-hands thing that performers do when seeking applause. "I also do Molotov cocktails—small, medium, and large." He bobbed to his imaginary audience. "Thank you, thank you."

"Take care, stranger." The guardsman raised his head from where it rested on his folded arms. "The Wizard is quite mad. The man claims he lives in a magic city by a bay, and that huge carts are pulled by cables up and down hills. He also swears that a gold bridge leads to the city. He even sings a song about it."

"If what you say is true," I said to the guardsmen, "then you would be safer back in the cell with your fellow soldier, the jailer. Come on, I'll even give you a couple free drinks."

Bockman led our pre-saddled horse back to the cottage. The guardsman and I followed behind. The man limped along and gave me no resistance. The soldier was ready to call it a day.

The sun was now low in the sky. Soon darkness would help cover our escape. The Spindledown coach station offered the safest sanctuary. Unless Old Penn had rented out my hidden room. Or Captain McAllen's men captured us on our way.

THIRTY

Hunkered Down in Spindledown

I was in a general funk as we followed the narrow road from the cottage towards Lord Weston's estate. Being dragged behind a horse had generated an overall aching body. My head throbbed, and both hands had rope burns. I shifted my rump in the saddle, trying to find a comfortable position.

Bockman rode double behind the saddle, both arms around my middle, the rope tethering the jailer's horse tied to his waist. He regaled me with tales of how Lord Weston allowed him to test market his aphrodisiac with the eager participation of Weston's occasional household visitors. I told him to knock it off.

"Just make sure the jailer's horse stays behind us," I said.

The ersatz wizard had a habit of gesturing with both hands when he got excited about a subject. I wanted to make certain our sack of trade goods, which we had brought from the cottage jail, didn't get lost on a straying mare.

The route curved around groves of trees and along a stream before straightening out at the edge of the woods. A heavy cloud cover guaranteed a black night. The first splattering of raindrops arrived unexpectedly in the darkness of Hangman's Forest and pelted my skin. I gave up trying to see the road, slackened the reins, and let the stallion find his own way.

I had no rain gear, not even a cloak to keep me dry. My clothes seemed to have an infinite capacity to soak up water. Every inch of my skin was cold. The promise of food and shelter at Penn's coach station kept me going. Then, for some reason, the stallion halted and refused to budge.

"Do you want to know why he has stopped?" Bockman's voice had that fake superiority of a preteen arguing with a friend.

"Enlighten me." I had tried to keep my temper under control by making mental jokes about my daffy landlord and our difficult situation, but Bockman was testing my limit.

"We're at the crossroads." He pointed left. "That is the coach road to Spindledown. Straight ahead would take us to Weston's estate. I should know. I walked this way many times behind a horse when being taken to the cottage and back."

"A horse's behind. That fits you," I said. "I don't see any stoplights. So why did the horse go whoa on me?"

"Elementary, my dear Vail," Bockman said. "This is the rest stop where riders meet to exchange gossip and the latest news."

"Yo, pilgrim," I tugged on the reins with my left hand and dug my heels into the horse's flank to urge the stallion forward.

My horse-riding skills were elementary at best, so I just mimicked John Wayne. The well-trained stallion hung a left and cantered towards Spindledown. The mare, laden with our bulging sack of Bockman's potions, dutifully followed.

The constant rain had shut Bockman's mouth. Either that or he had dozed off. After forever, we passed several small farms and an occasional cottage. Spindledown must be close. I reined the horse to a stop, woke Bockman, and dismounted.

"From here on, we walk," I said. "Take the supplies off the jailer's horse."

Bockman rubbed his eyes, mumbled a complaint, then dismounted. He untied the rope from around his waist, walked back to the mare, and removed the gunnysack from the horse's back. His eyes were all owlish again.

"Why walk?" Bockman said. "Weston's men could already be looking for us."

"They'll follow the hoof prints," I said. "I'm going to turn both of the horses loose to find their own way back to the stables. Perhaps we can mislead Captain McAllen and his bad guys."

Bockman didn't argue. He schlepped the gunnysack over to me. I swatted the stallion on its rump. The horse galloped off on the road toward Weston's estate, with the mare following. Maybe she hoped the stallion would share some oats and a dry stall.

"Elliot, I hate to be a pest," Bockman said. His mouth smiled, but the tone was critical, like a wife asking her husband if he was lost. "But are you sure of what you are doing?"

"No sweat," I said. "We're going to sneak into Spindledown to bribe an ancient innkeeper, hide in a secret room, and outfox Weston's elite guardsmen."

"And you think I'm loony?" Bockman circled his index finger around his temple.

We trudged through steady rain, both of us too tired to argue. Dogs in Spindledown Village barked our arrival. The rain tapered off, but the wind continued to chill us. I set the gunnysack down while figuring out the best way to approach the coach station. Bockman's teeth chattered and his lips were blue.

"Elliot, there's something important I have been meaning to ask you." Bockman didn't wait for my reply. "Did you bring a supply of

Particle Enhancement Liquid with you? I can't duplicate the formula with the chemical compounds available in these times."

"The good news is that I brought the leather bandoleer holding a supply of Particle Enhancement. There are enough vials for us to time travel back."

"I detect a problem." He reached out a shaky hand and clutched my sleeve. Drops of water dripped from the point of his Van Dyke beard. "Tell me the bad news."

"The bandoleer is stashed in the transport box at your London home. The computer decided to send it to your home address while I ended up in Lady Greyhurst's garden. I didn't know how to find your residence."

"Yes, separating the transport box from the time traveler. A slight programming glitch," Bockman admitted. "I meant to fix that before my last trip. It didn't seem important at the time. I didn't realize the London plague had broken out."

"Well, no harm, no foul."

I wasn't going to stress over a mere speed bump in our return plans. But Bockman dropped to his knees. He lifted his head toward me. Defeat and sadness were etched on his face.

"You don't understand," he said. "My home is near Saint Giles in the Fields church. It is the very center of the plague that is ravishing London. To go there is to risk a most horrible death."

Fatal diseases? I had counted on a round-trip ticket, not one-way to a seventeenth-century grave. A series of shudders racked my body, caused either by my bleak future or the cold night air. My mind stalled. I lifted the gunnysack and headed for the coach station. I'd feel better after one of Penn's hot meals and a good night's sleep. Tomorrow would be a better day to freak out.

— THIRTY-ONE —

Penn Station

Old Penn had stoked fires in iron braziers outside the entrance to the station courtyard to light the way for customers. I could hear noises from within the station. Bockman and I waited in the shadows.

The door opened to the hearty laughter of the last two patrons to exit. Their periwigs were askew above faces that glowed with the aftermath of heavy drinking. Penn waved them on their way before closing the door. I heard the bolt being drawn.

The two men crossed to the courtyard, then staggered out of sight. I moved forward, staying on the edge away from the flickering fires. Bockman tagged behind me, struggling to keep our sack of goodies from dragging on the wet ground. I rapped on the station door. The shuttered windows kept me from seeing inside. I repeated the knock.

"Go away." A protesting voice called out from inside the station. "I'm closed for the night." Penn's voice was distinct and clear. He must have been standing directly behind the locked door. "See me on the morrow."

"Penn, you old dog." I said. "Open up. It's me, Elliot. Lord Edward and I need to hide in your secret room. Weston's guardsmen are after us."

"So, the Watkins brothers didn't kill you after all?" Penn opened the door a crack. Penn's blue-veined hand appeared. He turned it palm upwards. "If you really are Elliot, give me back my little knife you borrowed in Hangman's Forest."

— — —

Old Penn made Bockman and me welcome in his own fashion. He offered to run a tab for the hidden room and charge us a modest sum for two meals a day. We offered three bottles of Bockman's Private Reserve in exchange. Bockman clinched the deal by throwing in a green bottle of the King's favorite passion potion. He suggested to Old Penn that selling a shot as a beer chaser could be highly profitable.

Penn laid out a cold roast-beef-and-cheese plate. Bockman and I sat in our skivvies in front of the fireplace while our clothes dried. Penn didn't press us for details until we had wolfed down the food. Then he became an eager listener when I told him about the Watkins brothers and my rescue of Bockman.

"Lord Edward." Penn doled out three beers and sat down at our table. "I wish you would work some magic and create more customers for my tavern."

"I already have," Bockman said. "By now, the alarm has been raised and soon the countryside will be crawling with Weston's men. Perhaps some of them will become customers."

I kicked Bockman's leg under the table. We didn't need Penn to be afraid of hiding us or tempted to sell us out for a reward. Penn exaggerated a yawn, a signal I took to mean my adventures were not as important to him as getting his sleep. Bockman and I gathered up our clothes and called it a day.

The glow from the burning candles in Penn's pewter candlestick lit the walls of the secret passageway that led behind the stone fireplace. He paused and pointed to a single brick with a u-shaped bolt attached.

"Spy hole," he said to Bockman. "I showed it to Elliot earlier. Lets a person see and hear what is happening in the waiting room."

The candles trailed smoke and dripped wax as he led us to the hidden room. Then Penn handed me a clay saucer holding a short candle. The innkeeper didn't trust any of his guests with his pewter.

Penn ignited my squat candle and bade us goodnight. Bockman curled up on his cot like a cat. All I remembered was my cheek hitting the pillow on my bed.

THIRTY-TWO

McAllen in Charge

I couldn't get enough air. Someone's hand was covering my mouth. I opened my eyes to find Bockman standing over me, a cautioning finger to his lips.

"Horses and men," he whispered. "They rode up a moment ago. I think it's Weston's guardsmen."

Hooves clattered on courtyard cobblestones. Harnesses jingled. A gruff voice issued orders—sounds of Captain McAllen's troops milling around in front of the building. Someone pounded on the station door, demanding entrance.

I led Bockman to the secret passageway behind the fireplace. My fingers found the u-shaped bolt on the back of the brick. I snuffed the candle, then eased the brick out.

"Coming, coming." Old Penn wore a dingy nightshirt and a striped stocking cap. His battered lantern cast flickering shadows over the empty waiting room. He shuffled to the door and opened it.

Captain McAllen, looking splendid and rugged in his uniform, brushed past Penn and marched into the room. Several of his guardsmen filed in behind. Their drawn swords flashed in the lantern light.

"How may I be of service to you, sir?" Penn bowed to the Captain.

"Tell me where to find the Wizard Bockman and his companion." McAllen towered over Old Penn who bent backwards as far as his aged spine allowed.

"But surely, sir," Penn said. "Lord Weston has command of that person. In God's truth, I do not know the man. If indeed such a person does exist. I have only heard wild tales."

"Search the building and the stables," McAllen said to his deputy. He turned back to Penn. "Innkeeper, awaken your guests and have them assemble in this room immediately."

"Gladly, Captain sir," Penn said. "Would that I be blessed with paying guests. The plague has ruined my business. No one travels to London. My coaches find few travelers these days and then only from Spindledown to distant villages."

"You had better be telling the truth." McAllen removed his polished metal helmet and handed it off to his deputy, then unfastened his red riding cape and tossed the rain-soaked garment over a nearby chair.

"My rooms are empty," Penn complained. "Go see for yourself. The dust lays undisturbed. I live hand-to-mouth by the grace of what few coins I eke from my tavern."

"Captain." A mustached guardsman stepped forward and saluted. "The innkeeper tells the truth. No one is here."

"Your mighty sir," Penn said. "Pray allow me to open my kitchen to feed you and your men. For I see your troopers are wet and weary. I will stoke the fire to warm the room. Make yourselves comfortable. I offer simple food that I prepare myself. I had to discharge my kitchen cook due to my failing business. I am all alone."

McAllen reached into his pocket and threw several coins onto a table. The gold glinted in the lantern's glow. Penn snatched them up before they had come to rest.

"Do the best you can." McAllen pulled a senior trooper aside. "I will make this my headquarters. Tell all squads to report to me here. Send men to capture the Watkins brothers and bring them here. Go fetch Grundle and say I command him to join us. The hangman has ways to coax the truth from those two cutthroats."

I hated hearing the Captain's orders to track down the Watkins brothers. Tom Major was severely wounded and would slow down the family's efforts to elude their pursuers. I pressed an eye to the spy hole.

Penn delivered a plate of leftover bread and moldy cheese along with a small basket of brown spotted apples long past their prime. The old innkeeper had provided Bockman and me with far better food than he had to McAllen. Was Penn silently thumbing his nose at the captain?

"I do not think this feeble innkeeper is capable of feeding us well," McAllen said as he walked his guardsman to the door. "Send a rider back to the estate and bring the maid, Lilly Swinden, to assist the innkeeper. She knows the ways of the kitchen. If Lady Greyhurst protests, tell her I act under direct orders of Lord Weston."

I slid the brick back into place. Things were getting complicated. McAllen had summoned the Watkins brothers and Grundle. Now he ordered Lilly to be brought here to the station. It would be delightful to meet her on the sly, if Penn would be coaxed into making arrangements. But having Grundle around was bad news. And I worried about Tom Major. Or more specifically, I fretted about Little Tom and Sister.

Skulking off to disease-ridden London didn't sound all that bad. Yes, it did. Bockman had described the plague symptoms: red blotches, raging fever, pus-filled sacs in the groin. Nasty, nasty stuff.

— — —

Lilly brought in stores of food to feed McAllen and his guardsmen. She worked wonders in the kitchen, transforming ordinary potatoes, onions, and meat trimmings into hardy stews for McAllen's soldiers. She fed the Captain and his senior guardsman the best cuts of beef and plumpest chickens. I could see it all from the spy hole and smell the food, all with envy.

Old Penn scurried around making the men comfortable and catering to their needs. I noticed the soldiers were content to linger around the fire with tankards of ale. Fewer and fewer search parties left the comfort of the coach station.

I grew bored being cooped up in our small hidden room. Bockman didn't seem to mind. Maybe because he had spent so much time locked in a jail cell. Penn needed a waiter to help him in the dining room. I volunteered to help. Lilly was dubious, but relented when I assured her I would keep my mouth shut.

Lilly seemed to be over the charms of the dashing Captain McAllen after seeing him order the village people around like a petty martinet. She got even with me though by having Penn tell everyone that the new waiter was a simpleton from a nearby village. I pretended to stumble, drool, and drop things. I was a natural. And, much to my delight, she and I had made peace.

I finger-combed my hair low over my forehead and made sure my upper teeth always showed over my lower lip. Thanks to the workman's clothing Penn had let me borrow, I passed myself off as a lowly servant groveling at the whims and orders of the guardsmen. I treated the whole scene like an actor's role and chuckled at my ease of moving among my enemy. In the process I gathered a treasure trove of material for future comedy routines, if I ever made it back to San Francisco.

On the third evening, I had again stationed myself at my favorite spot, the secret spy hole, and observed the soldiers' activity.

Captain McAllen was upbraiding three of his guardsmen who had returned from an all-day search.

"What do you mean, the thieving Watkins brothers are not to be found?" McAllen shouted. "Cannot three of my seasoned horsemen capture two scoundrels who are on foot? Why do I pay you?"

"By the time we located their house in Hangman's Forest, it was empty." The soldier braced to attention and stared at a spot on the wall to avoid McAllen's glare. "The Watkins family were last seen fleeing deeper into the woods. The wizard and his rescuer were not with them."

"Sir, may I offer a word?" the senior guardsman asked. Decorated marks on his sleeve indicated long military service.

"Join me for a tankard." Captain McAllen gestured toward one of the tavern tables, then gave curt permission for the man to speak.

"The Watkins are petty criminals," the senior guardsman chose his words with care. "Hired to do dirty work. They are not important. According to the jailer's testimony, they had already retreated before the prisoner was freed. The brothers could not know anything of the whereabouts of the wizard and the man who freed him." He ran one hand through his thinning hair then leaned closer to the captain. "The real danger is the stranger. He must be a very bold fighter to have captured two of our skilled men."

Bold fighter? Me? I pumped my fist and mouthed a silent cheer. Too bad I couldn't record the soldier's praise and send it to my ex. First time in my life someone admired my manly fighting skills. I pressed my ear against the spy hole to hear Captain McAllen's response.

"Hmmm, perhaps you are correct," McAllen said. "Yet I have received no word from my spies that such a hardened warrior has arrived among us. Has the French king sent a trusted lieutenant on a secret mission?"

"Captain," the senior guardsman said. "Perhaps we look at too distant a country. What Englishman would benefit most from securing the services of the wizard?"

"The one man who stands to gain the most has recently moved his court to Oxford." McAllen struck the table with his beer mug, sending foam splashing. "To escape the plague."

The older soldier signaled agreement by an almost imperceptible nod of his head. As if to say such dangerous words are best not spoken aloud.

"Talk of treason quiets the bravest of men," McAllen uttered. "If our mystery opponent is indeed an agent of King Charles, then I must alert Lord Weston. Have my horse readied."

I hurried from the secret passageway back into the tavern. Penn fussed at me for neglecting my waiter duties. He gave me a beer and pointed to the captain. I delivered it, and as I took the empty tankard away, I made sure to stumble against the adjacent table and open my hand. The empty tankard fell to the floor and rolled under the chair.

I bumbled around on my knees chasing it, but Lilly came by, took me by the ear, and jerked me to my feet. She led me back to the kitchen to the laughter of the guardsmen. As soon as we were out of sight, I gave her a kiss before she could cuff me. Her smile was reward enough. God, we had fun together.

"You delight in mischief," she said. "Take care lest you be found out."

Lilly was right, a new zest for life had emerged. Maybe it was due to being surrounded by danger. The worst that could happen to me at the What's Up? Comedy Club would be to get booed on the stage. A rotten tomato had never been thrown my way. In Spindledown I fought to keep my head attached. I realized Lilly, in her own way, watched out for my safety. No one did that for me in San Francisco.

A commotion stirred in the courtyard. Two of the sentries were challenging a new arrival. A brief scuffle ensued, accompanied by shouts. First, one guardsman was thrown through the doorway with such force that his body slid along the plank floor until it crashed into the stone fireplace. A second soldier fared no better. He sailed though the air, helmet flying off, and landed on a table, sending it toppling.

Captain McAllen put both fists on his tabletop and stood. He turned to the senior guardsman.

"Grundle has arrived," McAllen said.

I ducked behind the bar and crawled through the kitchen. Lilly stood at the kitchen door, blocking everyone's view while I hurried to warn Bockman. The hangman would recognize me. Even worse, Grundle knew about Penn's hidden room. Big trouble. I didn't feel at all like a mighty warrior anymore.

— THIRTY-THREE —

Grundle's Call Up

Grundle's arrival changed everything. My frantic rush to alert Bockman sent me pell-mell into the hidden room. If the hangman recognized me or searched our hiding place in the coach station, we could be captured. Captain McAllen might spare Bockman, but not me.

I found my wacky wizard sitting at the little table, quill pen in hand, making notations on parchment. He removed the various bottles and bins from the gunnysack and grouped them on the tabletop according to size and color.

"We have to get you out of here immediately," I said.

"Can't you see," Bockman said, annoyed, "I'm taking inventory?"

"Grundle has arrived. He knows about this hidden room."

"I'm not in the mood to receive guests." Bockman dismissed my warning with a wave of his quill. "Tell him to come back later." He jotted a note on the paper. "I should have brought more high-energy drink."

"In case you have forgotten"—I seized the pen from Bockman's hand and pulled him to his feet—"Grundle is the local hangman, your jailer's brother-in-law. Captain McAllen ordered Grundle to come here to make sure you are captured and punished for escaping."

"Jailed again?" Bockman's jaw dropped open.

He broke away from me and scurried around like a cockroach surprised by light. As a last resort, he flopped on the bed and pulled the covers over his head. I hauled him out of the bed by one ankle. Then I scooted the chair under the roof vent.

"Climb through the hole in the ceiling," I ordered. "Hide on the roof until I tell you to come down."

Bockman stood on the chair and made a feeble attempt to reach the ceiling. He couldn't do it alone. I clasped my hands.

"Put your foot onto my hands," I said.

I gave him a leg up and raised him high enough for him to wiggle through the opening. I had no sooner replaced the roof cover than the door to the room sprang open. I sent a quick prayer upwards and turned to face the intruder.

"Elliot, fear not," Lilly's voice soothed. "I have calmed Grundle. I slipped away from the kitchen and hastened to find you."

"The coast is clear?" I let my breath out, forcing the tension from my clenched fists.

"I know not about the seashore." Lilly gave me a puzzled look. "But here at the coach station, Grundle revels in his brother-in-law's embarrassment of losing Lord Weston's prisoner from a guarded cottage."

"I overheard the Captain order Grundle to find Bockman," I said. "You're certain we're safe?"

"Grundle cares not a fig for Captain McAllen's wishes." Lilly tossed her hair. "He suspects the handsome Captain brought me to Spindledown station to feast his eyes on me."

"And who put that idea in Grundle's thick skull?" I asked.

Lilly's enigmatic smile said it all. I also suspected that Lady Greyhurst had instructed Lilly to inform her of any news regarding Bockman's whereabouts.

"Elliot," Lilly said. "I have been waiting to give you something. Close your eyes. Hold out your hand."

Puzzled, I complied. In my past female relationships, there had always been more taking than giving. Something felt heavy and yielding in my hand. I opened my eyes to find both Le Mieux and Squarrels' money sacks. Penn had given her the money I gave him, knowing she would return it to me. Lilly had returned all my money—without my asking.

"Elliot, there be stories passed amongst the soldiers and servants." Lilly stood toe-to-toe with me and tapped her finger on my chest. "A mysterious man did cast a spell over the Watkins brothers, causing them to aid the stranger in freeing Lord Weston's wizard. The jailer swears the same man gave him a poisoned drink that paralyzed his body."

That would be me. A strange man. A man of mystery. I liked the idea.

"Another soldier claims a wild man flew from the sky and knocked him from his horse." Lilly continued her finger poking on my chest. "The same guardsman claims the wizard appeared suddenly with a flash of lightning and a clap of thunder."

"And what do Lady G and Lord Weston think of these weird tales?"

I decided on tit-for-tat. I tapped Lilly on her boob to punctuate my question. Lilly grabbed my finger and gave it a playful twist.

"They are in a frenzied state," Lilly said. "I overheard Lord Weston shout to m'lady that they would be ruined if the wizard fell into King Charles' hands."

I heard a muffled noise above me. Bockman was overhead, hiding on the roof. He must be overhearing Lilly's and my conversation. I stood on the chair and reached for the slate covering that concealed the opening. It was time to put on my own magic show.

"Hocus-pocus." I waved my hands and pulled the concealed cover free. "I command the wizard to drop down on us."

The soles of green satin shoes appeared, dangling from the ceiling, followed by Bockman's skinny legs. Bockman jumped down from the ceiling. I thought he would crash to the floor in front of Lilly. He surprised me by landing upright. Show off.

"Miss Lilly Swinden," I said. "May I present the former Hangman's Forest yard bird, Lord Edward Bockman of Wizard Town."

He bowed to her as if she were the queen. Then he gave her a hug that lasted a bit too long. His familiarity with Lilly annoyed me. Was I getting possessive?

"Dear Lilly," Bockman said. "Twice before, you have saved me. Now here I am again, placing my life in your hands."

What's with all this huggy-bunny familiarity? Bockman and Lilly had a lot of explaining to do. To me.

"Excuse me, kids," I said. "Is there a history here I should know about?"

Lilly placed one arm around scrawny Bockman's neck and the other around my waist. An impish smile lit her face. She was enjoying my petulance.

"I do believe gallant Elliot is jealous," she said, then gave me a kiss on the cheek.

"His nose is out of joint," Bockman said and laughed.

He pointed a narrow finger at my nose while he placed the forefinger of his other hand along side his own. He excused himself from Lilly's embrace and stepped to the bottles lined up on the table.

"When I was in the cottage jail," Bockman said, "I tried to

make champagne. But I couldn't keep the corks from popping. Let's celebrate with my version of Grand Marnier liqueur."

He passed the bottle to Lilly. She took a modest drink and handed the liqueur over to me. She lapped her tongue in and out of her mouth. Reminded me of a puppy trying peanut butter for the first time.

"I must return to the kitchen before I am missed," she said. "I'm certain Lord Edward's story will be better told without me here to confuse it with the truth."

Lilly curtsied and left. I liked the way she wiggled as she left the room. I hoped Lilly had made those moves for my benefit. I turned around and looked at Bockman. He didn't say a word, just grinned.

"First, there was my duel with Lord Weston," Bockman said as he snatched the bottle from me. He sat on the edge of the bed, crossed one foot over his knee, and chugged. "Suckered me into defending Lady Greyhurst's honor even though there was a high probability of my getting skewered on Weston's rapier."

"I sent you a book on dueling, but you never used it?" I said.

"The night before Weston and I were to duel, Lilly found me at the Wobbly Duck. I was fretting over my sure death. Lilly proposed that if Weston became ill, he wouldn't feel like fighting. That night I concocted my first potion. A mixture of honey and grated iris root. Makes a powerful laxative."

I rescued the liqueur from Bockman's clutches. He was hammering it down. He needed to keep his wits about him. If he had any remaining.

"Lady Greyhurst used Lilly to deliver private letters to Weston," Bockman explained. "So whenever she showed up at his country estate, he would send Lilly to the kitchen to assist his cooks."

"Arrogant SOB." I bridled at Lord Weston's high-handed attitude, since I already knew about Lilly's messenger service.

"Lilly slipped the laxative into his stew. Come morning, Weston was busy at his chamber pot. Never bothered to show up for the duel. I won by default."

"Lucky you to dodge the duel," I said. "But how did you end up in the dungeon?"

"Lady Greyhurst's message to Weston was a proposal that the three of us form a business venture based on my chemistry skills. She never imagined that Lord Weston would clap me in prison to make certain the King would not meddle." Bockman grimaced.

"Why would the lofty King," I asked, "meddle in a small private venture?"

"King Charles is always broke and eager for any money-making scheme. He even accepted money in secret from the French. I made haste to get away from Spindledown and return to London. By the time Weston recovered from his case of the trots, he had decided to throw me in his private pokey. He sent McAllen to shanghai me."

"So," I asked, "how did you send me the plea to rescue you if you were in the stony lonesome?

"When Lilly found out Weston had jailed me, she felt I had been betrayed by Lady Greyhurst. The whole thing turned into a complete mess, a dog's breakfast, as the English say."

Bockman mimicked drinking from a bottle. I surrendered the liquor to him. I propped one foot on the bed and rested my forearm on my knee. I motioned for him to continue.

"Lilly," Bockman said, "smart gal, talked Grundle into showing her the caged wizard in Weston's castle dungeon. While Grundle and his brother-in-law were snarling at each other over some family matter, I slipped my message to Lilly and told her how to launch the transport box."

"I figured you didn't send the last message in the box."

"Nope, nada. No way I could get to my London house to activate the computer for transmission." The wizard held the neck of the now empty glass bottle to his eye, hoping to find more orange liqueur at the bottom. "Lilly overcame all her fears of the unknown. Remember, she still thinks I have supernatural powers. She had the guts to enter the computer room at my London house all by herself, follow my instructions, and launch the box to you in San Francisco. That experience would freak out most seventeenth-century people."

Lilly was the most interesting woman I had ever met. Unpredictable but loyal. Not a fragile classic beauty like Lady Greyhurst. But there was something about Lilly that set her apart from others. An inner core of strength. Whatever she decided to do, she did with enthusiasm. I smiled at all my Lilly memories. Who knew dating an English peasant woman would be so intriguing?

But back to business. "Bockman, you need to stay here in the room," I said. "Captain McAllen is searching all over the shire for us. He doesn't know that we are under his nose. Can you remember to stay put?"

Bockman mumbled agreement. The problem was that his mind tended to wander, either pondering his latest product formula or drifting off onto unknown paths. I speculated that his repeated particle transportations in time had caused slight disruptions at his cranial molecular level. I asked him about my theory.

"Probably." He dismissed my concerns with a terse answer. "Right now I'm busy figuring how to enhance my antiplague product used in London."

"You have created something that will prevent people from getting the plague?" I said, incredulous.

"Sells as fast as I can make it." Bockman sat on the bed with hands in his lap. He seemed as deflated as yesterday's balloon. He worried his fingers like he was counting a string of prayer beads.

"What's the matter, Bock?" I asked.

"My product doesn't really work," he sighed. "It is so frustrating to live with seventeenth-century ignorance. Take the plague. The so-called experts believe the plague is caused by noxious airborne vapors. Doctors recommend strong scents to overpower the vile air. Others believe chewing tobacco is a preventive. Nonsense, of course, but I must cater to the market."

"I thought it was a disease carried by fleas on rats," I said.

"Oh, it is. But no one here is convinced by the truth. Folk wisdom decided cats and dogs carried the plague, so people went on killing sprees. That only removed the rats' natural enemies. Result? More rats with more fleas looking for something to bite. Ergo, more plague."

"Show me your antiplague product," I said.

Bockman selected a small yellow-colored tin from the tabletop. He removed the lid and held it under my nose. I jerked my head away from the pungent odor.

"What the hell did you make?" I sneezed, sneezed, and sneezed some more.

"Recall that old nursery rhyme?" Bockman asked. "Ring around the rosy, a pocketful of posies." He held the tin at arm's length. "The first line describes the circular red sores the disease produces, the second refers to the strong-smelling posy flowers people carry to ward off the plague. I combined tobacco snuff with flower-essence oils, then threw in anything I could find that had a strong odor. Final touch was to add a yellow dye for eye appeal."

"Do people eat, drink, or smoke your product to counteract the bad air?"

The whole idea preyed on people's ignorance. Bockman was

conning desperate people. I thought of Lady Greyhurst's circle of friends. The rich fled, the poor suffered.

"Some people have taken to wearing fancy facemasks filled with my powder," Bockman said. "Keeps the scent in front of their noses. Makes them feel safer."

"Bockman, at heart, you're a snake oil salesman," I accused.

"No, Elliot. At heart I'm a survivor," he said. "Lord Weston threatened to put me on the rack if I couldn't come up with an anti-plague product. I've always wanted to be taller, but being stretched didn't seem like the best way to go about it."

A noise in the passageway drew my attention. I held up a cautioning hand to Bockman. Old Penn stuck his head through the narrow doorway. His calm face neither smiled nor frowned.

"News to report," Penn said. "Though I mourn the loss of business, I rejoice that Captain McAllen and his guardsmen have departed. Lord Weston has recalled his soldiers to his estate. From what I overheard, Weston fears the King has sent a cunning secret agent against him. He readies his forces for defense. There are even whispers that Weston will set sail to seek refuge on the continent to escape the King's wrath. Perhaps Spain or Normandy."

"That's great news," I said. "We can show our faces. Get ourselves ready to return to the New World."

The innkeeper shrugged as if such weighty matters were not his concern.

"What about Grundle?" I asked. "Do you believe we are in danger from him?"

"Lilly hinted that the Captain had made advances toward her," Penn said. "Grundle wanted to pursue him, but Lilly asked him to stay close to her for protection."

"How did the hangman respond to that information?" I said.

"After he ripped away my station door, he seemed to settle down."

Bockman and I did a high-five. Old Penn copied our gesture by raising his right hand and pushing air.

— — —

The station returned to its quiet state after McAllen and his guardsmen left. The hustle and bustle of soldiers' boisterous clamor had been replaced with Spindledown locals meandering to the tavern for a quiet meal. Old Penn collared me later one afternoon while I was polishing my boots. His eyes twinkled in a rare display of exuberance.

"God's good grace has prospered my business," Penn said. "Aided by your stirring a wasp's nest of hungry soldiers by freeing the wizard. I have decided to celebrate my bounteous sales of food and beer. You, the wizard, and Grundle are my dinner guests. Lilly and I will host."

Lilly orchestrated our dinner-gathering with aplomb. So skilled, she could easily have handled a wedding party of mixed ex's, steps and formers. The lady had style and skills.

Platters of pigeon, roasted chicken, fish, fruit, and cheese filled the table. Conversation stopped as the five of us dove into the feast. The only tense moment occurred when Grundle stopped eating and pointed at Bockman.

"Are you the famous wizard?" Grundle asked. "I thought you were dead. Or was I supposed to kill you?" He tapped his teeth while he considered the question. Then he picked up a fork and speared a whole chicken. "No matter."

After dinner Bockman and Penn toddled off to the bar, leaving Grundle, Lilly, and me around the table. Grundle stood and rapped the table for attention like he was some after-dinner speaker on the banquet circuit.

"I have good news to share," Grundle said. "This morning a courier brought me an official letter from London. I have been elevated to chief executioner."

He took Lilly by both hands and twirled her around. Then he lifted her high overhead before he returned her feet to the floor. He grinned from ear to ear.

"Did you hear me, Elliot? I have been summoned to London, the big city. Goodbye to Spindledown Village."

"This is good news?" I said. "Excuse me, Grundle, but I thought the plague was rampant in London. You know, people dying right and left. Seems to me the future need for a hangman's services might be a bit limited."

"Well, yeah." Grundle gave me a playful fist on my bicep. "That's why there is an opening. The Chief Executioner died a week ago from the plague."

I rubbed my arm. The spot was going to be black and blue before morning. Lilly coughed into her hand to cover up a laugh at my expense.

Grundle had been called up from the minors. Couldn't fault a man for following his dream. How would I feel if I got an offer to be a headliner in a top New York club thanks to some New Jersey lowlife who bumped off the star comedian? Easy answer. If a deadly epidemic rampaged in the Big Apple, I would stay safe in San Francisco.

"Lilly, aren't you afraid for Grundle's well-being?" I said. "The black plague spares no one, no matter how strong."

"Grundle, I am happy for you," Lilly said. "But Lord Elliot speaks the truth. I would grieve if you died. But it is not only the plague I am fearful about. Bands of desperate brigands attack travelers on the roads leading to London. The law has broken down. No one man, no matter how brave, can fend off a gang of armed men."

"Ah, Lilly," Grundle pouted. "You know how important the

promotion is to me. Chief executioner has been my dream since I was a wee child."

"Even grain wagons dare not go into London city," Lilly said. "The farmers do fear to take their milled flour. Bakers cannot make bread, prices have gone up tenfold."

Lilly's last remark triggered an idea. I pounded my tankard on the table to get Grundle and Lilly's attention.

"So," I asked. "There is big money to be made if grain wagons can deliver milled flour to the city?"

"Yes," Lilly said. "But such a trip would be filled with danger. None are so foolish as to attempt such an effort "

"But in risk there is opportunity," I argued. "I have a bold plan. No matter how ill-advised the proposal, it is better than the wizard and me being hunted down in Spindledown by either Weston's soldiers or the King's men."

Lilly and Grundle turned their eyes to me and waited.

"I will lead a wagon train to London," I said. "Grundle, you will provide security. Lord Edward's medical skills will help combat the plague."

It was easy to volunteer Bockman. He was at the bar drinking with Penn. I waited for Lilly's approval of my new leadership skills.

"I will not let my brave knights go to London without a guide," Lilly said. "One who does know both the main streets and the back lanes."

"That would be very helpful," I said. "Who is this brave soul?"

"'Tis me." Lilly favored us with a bright smile.

"No, Lilly," I said. "You can't risk getting the plague. I would never forgive myself if you died because of me."

"And I would never ask you to go with me to London," Grundle said. "Lilly, I am not a total fool. You try to hide your true feelings.

It is a bitter truth to me. I see the light in your eyes when Elliot is around."

Lilly's face turned red. Far better for me than if Grundle's did. I'd seen him fired up before. But his showed no anger for me.

"Two grown men deciding my life," Lilly said. "I will not let that happen, no matter how sweet their intentions. I am going."

Avoiding decisions had been a lifelong trait of mine. But I had been forced to make tough decisions while mucking about in the seventeenth century. Now, I had a momentous one to deal with. If Lilly came with me to London, she could transport with me back to San Francisco. I realized that I wanted the two of us to shift our particles together. Forever.

I'd make my pitch to her during our trip to London. She might view my proposal as suggesting she become three hundred years older. Could be a tough sell. Then what would I do?

"It's settled then." Grundle clapped his hands together. "I'll convince two sturdy men to join us on our trip to London."

"They must be fools to face such a dark future," Lilly said.

"Not really," Grundle said. "They are both scheduled to hang in a fortnight. What a choice. Dead if they stay. Dead if they go."

The hangman horselaughed and slapped his thigh. I didn't think that was funny.

THIRTY-FOUR

Wagon Train to London Town

Every new plan needs a title so team members can relate to what's supposed to happen. I decided against Operation Flea Bite and went with Operation 2-3-4. The first two numbers represented the security men and the farmers. Grundle, Bockman, Lilly and me made up the four. It had taken over a week to pull everything together.

Much to my surprise, everyone undertook his or her part with minimum supervision from me. Lilly dealt with the farmers, Penn assembled the wagon teams, and Grundle trained his two pardoned prisoners as guards. Bockman, of course, stood around and criticized.

It was shortly after noon when I collared Old Penn at the bar. An assortment of mugs, glasses, and cups were strewn on the countertop. Several bottles of Wizard's Private Reserve hooch were arranged in front of him. Penn was practicing making cocktails according to Bockman's instructions. Puddles, spills, and empty glasses indicated the innkeeper hadn't mastered the mixed-drink formulas. Penn was appeasing himself by drinking his mistakes.

"Penn, have you seen Lord Edward?" I said. "He seems to have disappeared."

"Lord Edward said to shake, not stir." Penn poured several ingredients into a tankard, placed his palm over the top, and gave the vessel a vigorous shake. He grimaced as he sampled the mixture. "This potion is not to my taste." The innkeeper pushed the failed cocktail aside. "Now, what were you asking?"

"Bockman has disappeared. Do you know where he is?"

"Is that not what wizards do?" Penn slurred. "As the mood doth overtake them? I cannot fathom magicians' tricks. But you will take joy in hearing that Lord Weston has also disappeared from England. Sailed to some distant shore."

Bockman had developed the annoying habit of getting into mischief during the time we had been staying at the station. Three times I had to send Penn to retrieve him from trysts with the Widow Floss, who owned a local dress shop. Bockman contended his motive was merely to provide comfort for the newly bereaved. Penn wisecracked that Floss had been a widow for over ten years.

"Our wizard is best at conjuring up trouble," I said.

"Elliot, you do have a wit about you." Penn wheezed a chuckle. "We could attract new patrons to my tavern if you would entertain them with your mirthful stories. Do you perchance play the lute? Sing songs?"

Me? Doing a lounge act in Spindledown? Hippo would have fun with that idea. Maybe Lilly and I could form a duet.

"Lord Edward and I must return to our country." I leaned my elbows on the countertop. "How about a beer instead of all this fancy stuff?"

Old Penn filled two tankards, slid one over to me and hoisted the other for himself. I was going to miss the crafty innkeeper. I hoped his small business recovered from the calamity of the plague.

"Methinks you are wise to leave these parts." Penn wiped foam from his upper lip. "The wizard will always be a hunted man. Someone, somehow, will seek to capture him again."

"What's the status of the wagon train?" I asked.

"All arrangements have been made to depart for London," Penn said. "The three black-stone farmers and their wagons are now at the grain miller."

"Why do you call the drivers black-stones?" I asked. "Are they experienced and dependable?"

"The farmers drew lots from a bowl containing one black stone among many white ones. The men unlucky enough to pull forth a black pebble must leave their families behind and risk catching the plague while in London. If they get sick, they will never return. 'Tis the only fair way."

I didn't have the option of drawing stones. Returning to modern-day San Francisco required that I enter the danger zone, ground zero, or whatever we should call Bockman's London house. Why couldn't he have bought a place in the suburbs?

"As for Lord Edward," Penn said, "he is visiting with my friend, the physician." Penn nodded in the general direction of the street that paralleled Spindledown's main drag. "The good doctor's home is but a short walk along the back street. He maintains the only apothecary shop in Spindledown. The wizard took some of his potions to barter for special ingredients."

What was Bockman up to now? Keeping track of Bockman was like feeding my brother's cat. Unpredictable and annoying.

"What did the wizard seek?" I asked hoping Penn knew a good answer.

"I am not certain," Penn said. "He may have mentioned saltpeter."

Lilly stuck her head out of the kitchen. A high-bibbed apron covered her blouse. Sleeves pushed up on her forearms and a bandana protecting her hair evidenced she had been preparing food and supplies for our journey.

"Lord Edward returned a short time ago," she announced. "He borrowed some pots from my kitchen, then went to his room. He asked not to be disturbed."

"Nuts," I said.

Bockman was like a rambunctious kid that was suddenly too quiet. You wondered what he was up to. I started back to the hidden room to deal with Bockman, but the rumble of wagon wheels in the courtyard stopped me. Our three wagons filled with sacks of flour had arrived. Next stop, London.

Lilly came out of the kitchen and called me over. Even though she looked harried and sweaty, I had the urge to wrap my arms around her. I specialize in bad timing.

"Elliot, it is kind of you to carry these supplies and stow them in the wagon." Lilly enticed me with her amused smile.

"Oh, yes," I said. "I was just about to offer my services."

She handed me two baskets brimming with food. They smelled of baked bread, ripe fruit, and spiced meats. I carried the supplies out to the courtyard, resisting the temptation to sneak a tasty sample.

Bockman exited the station entrance, clutching his gunnysack over one shoulder. He carried a blanket-wrapped parcel tucked under his other arm.

"I hope you saved some flash-bangs in case we get bushwhacked along the way," I said.

"Sorry. All out," Bockman said. "But I do have a fresh batch of antiplague mixture. It will reassure our men."

Bockman's usual method of dealing with looming danger consisted of denial. I hurried to my room to retrieve the box of miniature paintings Lady Greyhurst had purchased for me. If I made it back to San Francisco, those little gems were to be my future fortune. I was finally on my way home, with a stopover in plague-ridden London. Would I be alone or would Lilly come with me?

Everything seemed to be coming together in the courtyard. I wasn't needed for the moment. I went for a short walk to say good-bye to Spindledown Village. I debated with myself about my honest feelings about Lilly. I decided nothing.

— — —

Our heavy wagons creaked and jounced through the English countryside at a steady pace. The two pardoned prisoners armed with halberds, a weapon with an axlike blade and a steel spike mounted on a long shaft, walked ahead of the lead wagon. Lilly sat in the high seat alongside the driver of the middle wagon. I rode shotgun in the third wagon, seated next to a taciturn black-stone farmer.

Bockman insisted that he sit in the back of my wagon bed to be our tail gunner. Grundle brought up the rear, walking a dozen paces behind our wagon. The hangman carried a long-handled, oversized axe slung over his shoulder. A tool of his trade?

Each hour brought our small band closer to the great city of London. Our trio of heavy-laden farm wagons rumbled through several abandoned villages. Vacant dwellings along the way had been looted. Broken furniture, smashed dishes, and soiled bedding littered weed-filled yards. Cottage after cottage had been burnt to charred skeletons. The local citizens had fled from the plague, putting maximum distance between themselves and the diseased city. The tiny village of Wynden Wide had been leveled. A bedraggled young man squatted along the roadside, hollow-eyed, his body gaunt.

"Young sir," Lilly called out. "Where is your family?

"Over there." He pointed to a pile of charred rubble on a barren rise. "In the church."

"Have you no one to care for you?" I asked.

"I dragged them all to the church. Stacked the bodies inside like cordwood." He wiped one hand across his eyes as if blotting out the memories. "Then I set it afire to stop the plague from spreading. A burden I shall carry forever."

He refused to join our traveling group, insisting he would stay to tend the meager family farm. I watched him standing bedraggled in the middle of the road, until we rounded a bend. And a new vista of debris replaced the previous.

We approached a timbered bridge over a narrow river just as dusk edged into the evening sky. The lead wagon halted. Sounds of loud arguing punctuated the air. Threats were exchanged. My driver reined our team to a stop, then stood in his seat to see what had happened.

"There be three armed highwaymen blocking the middle of the road, halfway across the bridge," he said. "Our men have come together to confront them."

Grundle heard the commotion. He headed forward from his rear position, his mouth turned up in a wicked grin. The hangman must have been yearning for some action.

"Elliot, protect Lilly," Grundle ordered as he sprinted past our wagon. "I will deal with our foes on the bridge."

Ahead of me, Lilly screamed. Behind me, Bockman shouted a warning. A bearded figure had arisen from a roadside thicket and attacked the middle wagon. He had both hands around one of Lilly's arms, trying to pull her from her perch.

"Elliot, we have a problem." Bockman pointed to the road behind us. Mounted men emerged from a grove of trees, two riding bareback, and one, a saddled horse. Four men ran alongside, brandishing farm tools as weapons. They yelled and whooped as they rushed forward.

Images of tattered clothes, filthy faces, wild gestures, filled my eyes. Ambushed. Bloody hell, we had walked into a trap. I drew my sword and rushed to rescue Lilly. Three strides brought me to the man attempting to capture her.

Lilly landed a sweeping right cross to the man's jaw. Her fist knocked his head sideways, towards me, his tongue halfway out of his mouth. His fingers let go of her arm, but he rallied to try again. I saw a flash of leg as Lilly stood and kicked him in his teeth. He tumbled backwards and landed in the ditch. I swatted him across his backside with the flat of my sword. He scrambled away.

"Lilly, are you hurt?" I said. She had a fierce look in her eyes but didn't appear to be injured.

"I am unhurt," Lilly shouted. "Help Lord Edward."

I spun around and raced back to my wagon. I grabbed the sidewall and vaulted over the railing into its bed, landing amid the bulging sacks. Flour billowed into the air.

The vicious gang behind my wagon was closing the distance, their weapons raised. They yelped like a pack of wolves eager for the kill. No mercy for their victims.

Bockman pulled the covering blanket off the rear wagon gate. Foot-long rolls of tubing tied onto the wood railing were aimed toward the men and horses attacking us. Bockman stood like a Royal Navy seaman manning a ship's cannon. Smoke rose from a lighted taper he held in his hand. He whooped a banshee yell as he lit fuses.

Balls of fire shot from the tubes, then arched in a flaming trail that landed in the midst of our pursuers. Each ball exploded in a star of green and red. Sparkles zoomed and whizzed. Their horses bucked and reared to escape the noise and flaming missiles. Riders were thrown from their mounts. The mob scattered.

"How do you like my Roman candles?" the wizard taunted the fleeing men.

Our wagon drivers struggled to keep our horses under control. Grundle had run back from the bridge to order the wagon train forward. The lead driver shouted at his team, flicking the reins.

"Get moving." Grundle slapped our wagon's side. "The bridge is now clear."

Our driver whipped the horses. The wagon jerked forward to join the others.

"What happened to the rogues on the bridge who were blocking us?" I stepped over the front rail and slammed myself onto the seat.

"They have gone for a swim in the river." Grundle had a bloody gash down one arm. He turned and ran back toward the lead wagon, laughing into the wind.

"Wizard, I'm so happy I did not capture you as Captain McAllen ordered me to do," Grundle exclaimed.

I twisted in my seat to see what Bockman was doing. The wizard had dropped his drawers and was mooning our pursuers, who now milled about in confusion behind us. If there is such a thing as a second childhood, Bockman was enjoying his.

I glanced ahead at Lilly's wagon to make sure she was still okay. She sat straight-backed in the wagon seat, unfazed by the attack. A vivid memory had surfaced. I whistled to get her attention.

"Lilly, I need another bath."

She turned around and waved at me, her laugh bubbling up.

"Thank you, my brave Elliot, for saving me."

Lilly blew me a kiss. She had not needed my help, but I appreciated her gesture. My feelings toward her had taken a new turn. Fight or no fight, I liked her at my side.

THIRTY-FIVE

Comes the Blackbird

News of a wagon train delivering scarce flour to London had arrived before we did. A pudgy officer clad in breastplate and metal helmet met us at the city gate. He and his detachment of King Charles' soldiers were, he said, to escort us to the main bakery a short distance away. Our two weary guards welcomed the added show of force.

A pack of hungry men, women, and children trailed behind us, keeping well clear of the soldiers. The King's men had no qualms about repulsing them. The officer's attitude seemed to be that if some were killed, they could have died anyway from the plague.

The black-stone farmers pulled their wagons into an interior courtyard. Iron gates were secured to keep the flour safe from theft. The farmers delighted in the premium paid for the flour, counting it a just reward for the risks taken. The King's officer promised to escort the farmers back to Spindledown as soon as he received official permission. In my opinion, his offer had more to do with getting him out of plague-ravaged London than any concern about the farmers' well-being.

Grundle gathered Lilly, Bockman, and me in front of the bakery. The hangman spiffed his mop of red hair by spitting on his hands and slicking down the sides of his pageboy cut. Then he raised his axe to his shoulder.

"I must take my leave now," he said. "My orders are to report as soon as I arrive. I am most eager to start my new duties as high executioner."

What perks went with that promotion? More money, more heads, and a rope allowance? The possibilities were endless.

"Lilly, I know you are sad at my departure." Chin down, Grundle's lower lip protruded. Even his axe drooped from his shoulder. "Do not think ill of me for leaving you. Elliot will take care of your needs."

Lilly's demeanor gave no clue as to her inner feelings. I hoped her thoughts were shouting, "Yahoo. See ya later, big boy. I'll be in touch."

"Grundle, I am proud of you," Lilly complimented. Her fingers fiddled with the ties on her bonnet. "You delivered us safely to London."

Grundle aw-shucked and handed his axe to Bockman, who clasped it as if he were an honor guard at a coronation. Grundle rubbed his right ear. His lobe had a chunk missing. A new battle scar? I'd have hated to see the other guy.

"Elliot," Grundle said, "promise that you will look after Lilly."

He draped one big paw over my shoulder, lowering my clavicle a couple of inches under the pressure. What could I say to the hangman? Excuse me, but I'm about to abandon Lilly and take off for San Francisco with my box of valuable paintings. Grundle mistook my hesitation for emotion. He pulled my head close to his oversized chest.

"As long as I'm around, I will watch over her," I hedged. "Every day . . . I'm here in England."

"Tell your grandchildren," Grundle's voice clutched, "you were friends of the famous London hangman, Two-Chop, before he became high executioner. Tell them we fought bad robbers together."

Grundle wiped a smudge of moisture from under his eye. Then

he gave Lilly a big hug that enveloped her from waist to neck. She held onto her bonnet to keep it from falling off.

Bockman returned Grundle's axe like a soldier responding to the order to present arms. The wizard saluted him. Then the hangman strode down the street and paused at the corner. He turned, waved, and walked away.

"At least he didn't whistle heigh-ho, heigh-ho," I quipped.

Bockman's only response was a spastic twitch. The wizard hadn't been himself the last few hours. His speech was halting at times. His skin color was off. Had he caught the plague? Became infected so suddenly? Were Lilly and I exposed? Most likely, Bockman was simply stressed out. Being imprisoned could do that to a person.

The wizard picked up his gunnysack. I noticed that his left hand was bandaged. I didn't recall him being wounded in our fracas at the bridge.

"You hurt your hand?" I asked.

"A scratch. None of your concern." He forced a smile. "By the way, Penn's physician told me he had been summoned to administer aid to one of the Watkins brothers. The doctor had to keep mum about it for fear of Captain McAllen finding out."

"Was it Tom Major? He was seriously wounded helping me rescue you," I stammered. "Is he okay?"

"Yes, to your first question," Bockman said. "As to his wounds, Major is still alive, but it will be a difficult recovery. The younger brother waited too long before seeking medical help. He was afraid the family would be captured."

"That's terrible news," I said. "I feel like hell."

"I sympathize with your feelings, Elliot," Bockman said. "But now we go into the real hell."

— — —

Lilly led us into the area west of London's venerable city walls. Bockman admitted he had limited knowledge of the area. He had traveled only the one route between his St. Giles in the Fields house and Lady Greyhurst's home. His mind had been more on fooling around with her than paying attention to the map.

"Be alert for marauding ruffians," Lilly warned. "I will avoid the main streets, where criminals often lie in wait. Instead, we three will slip along back lanes and tread narrow walkways."

We were about a half-mile from the bakery when we turned onto a side street lined with miserable tenements that symbolized London's slums. Bockman tugged my arm, then stepped in front of Lilly.

"See that door?" he pointed across the littered street. "The one with a red cross on it?"

A low stoop led to a weathered door. Splashed across the paneling was a red-painted cross. Rough planks secured the door.

"Someone inside is dying of the plague," Bockman said. "The authorities have nailed the door shut and left everyone inside to die or live, as God judges. A draconian action, but they felt it was the only way to stop the plague from spreading."

"Can't the people inside just escape somewhere?" I asked.

"How do they find food?" Lilly protested. "Does no one care for the sick?"

"Soldiers enforce the authorities' decree," Bockman said. "Anyone caught outside their sealed home can be executed on the spot. As for care, those in charge have hired untrained nurses to bring in food. Even worse, unscrupulous men appoint themselves as doctors."

"A bunch of ghouls preying on the sick," I protested. "A license to be a grave robber before the body is in the grave."

Bockman leaned against the building wall. His face was ashen.

He held his bandaged hand in front of his face. It trembled like he had Parkinson's disease. I was right, the wizard was sick. We hadn't been in the city that long, so logic said he hadn't had time to show signs of the plague. Something odd was going on. I reached out to help him, but he rejected my offer with an angry wave of his hand. Had time travel caught up with my landlord?

"Perhaps I am a bit weak," Bockman relented. "Elliot, please carry my supplies." He rested the sack on the pavement, where the contents settled to the sound of clinks and clunks. "Wait, I do have something to give our tired bodies a boost."

Bockman spread open the drawstring and pulled a pint-sized, tan-colored bottle from his sack. He removed a stopper from the neck, sniffed the contents, and held the bottle out for my inspection.

"High-energy drink," he said. "Full of sugar, caffeine, and a couple of herb extracts that will probably be illegal in the next two hundred years. Instant energy. For an hour or so."

Bockman's elixir had the appearance of brown sludge and tasted as bad as it looked. Lilly, Bockman, and I huddled and passed the bottle around as if we were homeless people under a bridge on Saturday night. I yearned for good old Particle Enhancement slime—which had better still be napping in the transport box at Bockman's house.

There should be enough vials stored in the bandoleer for all three of us to transport back into modern times. If Computer Blue were still functioning. And I enticed Lilly to come with me. Bockman pulled the gunnysack over to the curb to take inventory before we proceeded. I took advantage of Lilly and me being alone.

"Lilly," I said. "You know I think warmly of you."

"Oh, is that so?" she said. "You have not been forthcoming and told me of your true feelings."

I hadn't? I had hinted, implied, and suggested. You would think that was enough. Oh, she wanted to hear the "love" word. Years ago, I had bared my heart to my then wife and ended up with my male ego being stomped on.

"Remember how the box disappeared?" I said. "Bockman and I will do the same thing and return to our distant home."

"Is it far?" Lilly asked. Her brow furrowed as she mulled over my remark. "I have not been more than five days' journey from Spindledown."

"Far away into future time. Bockman's magic will send us to the edge of the western ocean, to a wondrous land. Ask me a question and I will try to give you an honest answer."

"Does another woman wait for you in the New World?" She leaned close, alert to any nuance.

"No." I said, unsure of how specific I wanted to be about my past romantic relationships. "Come with me on a grand adventure, traveling in time."

"Is it harder to go forward in time or back in time?" Lilly asked. "I know not what you do for a living. You know little of craft or trade. Farming bores you. And while you are brave, I do not see you as a military man. Your hot blood tells me you are not a churchman."

I tried to recall the small shops we had passed along the London streets. Cobbler, blacksmith, barber. I couldn't claim any of those skills. My list of previous jobs consisted of lifeguard, bouncer, pizza delivery man, cell phone salesman, and telemarketer. None were relevant here. I would take a chance and tell Lilly the truth.

"I make my living as a stand-up comic," I confessed. "I make people laugh. They pay me money."

"You are barmy," Lilly said. "I would be wise to keep my distance from you."

Her lopsided smile took the sting from her comments. She was more careful of hurting my feelings than Hippo had ever been when I shared my thoughts with him.

"Will you come with me?" I pressed her for an answer. I could deal with either a "yes" or a "no."

"Perhaps," she said. Lilly raised one hand to her mouth and tapped her lips with a raised finger.

The word "perhaps" was not an answer. It was confusion. In the male mind this often leads to false positives. Hope raised and successful conclusions projected. Most often not shared by the female mind.

"Elliot," Lilly said, "Let us both think on this matter. I do believe you make up fairy tales. I do not believe in fairies."

"Just wait until you get to San Francisco," I said.

I waited for her to laugh, but my joke went over her head. Yet here we were in London, on our way to Bockman's house, taking a break, talking about our future together, and sharing a drink.

"Are the two lovebirds through billing and cooing?" Bockman said. "We shouldn't tarry any longer. Time is against us."

My mad chemist landlord hadn't lost his special touch. The bottle of Wizard's Wonder Tonic had jazzed my energy just as Bockman had promised. I made sure my box of miniature paintings was inside the sack along with Bockman's elixirs and potions. With or without Lilly, my investment promised a brighter financial future than making people laugh at me.

We started off at a brisk pace towards Bockman's house. I took pity on Bockman and carried the heavy sack. The tin boxes, glass bottles, and my container of miniature paintings bumped in rhythm against my back as I walked along. London had taken on a strange quiet. Citizens avoided each other. Here and there, solitary figures hurried along the streets.

Lilly led us to a small cobblestone square lined by wooden houses that leaned toward each other like old folks at a family reunion. Faded shop signs jutted over the storefronts: a cobbler's shoe, a barber's striped pole, and a tailor's oversized scissors. Signs shaped to show the craft so that illiterate people could recognize the goods or service for sale.

Something bothered me. I was nervous, freaked out, whatever. My intuition screamed danger. I looked for something to validate my unease. Right, left, front, back. Nothing. Silent streets, deserted lanes, vacant courtyards, empty shops. Most people were holed up in their homes and intended to stay there until the plague abated or they died.

An erratic gust spun a dusty vortex. I heard muffled sounds from boarded buildings. The voices of doomed people waiting for the release of death? No, my imagination was running roughshod over my common sense. My ears had heard only the wind moaning through broken windows. Then I saw it.

A dark image stood on the edge of a cabled roof. A raven tall as a man glowered down at me, waiting, watching. A protruding ivory beak affixed on top of an inky body. Wings folded. Brooding over our intrusion. That omen of death spread his monstrous wings. I rubbed my eyes. Looked again. Nothing.

"Backwater Lane," Lilly whispered as she pointed to the entrance of a gloomy alley leading away from the square. "We are near to the rear of Lord Edward's house."

I put a protective arm around Lilly and hurried her across the cobblestone square to the narrow opening. From there on she led the way. The sound of Bockman's shuffling feet followed us. I turned to make sure he was okay.

Bockman trudged along head bent as if he willed each step forward. Bockman's image oscillated in and out of focus. What had been in that energy drink? I shook my head. The image cleared. Bockman looked up at me.

"I was daydreaming about Lady Greyhurst's favorite position in bed." He made a failed attempt at a leer. "She called me her little cockerel. I shall miss her."

Each step closer, each passing minute, Bockman became more aberrant. Were his particles being twisting by some unknown effect? Was he going to do a Jekyll and Hyde on me?

Lilly halted next to a wooden fence whose stained boards walled off a small yard behind a two-story house. Cobwebs filled the corners of shuttered windows. She rested one hand against a rotted fencepost.

"Here is your house, Lord Edward," Lilly affirmed. "Sure as where I knew it would be. Now, I have done my part. Ask no more of me."

Lilly puffed her cheeks and slowly exhaled. Her gaze went to the spacing between Bockman's house and his neighbor's adjacent home. A wide flagstone footpath led to Bockman's tiny yard overrun with weeds. Hard to mow the lawn when you're shackled in a dungeon out of town.

"You will have to break in." Lilly blushed and turned her head away.

"But I told you where to find my key," Bockman protested. He expected logic where there was none. "You sent the box to Elliot."

"I swore," Lilly countered, "I would never go near this evil place again. All your magic frightens me." She bit her lip. "After I saw the box disappear, I fled from the house and threw away the key. 'Tis ungodly to possess such power. I will have no truck with it anymore. I fear little in life, but I fear eternal damnation."

Lilly folded her arms in a show of stubbornness. Now was not the time to argue with Lilly. I would have to leave her if she didn't transport with me. That decision pricked at my conscience, making me feel like one.

"Elliot, you are strong," Bockman instructed. "Force the back door. Then it's up the stairs to the second floor, the room on your right. The computer launch pad is the modest walk-in closet."

"Step aside, Lilly," I ordered. "I'm about to spring one oak door."

I lowered my shoulder, then rammed it against the solid door. Ouch, that hurt. After three attempts and one hurting shoulder, I managed to pop the door from its lock.

Bockman entered first, I followed close behind. Lilly stood outside and refused to enter the gloom. I reached out, seized the ties of her bonnet and jerked her inside like you would tug a reluctant dog.

"Damn it, Lilly," I said. "It is not safe outside. Don't be a stubborn ass."

I got a heel of her shoe on my toes for that analogy. But I was right. Bockman's magic would cause her less harm than the plague. Not only that, but who knew what scoundrels roamed about when night came.

"Bockman, does your magic include a little light?" I grumbled, groping in the dark room.

A moment later he held a lantern in front of my face. The feeble glow from the candlelight bobbed up and down the walls as the lantern swayed in his bandaged hand. Steep stairs ascended to the upper floor.

Bockman led us up the curved stairway. The musty smell of a long-closed house permeated the air. Stair boards squeaked under my boots. Something scurried from the edge of the pale candlelight into the darkness. Lilly yipped and paused, one foot on the tread. Damn, I hoped that wasn't a rat. I didn't need home delivery for the plague.

The three of us crept down the hallway and gathered in front of a solid door. Lilly squeezed her rough hand over my other hand. She wanted to stay close. Bockman handed me the lantern.

"Hold this," Bockman said. "I need to retrieve the room key. I hope Lilly didn't toss this key out as well."

His knees creaked as he stooped to the floor and lifted a rug. He pressed a finger into a knothole. The board popped open. He slid one hand under the edge, lifted the board, and folded it back on itself. Then Bockman reached inside the hole and pulled out a matchbox-sized metal container, the magnetic kind people used to hide car keys under the fender.

"The transport box should be in front of the closet," Bockman said. "I need . . . I must drink the Particle Enhancement Liquid immediately."

He handed me the key and motioned for me to unlock the door. His hand was shaking. I held the lantern up to his face. Bockman now had four eyes, two noses, and a double mouth. He covered his face with his bandaged hand. Lilly gasped in shock. She backed away from us, palms covering her mouth.

"Bock. What's happening?" I said. "You're spooking me."

"You guessed right, Elliot. My particles are unstable and shifting. The Enhancement Liquid should repair the damage. I must drink a double dose to survive the return trip to San Francisco. I'm afraid my time-travel days are over. Too many trips."

I twisted the key, turned the handle and pushed the door open. Lilly's eyes were squeezed shut, blotting out the strange sight. She refused to enter. Bockman and I left her in the hallway and entered the dark room.

"Find the candle sconce on the right wall" Bockman instructed. "Turn it counterclockwise and then push inward. Hurry."

I held the lantern high. Took baby steps along the wall so as not to trip.

"Found it," I announced.

My fingers closed over the brass arm that jutted from the sconce. I rotated the fixture, heard a faint click, and pushed inwards. Machinery coughed before settling into a steady purr. A ceiling fixture flickered, then filled the windowless room with light.

Bookshelves lined one wall, a table served as a desk. A couple of chairs completed Bockman's plain office. The forlorn transport box, edges coming apart, sat there on the floor.

"Portable power generator." The wizard's mouths gave me lop-sided smiles. "Provides electrical energy for the remote computer station. As we speak, the closet computer is alerting home base in San Francisco to initialize the synchronization program. The primary coordinates are to this house. Default location is to Lilly's family farm where I first landed."

I wanted to ask a million questions, but Bockman stopped me. Two versions of his right hand waved in my face. I got his message. Get on with it.

"The box," he whispered, "get me the Particle Enhancement Liquid." His legs gave out and he face-planted on the floor. Or should I say faces-planted. I rushed to the box and lifted the lid. I ignored all the important stuff I had packed in anticipation of my time travel. Only one item mattered, the bandoleer of vials filled with Particle slime.

I jerked the leather belt out of the box. The half dozen glass vials glowed with the greenish-yellow liquid. With nervous fingers I pried a vial free from the loop that secured it. Be careful, klutz. Don't break it.

I rolled Bockman onto his back, lifted his heads. Crap, which mouth should I pour the fluid into? I aimed the stream of Particle Enhancement Liquid between the two openings.

— — —

Two vials and twenty minutes later, Bockman's doppelganger images had merged back into a single shape. My landlord was starting to look like his old self. Lilly stood in the open doorway, still afraid to enter the room.

"Elliot, give me the lantern," Lilly demanded. "I shall stay away from you two until you finish this dangerous magic. You are inviting trouble upon us."

I handed her the lantern. She flounced out of the room, leaving me to tend Bockman. I examined the deteriorating transport box. A fragment had splintered off. When I held it in my hand, the wood crumbled into sawdust. Not good. I couldn't transport paintings in a sawdust container.

"The box's special coating is wearing off." Bockman had revived and was sitting upright. "I soaked the boards in Particle Enhancement Liquid for a month until the wood was saturated. Like me, the box has just about made its last journey through time."

"Well, well, well," I said and looked at Bockman. Would I end up that same way? "Feeling better? Nice to see only one of you."

"You might say I have my acts together," Bockman chortled. He stood and tottered on unsteady legs.

I secured the miniature portraits inside the transport box, then fist-pounded the lid tight. Ready for delivery.

"I'm curious," Bockman said. "What are you going to do with the miniature paintings of Lady Greyhurst's social circle?"

"Sell them through a friend of mine," I confided. "Hippo

Hyman. Works with me at the What's Up? Comedy Club. Newly discovered lost royal portraits bring big bucks from museums."

"And what are you going to do about Lilly?" Bockman asked. "Have you convinced her to come with you?"

"I'm working on it."

Bockman opened the walk-in closet. Straight ahead was a bank of monitors and controls, neatly clustered around a green circle painted on the floor. A person standing on the circle could easily reach the controls.

We positioned the transport box in the center of the green-painted area. Bockman gave me a brief run-through of the essential steps.

"This remote station is controlled by the home computer's program, so all you need to do is push this one button and say the launch password."

"The same as the San Francisco computer?" I said. "Catapult."

"Close, but no." Bockman hummed and talked to himself as he activated the launch sequence. "The code word here is"—he hit the button on the console—"Slingshot."

The shimmering blue aurora formed along the walls, moved to the ceiling, spinning. The transport box became transparent. I could see ghostly images of the paintings. Then the box was gone, winging its way from seventeenth-century England to modern California. Spooky.

I heard the faint jingle of metal in rhythmic cadence. Chains? Lilly stood in the doorway face tilted upward, the lantern held low along her side. Apparently she had changed her mind about being with me. I smiled her a welcome. She stumble-stepped into the room, almost falling before she righted herself. A huge black raven, tall as a man, had pushed her into the room.

THIRTY-SIX

A Trail of Particles

The masked man's fingers clutched a handful of Lilly's hair, forcing her chin up. He shook a leather bag, jingling the contents. A stench filled the room, cloying floral scents, pungent tobacco, and the sticky sweetness of decay. The long ivory beak turned in my direction. Bloodshot eyes fixed onto mine.

"Monsieur Tanner," the birdman said, "or whatever your real name eez. We meet again."

He released his grip on Lilly and pulled the bird mask away from his face. Shoulder-length hair straggled from his bald crown. Mucus ran from the nose on his beet-red face. He wiped the snot away with the long sleeve of his enveloping black garment. The man stood facing me, one foot twisted inwards. Lame Le Mieux, my nemesis.

"Coins, wedding rings." Le Mieux smirked. "Lovers' tokens, family heirlooms, grandmothers' jewelry. It eez all here, except zee money you took away from me in Spindledown."

The Frenchman toyed with his leather sack, then shoved Lilly toward me. I pulled her to my side. Bockman shielded himself behind us. Lilly swiped her hand through her hair, brushing off Le Mieux's touch as if it were a creeping bug.

"Let me introduce you to my associates."

Le Mieux did a double-loop flourish with his free hand and

bowed while extending one foot. He waggled the fingers of his extended hand at me. Two thuggish men and an ugly old woman paraded into the room, a sordid gang of misfits. Their soiled clothes were a patchwork of ill-fitting castoffs. The dirtiest bunch of curs I had ever seen.

"This hairy ape eez Rupert," Le Mieux said. "You do remember your coachman, Monsieur Squarrels."

"The last time I saw Squarrels he was hauling ass out of Spindle-down," I said.

"I pay them to gather up zee dead and cart zee bodies away to dump them in common graves. They prefer no one knows their names, seeing as how zee unsavory tasks they perform taint their acceptance among zee bourgeoisie."

Curb service for plague victims. The whole idea was revolting, but someone had to do the dirty job. Le Mieux's gang would be my first pick.

"I secured a charter from the London authorities." Le Mieux stowed his money sack into a side pocket, then rubbed his palms together. "They do not want to soil their own hands, so they pay me to dispose of zee human debris left by the plague. I hire my own workers."

"We empty dead men's pockets," Rupert declared, "as a reward for our service. Wedding rings are ours to keep. Wealthy souls don't mind when we pull fillings from their mouths either."

"I have titled myself Doctor Le Mieux—an honorary degree." Le Mieux chortled. "When they need a doctor, London's desperate people fancy zee illusion of medical skills in zee man they pay for treatment. Some stupid fools even place extra value on my French accent. I pretend to be a former court physician in service of King Louis."

Le Mieux's female associate, the old hag, coughed up malicious laughter. Lilly shivered as she pressed close to me. My anger at Le Mieux rose a couple notches.

"My nurse eez a bit scraggy, I admit," Le Mieux purred. "Pray you never need her tender mercy."

The so-called nurse had mousey hair with patches missing on the sides as if she had mange. Her sharp face highlighted a skin tone best described as pallor. Flat breasts sagged halfway to her stomach under a loose blouse missing two buttons.

"Miss." I acknowledged her with a perfunctory nod and a sarcastic smile.

"Don't mock me," the geriatric retorted. "I bring food to the house-bound sick."

"I swear she speaks zee truth," Le Mieux interjected. "Zee food is potage, simple gruel. And we give zee first soup bowl free." The Frenchman wiped a dirty sleeve across his perspiring brow. "Of course, zee second must be purchased at a price I deem proper."

The hag chortled. All that the witch needed to complete her image was a pointed hat and a caldron.

"I see you brought a pretty femme with you," Le Mieux said as he turned his attention again to Lilly. "An unexpected treat." The Frenchman grinned open-mouthed like a moray eel. "I look forward to getting to know her better."

Rupert nudged Squarrels and snickered. Lilly moved her hands to cover herself in the classic female one up, one down pose, then turned away. Such behavior was contrary to Lilly's usual feisty spirit. I stepped forward, hand on my sword pommel. Rupert and Squarrels positioned themselves next to Le Mieux. They each slapped seventeenth-century versions of blackjacks against their palms, eager to bludgeon me at the Frenchman's command.

"Monsieur Le Mieux." Bockman leaned his head from around

my back. "I detect the odor of Wizard's Antiplague Medicine emanating from the nose of your bird mask."

Bockman stepped out from behind me, his bandaged hand holding the gunnysack. He gave it a shake. He pointed his index finger in the air like some lecturing professor.

"However," he scolded, "I discern that the medicine has lost its potency. You need to refresh the supply or risk being infected."

"And who are you who acts so full of knowledge?" the Frenchman sniped.

"I am the true wizard, Lord Edward," Bockman said with puffed chest. "You can be a fool or you can be alive. The choice is yours."

Good for Bockman. The little runt was strutting his stuff. Exuding confidence. Lilly gave him her best atta-boy look of support. She slid one arm around my waist, her hand lingering on my back. Then I felt a sharp prick against my spine. I reached behind me. Lilly palmed a knife into my hand. She had pulled the weapon from some hidden pocket in her clothing while pretending fear. Someday I intended to investigate all her hiding places.

"Well, Little Lord Puffball," Le Mieux said. "I do not care who you are," He patted the pocket containing his money sack. "I can buy anything I want."

"Except immunity from the plague." Bockman flipped the back of his fingers under his chin in Le Mieux's direction as a gesture of disdain. "Kills rich and poor alike."

He shooed Le Mieux aside and moved to the table. Bockman pulled three yellow tins from his gunnysack and stacked them into a little pyramid. The smile on his face radiated pride.

"I cannot believe my good fortune," Le Mieux exclaimed. "Trois tins of Wizard's Plague Medicine." He seized the top tin. Eager fingers pried off the lid. The pungent odor leaped into the air. "Zee best. And very fresh. It will keep zee disease-ridden miasma vapors from my nose."

Le Mieux gleefully passed the open tin under the nostrils of his gang members. They grinned in feigned delight. If the boss was happy, they were happy. Le Mieux tapped the beak of the raven mask against the tabletop. A dark brown gob, resembling used chewing tobacco, rolled out.

"Ahh, you were correct, Lord Wizard." Le Mieux pinched his fingers into the yellow tin, gathering a portion. "Mine was spent." He stuffed the bird beak with the pungent mixture. "I know men who would trade their wives for a fresh tin of Wizard's Plague Medicine."

"Like your bowl of gruel," Bockman said. "My first one is free to you."

Bockman turned his back on Le Mieux, then raised one hand to his mouth, mimicking drinking. I nodded understanding and yanked vials of Particle Liquid free from the bandoleer. Bockman's hand trembled as he pulled out the stopper and gulped the vial's greenish-yellow contents. I followed suit, shuddering as the awful stuff ran down my throat.

"Here, Lilly, drink this. Now," I ordered as I handed her the third vial. "For once, don't argue."

"No." She pushed the open vial away and scrunched her face to reject my offer. "I fear that strange potion will poison my spirit."

"Mon amis. We will take the wizard's medicine supplies," the Frenchman announced. "Let us see what other treasures he hides."

Bockman clutched the sack to his chest and backed away. He bumped into Lilly. She stumbled aside, almost losing her balance. I backhanded Bockman out of my way.

"Nurse, get zee woman." Le Mieux pointed at Lilly. "Rupert, Squarrels, you take the big man. The wizard eez mine."

The harpy swarmed over Lilly, tearing at her clothes with tal-onlike nails. The sudden assault stunned Lily. The nurse twisted Lilly's arm and forced it behind her back. With one hand the witch picked up the lantern and with the other she force-marched Lilly from the room.

I drew my rapier. In my other hand I held the knife Lilly had given me. Rupert and Squarrels rushed at me, attacking my sword hand, flailing away with their clubs. A sharp pain lit up my knuck-les. My fingers went numb. The sword fell. I jabbed Lilly's knife into Rupert's forearm and drew blood. He let out a yowl.

"I have zee wizard's sack." Le Mieux held his trophy aloft. "Retreat."

The three men backed out of the room and into the hallway. Le Mieux was first over the threshold.

Bockman, on all fours, struggled to recover from Le Mieux's blows. I snatched my fallen sword from the floor and went after the Frenchman's gang. I caught up with them at the top of the dark stairs. The lantern in the nurse's hand provided the only light.

Lilly, hands clutched tight around the banister, had recovered enough to resist the hag's attempt to force her down the stairs. The lantern swung back and forth as the nurse tried to pry Lilly's hands off the railing. The light swung away. I lost Lilly to darkness.

Le Mieux was the first person visible in the swaying light, then Squarrels. But where was the wounded Rupert? The coachman stood on the top landing, blocking my way, while Le Mieux backed down the stairs. The Frenchman's arms were wrapped around the sack, shielding his chest. Squarrels raised his blackjack to attack me. I thrust my sword toward his head. He dodged my blade, only to plunge over the railing. He yipped for help as he fell to the floor below.

All seemed dark now until the lantern light swept across Le Mieux's face. The Frenchman's terrified eyes focused on a spot behind me. A strange blue glow illuminated the stairwell beyond the light of the lantern. I turned my head toward the glow.

Bockman stood behind me at the top of stairs, his hand extended like that of an evil magician casting a spell. The unwound bandage dangled from his wrist. Luminous blue vapor outlined his hand. Bockman's skull showed through his transparent flesh.

Le Mieux's mouth opened in a voiceless scream. He threw himself backward away from the apparition and plummeted into his nurse, knocking her down the stairs. The lantern flew from her hand. I glimpsed Lilly, one fist flailing away, the other hand still holding onto the railing. My fingers circled Lilly's wrist, and I pulled her to me.

Bottles in the sack smashed together at the bottom of the stairs. Glass broke, spilling liqueur, soaking the cloth. For a brief moment, the lantern light disappeared. Then a blue flame erupted as the spilled alcohol ignited.

The nurse gasped, then tumbled out the door in a tangle of skirt and thrashing legs. Squarrels hopped on one foot, his pant leg engulfed in flames. He shed his trousers and fled bare-bottomed. The sides of Le Mieux's long cloak burned like flaming wings as he ran from the house, the cloth trailing red tongues of fire into the night.

"Don't leave me." Lilly put both arms around me, her head pressed against my neck. I stroked her hair, then held her face between my hands.

"Lilly. Darling." I said. "We must transport to San Francisco before the fire reaches the upper floor."

She pulled her head away from my grasp, grabbed my arm and turned me around to face Bockman. Lilly stifled a scream. The wizard beckoned us with his translucent hand. The vivid outline pulsed blue. Particles smoked off his fingers.

"Your hand . . ." I didn't know what to say.

"Wild and crazy, isn't it?" Bockman's mouth twisted in a mischievous grin. "It should restore on the other end of time. We must activate the return sequence. Now."

Bockman hurried into the room, leaving Lilly and me in the hallway.

"Lilly, come with me." I yanked her to me. "It is now or never." A cliché. I didn't have time to be eloquent. "San Francisco is a marvelous city full of things you can't begin to imagine."

"Never." Her jade eyes flashed, then softened to a plea for understanding.

"Return with me," I begged. "Back to my time."

"Your time?" she cried. "Back to a foreign place where I would forever be a stranger?"

"A place without the plague. A place where a treasure chest of things will make your life easier."

"Elliot. Things are not important to me." She took my hands in hers. "Stay with me. Please. We can have a good life here."

"But you don't understand. You can't understand. I need to get back to . . ."

To what? Being a struggling comedian who couldn't even pay the rent? Eating take-out Chinese by myself? Where else would people respect me as a mighty warrior? Where would I find another Lilly? A woman . . . I loved.

Flames now consumed the staircase. The lower steps fell away with an explosion of smoke and flaming embers. A wall of hot air hit us. All oxygen seemed to be sucked away.

"I must help Bockman," I pleaded.

Lilly let me pull her into the computer room. Bockman stood in the center of the closet's green transport circle, his finger poised above the command console.

"Are you and Lilly coming with me or not?" Bockman's arched eyebrows accented his question. "You're lucky to have Lilly." He pouted. "I'll never have the opportunity to ask Lady Greyhurst the same question." He brightened. "Ah well, wouldn't have worked anyway. A King's ex-mistress is too high-maintenance."

He looked at me with those owlish eyes. He had a cockeyed grin.

"Go," I said. "I'm staying with Lilly."

The words came out with more reluctance than I intended. I surprised myself again. I didn't recall any logical internal debate.

"Elliot, thanks for rescuing me," Bockman said. "Now, I'll return the favor. The bedroom window. Escape to the next house. Run back to the bakery." He pressed the launch button. "Care to say the magic word for me?"

"Slingshot," I said.

The launch command word came out of my mouth more sad than exhilarated. I surprised myself, again. But I felt okay. The aurora glowed blue. Light crept up the closet walls.

"Find Hippo at the What's Up? Club. Sell the paintings," I yelled in a burst of enthusiasm. "Send me my money. I'll settle the debt to Lady Greyhurst. She'll be fine."

The wizard gave me a thumbs-up. Particles spiraled from his body. His legs disappeared, then his waist.

"Look for the box," he said. "Lilly's farm."

The force moved upwards until there was nothing but his head suspended in air. Bockman's face evaporated. Only an echo of his gleeful laughter lingered behind. I stood, dumbfounded by my illogical decision. What had I done? Arms hugged me.

THIRTY-SEVEN

The Spindledown Run

"You stayed." Lilly beamed at me. "Remind me to thank you proper if we get out of here alive."

"I prefer an improper reward."

"Same as you said about that time travel." She gave me a saucy look. "'Twill be more than you can imagine."

A gray blanket of choking smoke invaded the transport room. I grabbed her hand. Overhead, the light fixture dimmed, flared, then failed. We ran towards the red glow that lit the hallway. But the lower floor of the house had become an inferno.

"Bedroom window," I shouted as I tugged Lilly down the hallway. "Bockman said we could jump from the bedroom across to the neighboring house."

I slammed the door behind us to keep the smoke at bay, but whitish fingers crept underneath. Lilly leaned her head against the bedpost, coughing, trying to catch her breath. She tore a piece of the bed's drapery from the overhead railing and held it over her mouth.

I rushed over to her side and guided her around a thick-cushioned chair, past Bockman's old movie poster, and to the wide window. I yanked opened the shutters, grabbed an end table, and broke out the windowpane. The house next door, the one that I had thought almost touched Bockman's home, stood five feet away. A narrow baroque balcony with fancy curves fronted its closed French doors.

"Stand back, Lilly."

I brushed her aside, lifted the chair, aimed at the French doors, and hurled it though the air. The chair smacked dead center into their handles, popping the doors inward. The chair rebounded, teetered on the balcony's edge, then plunged to the ground.

"Lilly, jump over to that balcony and into the room," I said. "Do it now."

Her hands on the sill, she leaned her head out the window. She tilted her head this way and that. Evaluating the risk.

"You go first," she protested.

I felt a rush of air hot on my back. The door behind us had opened. I took a quick look. An apparition from hell loomed in the thick gray smoke. Rupert. Lilly shrieked as I picked her up and tossed her out the window. Her body flew across the open space, over the balcony railing, and into the opposite room.

I turned to face my attacker. Rupert charged me, head down, arms outstretched. His singed beard and hair trailed smoky streamers as he thundered across the room like a mad bull. I pirouetted aside in a move that would have done a matador proud.

Rupert barreled past me. I planted my boot in his butt and propelled him out the open window. A loud thump followed by a plaintive plea rewarded my effort. I leaned out my window. Rupert dangled from the balcony on Lilly's side. His fingers clutched the far railing as his feet bicycled in a vain attempt to secure a footing.

Lilly reappeared on the balcony, sputtering angry words. Then she pointed to the hands clutching the railing. Her face perplexed. Eyebrows gathered in a question.

"Those fingers belong to Rupert," I said. "When the bedroom door flew open, it was him about to assault us."

"Well, Elliot," Lilly chided, "you could have explained yourself before pitching your lover through the air."

"Didn't have time," I retorted. "Do you want to take care of him now, or do you want me to?"

She raised a finger and withdrew into the room.

"Hey, Rupert," I called. "I hate to tell you this, but Lady Lilly has a mean temper when people treat her badly."

"It's Le Mieux's fault, not mine," he whined.

Lilly reappeared through the open doors, a heavy brass candle-holder raised over her head, poised to whack Rupert.

"Sir, would you prefer head or hand?" she asked with mock sweetness.

"Don't really matter, miss." Rupert winced. "Really, I prefers to do my own self in."

He released his fingers and dropped from sight. Lilly and I looked down from our separate vantage points. *Kerplunk*. Rupert landed in the upholstered chair before spilling to the walkway path. Turtle-slow, he crawled away.

"Lilly. I'm in danger of being roasted." I said. "Watch out. Here I come."

"Hurry before you burn your cute bottom."

I cast one last look behind. Flames devoured Bockman's bed. I patted Bockman's Robin Hood poster for luck, yelled my best Tarzan imitation, and leaped out the window. Lilly hop-stepped backwards as I crash-landed at her feet.

— — —

A carved headboard, a mattress piled with plump pillows, a dressing table, an armoire. We had landed in someone's master bedroom. I wanted to laugh. Maybe later, when I recalled these as fun times.

"With all the commotion," I said, "we probably scared the wits out of the occupants below."

"Plague or no plague, wild things always happen when I'm

around you," Lilly said. "Like sword fights, a human hand you could see through, and now a burning house. Elliot. I shall never be bored with you."

"Don't forget my jokes," I said. "Lots of laughs together."

"Time for us to flee from here," Lilly insisted.

We clattered down the stairs to the lower level and encountered an elderly couple creeping up the staircase to investigate the noise. They took one look at our rapid descent and pressed themselves against the wall as we rushed past down the stairs.

"Fire." I waved in the general direction of Bockman's house. I mimicked a cell phone by sticking out my thumb and little finger. "Call 911." Lilly and I burst through the front door and dashed outside.

First, one door opened, then another along the street as residents reacted to the plume of black smoke billowing skyward. People swarmed into the street. Danger from an all-consuming fire must have overcome their fear of the plague. Alarms were shouted. Doors pounded. Citizens rallied to their neighborhood threat.

"Back to the bakery," I said. "We'll join the Spindledown wagon train with its armed escort."

I felt alive. My new life was going to be a blast. It would be great to see Old Penn again. Perhaps we could figure out a way to help Sister and Little Tom.

Lilly gathered her skirt and broke into a run. I tried to pass her to show off my athletic skills, but she just laughed and shifted into another gear. I admired her swaying rump in front of me. Maybe the view was my reward for letting her lead the way.

"Anywhere you go, Lilly," I declared, "I'll be sure to follow."

Lilly rewarded me with lilting laughter.